"This story is simply sublime. . . . The story itself was gorgeous. The characters are complex and unique, and the sacrifices each one made for the other were heartbreaking."

—Fresh Fiction

"Dahlia and Josie are rich, complex characters. . . . The plot pulls the reader right along, trying to figure out what really happened between the two men, as well as what might still happen for the sisters and their love interests . . . recommended."

—Devourer of Books

"*Little Gale Gumbo* is written in the spirit of Adriana Trigiani's bighearted family sagas. . . . The relationships are complex, substantial, fraught with complications and uneasy answers, but ultimately satisfying. . . . While food plays a central role in this novel, in the end the strength of the story is in how it portrays the healing love between broken hearts, the power of that love to heal in unexpected ways."

—Reader Unboxed

Also by Erika Marks

Little Gale Gumbo

The
MERMAID
COLLECTOR

ERIKA MARKS

NAL
ACCENT

NAL Accent
Published by New American Library, a division of
Penguin Group (USA) Inc., 375 Hudson Street,
New York, New York 10014, USA
Penguin Group (Canada), 90 Eglinton Avenue East, Suite 700, Toronto,
Ontario M4P 2Y3, Canada (a division of Pearson Penguin Canada Inc.)
Penguin Books Ltd., 80 Strand, London WC2R 0RL, England
Penguin Ireland, 25 St. Stephen's Green, Dublin 2,
Ireland (a division of Penguin Books Ltd.)
Penguin Group (Australia), 250 Camberwell Road, Camberwell, Victoria 3124,
Australia (a division of Pearson Australia Group Pty. Ltd.)
Penguin Books India Pvt. Ltd., 11 Community Centre, Panchsheel Park,
New Delhi - 110 017, India
Penguin Group (NZ), 67 Apollo Drive, Rosedale, Auckland 0632,
New Zealand (a division of Pearson New Zealand Ltd.)
Penguin Books (South Africa) (Pty.) Ltd., 24 Sturdee Avenue,
Rosebank, Johannesburg 2196, South Africa

Penguin Books Ltd., Registered Offices:
80 Strand, London WC2R 0RL, England

First published by NAL Accent, an imprint of New American Library,
a division of Penguin Group (USA) Inc.

First Printing, October 2012
10 9 8 7 6 5 4 3 2 1

 REGISTERED TRADEMARK—MARCA REGISTRADA

LIBRARY OF CONGRESS CATALOGING-IN-PUBLICATION DATA:

Marks, Erika.
    The mermaid collector/Erika Marks.
        p. cm.
    ISBN 978-0-451-23792-7
    1. Wood-carvers—Fiction. 2. Mermaids—Fiction. 3. Man-woman relationships—
Fiction. 4. Family secrets—Fiction. I. Title.
    PS3613.A754525M47 2012
    813'.6—dc23   2012013248

Set in Cochin
Designed by Catherine Leonardo

Printed in the United States of America

ALWAYS LEARNING   **PEARSON**

To my little mermaids, Evie and Murray

THE MERMAID COLLECTOR

Letter to Lydia Sprague Harris, wife of lighthouse keeper Linus James Harris, dated August 2, 1888: (Property of the Cradle Harbor Historical Society)

My dearest Lydie,

By the time you find this letter, I will be returned to the sea.

These last months back on land have been filled with an unbearable duplicity. I have tried my best to remain your devoted husband, to tend to you as a man should tend to his wife, as I did without question and with absolute joy in the days and years before my voyage, but I can see that my charade has not served either of us well.

Some of what we told you all, our dear and most precious wives, about that bright and flawless day we set sail was true; we did indeed chart a course for Hope Island, and we did find the seas calm and forgiving. We did dine well on the ham and Indian pudding you packed for us, and we did ponder the future and all its promise under the vast periwinkle sky.

But it is there that the truth stops. What transpired next, and for all the time afterward, we have hid from you, certain that our rapture would fade, or prove only the stuff of an extended dream. But we four now know that we cannot bury the truth of our hearts any longer. What has happened to me and my fellow sailors since that strange day can never be explained, let alone understood, for I myself can barely do either; yet there is no escaping it, any more than we can escape the beckoning of the sea, or the songs of our saviors who dwell just beneath its mighty waves and plead nightly for our return.

My dear wife, you know I am not a foolish man, nor one bereft of the truths of science; yet every rational thought has abandoned me. I have left you my log book, for the confession that it contains is an unspeakable one, which is why I can only put it to paper and hope that it will offer you and our son a modicum of peace after I am gone, even if it is only as a lasting tribute to my madness. Whatever the reason, you and Henry deserve better than a man whose heart has been torn from him and left to float among the waves like driftwood, sunbaked and weathered, parched of all its weight and worth.

I do not expect forgiveness in this lifetime or the next. But know that while I was on land, dry and human, I was truly blessed to be a husband and father.

Good-bye, dear Lydia. May we all find our place on this earth, by land or by sea.

Linus

It is a sad fact that mermaids are often
drawn to human men, falling deeply in love
with them, then forgetting with equal speed, and
dire consequences, that no matter their devotion,
human men cannot breathe underwater.

—*The Mermaid Mutiny and More:*
A Complete History of Cradle Harbor

To: tgrace@chicagocentral.org

From: ehawthorne@chhs.me.com

Dear Mr. Grace,

As we have indicated in our many phone messages, this news of your inheritance of the lightkeeper's house has all of us at the Cradle Harbor Historical Society shocked and alarmed.

For years we have been under the impression that Frank Hammond intended to bequeath the historic building to the town in the event of his passing. While I do understand that the prospect of opening one's home to tours might seem intrusive, surely you can appreciate our wishes to see the Harbor's heritage preserved and displayed. With the Mermaid Festival just weeks away, it is of the utmost urgency that we speak with you as soon as possible about the matter.

We have a wonderful and comprehensive history of our town, which I wrote my first year as president of the historical society, entitled *The Mermaid Mutiny and More: A Complete History of Cradle Harbor*. If you would be so kind as to forward me your address, I will have one sent to you promptly. I think you will find the book enlightening. I also implore you to visit our online archives and learn more about our town's precious heritage, as well as that of our beloved keeper's house, in the hope that you might reconsider your position on prohibiting future visitors to the property.

We very much look forward to your response, as well as your impending arrival. I have no doubt we can work together and come to a fair and mutually agreeable solution to this problem.

Sincerely yours,

Edith Hawthorne, President

Cradle Harbor Historical Society
212 Main Street
Cradle Harbor, ME

Monday

Four Days before the
Mermaid Festival

THE MATERIAL OF THE CHIMES isn't as important as their placement. Most any material of a sturdy and mountable nature will do, such as hollow stalks or copper piping. What matters most is that the chimes be situated on all homes that face the water. When possible, every home in such a location should hang at least one set, if not several. The louder the tones, the farther out to sea the sound will carry and the more protection will be guaranteed for every shoreline community and its male residents.

—*The Mermaid Mutiny and More:*
A Complete History of Cradle Harbor

One

THE LITTLE GIRL WAS BREATHLESS with excitement as she pushed through the fence of hedges toward the water's edge, skinny freckled legs and lopsided red pigtails spinning in opposition as they disappeared into the fog.

Tess Patterson stood at the window and watched her nine-year-old neighbor make the same pilgrimage she'd been making almost every morning for the past week, but it was always the same at this time of year in Cradle Harbor. With the Mermaid Festival just five days away, every girl under the age of twelve—and a few girls above it—found herself helplessly swept up in the excitement of the town's impending celebration, rushing to the surf to make sure she would be the first of her friends to find a mermaid's purse washed up on the shore or to catch the faintest chime of what surely had to be mermaid song and not simply a mourning dove's faraway call.

It was a feverish time in which for one long weekend the smells of blueberry custard and bonfires built with cedar starters would fill the air of the coastal village with such an insistent thickness that not even the sour scent of the lowest tide could overtake it. It was a time when the ocean was the warmest it would be all year, a time when inns teemed with guests and Puffin's Good Basket would always run out of its famous whoopie pies before noon. Impetuosity ruled like some kind of stalled weather system, casting down showers of romantic stirrings that would quiet even the most notoriously discordant couples for a time and make friends of lifelong enemies. No wonder so many flocked from so far away to stand in the path of the storm.

Tess raised her coffee to her lips, blew across the top, then took a long sip, tasting the hint of clove she'd lately started to mix into her grounds. Even at twenty-five, she was still every bit that fanciful girl; her own heart still pounded while, ears perked and eyes wide, she crouched on the cold sand in the liquid light of dawn, turning at every tossed pebble, every gull's squawk. But of course she'd been raised on the promise of fantasy and the certainty of fate. Nine years after losing her mother, Tess knew her belief in life's magic was the legacy Ruby had left her with, one she treasured, no matter what the locals still whispered in her wake. And anyway, not everyone in Cradle Harbor thought she was a bad apple that hadn't rolled far enough from the family tree.

Bedsprings groaned behind her. Tess turned from the window and smiled with relief at the sight of Pete Hawthorne, his broad back rising and falling with sleep.

Several times in the night, she'd felt the pangs of panic shake her awake, and she'd reached across the bed to make sure he was still there. Now in the soft light of early morning, there was no mistaking it. But it was always the way when they'd been apart too long. Her brain would need a few hours to catch up to her heart.

She hadn't been in love with Pete forever, but most days it felt that way. In the months after her mother had drowned, Tess had been so lost, feeling so untethered and yet so desperate to attach herself to someone; then there he was—Pete Hawthorne, the golden boy of Cradle Harbor, the object of lust for every girl in town. And he'd chosen *her*.

Not that theirs had been a smooth road. The past year had been a particularly hard one. In January, after months of what Tess had been certain were advances toward a real commitment, he'd blindsided her by moving in with Angela Whelan. Sure that he'd regret the decision and come back to her, Tess had waited through their affair, much to the frustration of her stepfather, Buzz, busying herself with work through the coldest winter months and an unusually wet spring.

But it had all been worth it. Just two nights before, Pete had arrived on her doorstep with the news that he and Angela weren't working and that he was moving out of their apartment on Mercy Road. Tess had cooked him a mushroom omelet, and they'd made love three times. Tonight, she was making his favorite meal—seafood lasagna and pumpkin cheesecake. She'd special ordered the scallops and lobster meat from Russell's Market. She'd cleaned her bathroom. She'd emptied the biscuit tin on her dresser and managed to find a pair of earrings that matched. After all these months of waiting, she had a date—a real, live, honest-to-God, shave-your-legs-all-the-way-to-your-ass date, the sort of date that came with a promise, an assurance of something more, something binding.

It was all the more reason Tess wanted to get an early start on the day. She would need most of the afternoon to prepare, and there were still three cottages that needed cleaning for incoming guests. Buzz would tell her that she didn't have to help him. He'd insist that she finish her sculpture instead of sweeping out windowsills or scrubbing sinks, but Tess knew her stepfather could never manage the rentals on his own. It was the least she could do, considering that he never charged her rent on her cottage, or the shed he'd helped her turn into a woodworking studio when she'd lost her lease in town.

When Tess stepped out of the small yellow house, the morning air was damp and crisp with chill as it always was by the sea. The fog was still thick enough that she could barely see the tops of the rental cottages that stood on the other side of the driveway, each with an unobstructed view of the cove. The early mist would lift in a while, burn off like smoke, and give way to a humid August day. Until then, she would need more than just a thin T-shirt. She saw Pete's navy sweatshirt draped over the arm of the wicker couch, and she tugged it on, sliding her bare feet into her unlaced sneakers. Above her, the collection of wind chimes dangled without touching, the air too still to incite their usual symphony, so she tapped them on her way down the stairs for good measure, and they rang out a brief but clear song.

She took her time crossing the lawn, through the dew-dusted grass to reach the shed, not caring that her toes were quickly soaked, squishing against the canvas with every step. Even cold feet wouldn't bother her this morning. When Tess reached the garden shed at the bottom of the slope where her sign rocked gently on its bracket, she pulled the heavy door along its rusted rails and revealed her studio. The warm, coppery smell of her tools, followed by the leafy scent of fresh wood, rose up to greet her as she stepped inside. She pried off her sneakers, leaving them in the doorway to dry for when the sun came up in full, and moved to her cluttered workbench where her most recent order—a sign for Poe's Landscaping—lay buried, neglected, under weeks of dust.

The company had called twice to inquire about its status. Tess had promised it to them more than a week ago, and she was nearly done carving it, only one daylily to go, but in the past month her sign business had taken a backseat to another project. She picked up the chisels she'd sharpened the night before and crossed to the other side of the room where an ivory sheet hung over a bulky shape. Carefully, she pulled off the sheet to reveal a two-foot-tall wooden sculpture of a mermaid. Its form was still rough in places, looking more fish than female, but as she ran her fingers over the wood, Tess imagined it complete—how smooth the wood would become after she'd sanded it, how it would glow to a creamy tan with its finish coat of tung oil. For now, though, it was carved out just enough to create a basic shape, the only discernible part of the mermaid's body being her curving crescent tail and the upturned round of her still-featureless face.

Tess had debated for almost a week which wood to use. The old figurehead carvers, among them Buzz's great-great-great-grandfather, a black-haired Scot who'd carved for clipper ships, had always used a softer wood such as pear or pine for their mastheads, since those pieces would always have been painted. But she'd needed a harder wood. Aspen had a fine grain and sanded easily, but Tess loved the dark color of walnut and mahogany. In the end, she'd settled on basswood. With its grainless appearance, it certainly wasn't the most interesting wood to look at, but it was lightweight and ideal for intricate carving.

Tess picked up her chisel and mallet and began to cut away thick curls, savoring the grassy smell the fresh wood released into the air. She'd been struggling for the past two days to get the torso just right. She'd checked her own body in an old mirror she'd propped against the wall, tugging up her T-shirt to study the curves of her own breasts, the contours of her ribs, and arching her body as she'd outlined the reach of her maiden, places where the hard edges of bone melted into soft flesh, then into scales.

For any other piece, she might have been less fussy, but not for this one. This sculpture had to be perfect.

"She's looking good."

Tess turned to find Pete standing in the shed's opening, his light blond hair tidy now.

"You really think so?"

"Absolutely." He came up behind her. Tess guided his arms around her waist and leaned into his chest.

Still, the knot of doubt twisted in her stomach.

"What if they hate it?" she asked.

"No one's going to hate it," Pete said.

Tess lifted his hand to her lips, kissing his fingers one by one. "Your mother will."

"No one cares what my mother thinks."

"Liar. Everyone does." Which was exactly why it pleased Tess—and why it always had—to think on Edith

Hawthorne spitting nails over their romance. After all, Pete's mother had always been first in line to spread fresh gossip about that "bohemian" woman from California and her "ragamuffin" daughter. How Tess had wished she'd been a fly on the wall when Edith was told that Tess's entry had been selected out of the ninety-six submitted, the panel of judges—Edith Hawthorne among them—having been kept blind to the identities of the artists involved.

Just last night, while Tess had fixed him a second rum and Coke, Pete had confessed that in her fury, his mother had insisted on a recount, but the panel's choice had prevailed.

"This commission is a big deal," Tess reminded him, tracing the lines of his palm.

"I know it is. You won it."

"It's not just that." She turned in his arms to face him. "Now they all have to admit it."

Pete frowned down at her. "Admit what?"

Tess saw the genuine bemusement in his narrowed eyes. She didn't expect him to understand. Pete was Harbor royalty. He had no idea what it was like to be the source of town gossip, to have to prove your worth, your innocence. Tess's grudge match with the Harbor's old guard had been going on from the moment she and her mother had rolled into town in Buzz's truck sixteen years earlier and wandered into Puffin's for a bite to eat, both of them stinking of bonfire smoke and incense, unwashed and uncaring. It had been a first impression that would seal their fate as outsiders. It had outraged Tess—and it still did—that in all the years her mother had lived there, the residents had never given her talents their due, never acknowledged what an accomplished painter Ruby was.

But all that would change now. This sculpture, and its prominent display in the foyer of the library, would finally secure those long-denied accolades. Tess had entered the competition as much for her mother as for herself—and winning it had been a victory for both of them.

"Speaking of parents . . ." Pete nodded to the door. "I was sure I'd wake up and find your old man had slashed my tires in the night."

"I wouldn't worry," said Tess. "Buzz isn't in much of a tire-slashing mood these days."

She glanced reflexively to the window where her step-father's red trailer was visible, his porch light blooming in the mist. Losing Frank had taken so much out of him. The brothers-in-law were close, closer than many would have guessed. They were as different as could be, but still a friendship had blossomed when Joan, Buzz's younger sister, had married the successful businessman who'd grown up in Cradle Harbor. When everyone else in town had judged Buzz harshly for bringing Tess and her mother back from the music festival and moving them into his home and his heart without hesitation, Frank had been kind and welcoming.

Buzz had never forgotten that. Neither had Tess.

"I would have thought he'd be *exactly* in that kind of

mood," Pete said, "after the whole thing with the keeper's house."

"Why would he be pissed off about the keeper's house?" Tess asked.

Pete shrugged. "Because he and Frank were family. And Frank goes and gives it to some guy nobody's ever heard of."

"Buzz didn't want it. He and Frank talked about it."

"Then you and Buzz must know this Tom Grace guy."

"I'd never even heard of him until last week," said Tess.

"What about Buzz?"

"He knows he's a teacher from Chicago."

"Yeah, but how did he know *Frank*?" pressed Pete.

"God, you sound like your mother; you know that? Where's the microphone?" Tess playfully searched him, peeking through his shirt buttons and lifting one arm to inspect his armpit. "Come on—I know it's here somewhere. . . ."

Pete chuckled, easing her hands off him. "Very funny."

Tess stretched to link her arms around his neck. "I don't want to talk about Tim."

"*Tom*."

"Whatever . . ." Tess kissed his chin, then his throat.

"I just think it's weird that no one knows who this guy is," said Pete, breaking their embrace.

Tess groaned. "Please don't tell me you're taking up your mother's crazy campaign too?"

"Of course not. I'm just curious, like everybody else. Aren't you?"

"Oh, I'm curious, all right." Tess slid her arms around him again, her hands riding up his spine, then coming around to his zipper. "I'm curious what would happen if I undid this button. . . ."

"Hey, now." Pete grinned. "I'm already late. . . ."

"They'll understand," she whispered, freeing the button. "Everyone knows nothing gets done this close to the festival."

"Everyone except Vic Marshall." Pete gently removed her hands, buttoning himself back up. He dropped a kiss on her forehead. "I think you can wait a few hours, don't you?"

Tess smiled. "Don't be so sure."

Still smiling after she waved him out of the driveway, she came back inside her woodshop and pulled the heavy door closed behind her, feeling as light and unfettered as the paper-thin wood curls that blew across her floor like sand-colored snow flurries.

Maybe she *had* waited forever for Pete Hawthorne.

But that was the thing about life on the water: Tides went out and, eventually, they came back in.

TOM GRACE SMELLED THE OCEAN long before he saw it. It had crept into the old blue Volvo like smoke, thick and wet and salty, and he was grateful for it. Sixteen hours on the road and he had grown tired of breathing in fast-food grease and restroom lemon soap. On either side of him, long stretches of white pines rose up like fence posts, straight and even, trimming a road that twisted like a string of black licorice.

When he saw the sign for Cradle Harbor at last, a tidy painted square nestled behind loose-petaled roses, he thought for a moment he could still turn back. But he couldn't, of course. He'd moved them out of the apartment on Webster, and Dean wasn't far behind, his younger brother having no way of reaching him except for his cell phone, a fact that had kept Tom in a constant state of panic for the entirety of his twelve-hundred-mile drive from Chicago. His panic seemed only to grow the closer he got to his final destination. In the seventeen years of caring for Dean since their parents' death, Tom had never liked to let his younger brother out of sight for too long. The last thing Tom had wanted was to leave Dean to come a few days behind him, but what choice had he had? Tom knew he couldn't risk losing the house Frank had given them, knowing how contentious the gift had been.

He reached for the foam cup wedged in the holder beside him, remembering as soon as he did that it was empty. God, he was thirsty. He tugged at his tie, feeling foolish for wearing it. Ten years of being a teacher had conditioned him to wear a tie every day. Out of habit, he'd even worn one on the weekends, much to Dean's endless amusement.

Slowing as he neared the center of town, he found his thoughts drifting restlessly to the lines of Frank's last letter, the instructions Tom had pored over so many times. *I've left the keys to the keeper's house with Buzz Patterson at Birch Point Cottages on Birch Road. He'll be expecting you.*

Expecting him. The very idea rattled Tom to the core, filling him with a chilling image of wide-eyed faces and shaking fists, demanding to know why Frank Hammond had willed their historic Cradle Harbor lightkeeper's house to someone they believed to be a perfect stranger. Tom knew little about small towns, but he imagined they were filled with people much like the hordes of seagulls he'd encountered all his way up the coast: sharp-eyed and insistent, unwilling to retreat until they'd gleaned a tasty morsel.

Already he'd endured a slew of e-mails from the town's historical society, demanding that he agree to allow them access to the keeper's house for tours. Tom had replied only once, curtly and firmly, but still the e-mails and phone calls had continued. He'd ignored them, and he had the feeling they weren't women used to being ignored. Making matters worse, he'd refused to let them send him a copy of their precious town manifesto. He had little interest in the folklore of this place, in whatever foolish legend they all dusted off every summer for their famous festival—or so Frank had referred to it in his letters over the years.

Tom gripped the wheel with both hands, the plastic hot beneath his fingers, his scalp feeling the same fever under his wavy chestnut hair. He had meant to get a haircut. He needed one desperately; it wasn't like him to go so long without one. He felt shaggy and crass. He could smell himself, and God, he stank. Even his fingers smelled— hamburger grease and motor oil (the car had been burning it copiously since Erie, and he'd left a constellation of droplets on one pant leg while checking the stick in Katonah). He only hoped the old house had running water. He didn't care if all the windows were missing, even the front door. It could be without a stove or a fridge, infested with ants. Just as long as there was water. He wanted a shower, a shave, a bar of soap with corners.

There was always the sea, he told himself as he arrived on the other side of the village, seeing the pines thin just enough to reveal fields of marshland, spotted with shingled sheds bleached as white as bone. If he grew desperate, maybe he could climb down the ledge of rocks below the lighthouse and splash himself clean. But then he'd smell of salt, wouldn't he? No, not much of an improvement.

Dean wouldn't care, though. Tom knew his younger brother would rush to the water's edge the minute he arrived; he would swim in the frigid ocean at all hours. Tom only hoped the current wasn't too strong at the end of the Point. Dean wasn't used to such rough waters, and Tom would be powerless to stop him.

When the sign to Birch Cove Cottages finally appeared on the horizon, Tom had to squint to read it behind a veil of pine needles. He came to a stop, surveying the long driveway in front of him before starting down it. After swerving around several bends, he saw a stretch of cleared land and a handful of gaudily painted cottages. On the other side of the road, farther up a rise and right on the edge of the woods, stood a lemon yellow cottage with a watermelon door, and a ways beyond that, at the top of the hill, a fire-truck red trailer. Tom pulled the Volvo into the turnaround and killed the engine, not sure where to go first.

Out of the car, he caught at once the clear sounds of wind chimes to his right. He glanced up at the yellow cottage and saw several sets hanging from the porch over-hang, knocking together in the breeze. More sounded farther up the hill. Looking at the trailer, he could see a row of the metal rods hanging from the deck railing. The wind strengthened, and soon the air was filled with the cacophony of their bells, only for an anxious moment, then quieting remarkably seconds later as the breeze thinned.

As if feeling somehow released in the quiet, Tom turned to the water and saw one more building he'd missed on his first survey, a shed with a hand-carved sign hanging over its door: TESS'S WOOD CARVING AND SIGN SHOP. Surely someone inside could direct him to Buzz Pterson.

There was a window on one side, the

23

him, and he walked to it, having to navigate his way over a stack of logs to get there. Once he had, he cupped his hands around his face and pressed his nose against the glass. Squinting in, he could make out the shape of the interior, cluttered surfaces lit by a window on the opposite side. He scanned the room, almost all the way to the end before he saw her.

A woman sat in the cone of a spotlight and facing a mirror, one hand posed at her hip, the other reaching out to draw on what appeared to be a wooden dolphin. Tom squinted harder, shifting against the pane for a better view and got one. Now he saw clearly, too clearly to look away, though he knew that would have been the right thing to do. After all, the woman had drawn up her shirt on one side and gathered the cotton just above her breast, high enough that he could see the pale fullness of one side, the creamy skin in stark contrast to the rough wood of the shed's walls. She was posing, he was certain of it, being her own model. But why, when she was sculpting a dolphin? Now she reached her arm behind her, arching her back, her dark hair washing her shoulder blades. She watched herself as her torso curved, causing more flesh, a crescent of nipple, to be exposed.

At that instant, Tom caught his own reflection in her mirror, then the woman's eyes shifting to meet his and rounding.

She twisted to face him.

"Shit—" He darted backward so fast that he knocked

his head on a set of wind chimes—*Christ, how many does one person need?*—causing them to ring out in alarm. He grabbed the bamboo sticks to quiet them, rubbing his head with his other hand.

From the front of the shed came the creak of the door being pushed open and then the woman, barefoot, her hair wild and coppery in the sunlight, her eyes the color of freshly cut limes. Her T-shirt was down now, hanging nearly to the hem of her lopsided shorts. It was a man's undershirt, there was no mistaking it, oversized and worn and low on one shoulder. She held a chisel in her left hand. More like *wielded* it, he thought. What had he gotten himself into?

"If you wanted to spy on me," she said, "you should have gone around to the other window. The view's much better from there."

"I wasn't spying," Tom defended hotly, already feeling the color seep up his cheeks as he struggled to untangle himself from the precarious stack of logs he'd climbed over. "I was just trying to find someone to ask directions."

"You could have knocked."

"You could get curtains."

"It's private property."

He cleared his throat, succeeding at last in finding level ground. "I'm looking for Buzz Patterson. Is he here?"

"I suppose he's somewhere."

"He's expecting me."

"I doubt that." She dangled the chisel by its handle.

25

"Buzz isn't expecting anyone today. Cottage reservations don't start until Thursday."

"I'm not here for a cottage," Tom said, tugging on the knot of his tie, which seemed tight suddenly. "I'm here for the keys to the keeper's house. I'm Tom Grace."

"Oh." She looked him over for a long moment before her eyes lifted to the hill. She pointed behind him with her chisel. "Guess you're in luck."

Tom turned to find Buzz Patterson marching down the hill, the sixty-five-year-old dressed in his uniform of jeans and an unbuttoned flannel over a tie-dyed tee, his long red hair, which, along with his beard, had become increasingly threaded with gray in the past few years, pulled into a ponytail that fell to his shoulders. He arrived and thrust out a meaty, freckled hand. "Tom Grace, right?"

Tom cautiously extended his own. "How did you know?"

Buzz nodded to the Volvo. "Saw the Illinois plates. Buzz." He gave Tom's hand a rough shake. "I wasn't expecting you until tomorrow."

"I decided to drive straight through," Tom said.

"I see you've met my daughter, Tess."

Tom turned to Tess but found she'd already returned to her shed. Buzz squinted up at the sky, then gestured to the woodshop's open door. "Let's get out of the sun a minute." Tom followed Buzz inside, his lungs filling at once with the spicy smell of wood, so sharp his eyes watered.

"Tessie's working on a big commission." Buzz pointed

to the large sculpture at the other end of the room where Tess had returned, moving a chisel over a newly outlined curve. "They're going to put her mermaid in the library. Going to have a big unveiling this weekend."

Tom offered up a brief but polite smile, feeling dim. He'd thought it was a dolphin. No wonder she'd been studying herself. Breasts on a dolphin. Idiot.

"She's crazy talented, Tom. You should see the stuff she's done."

"Don't believe a word of it," Tess said without turning. "He's hopelessly biased."

"Damn straight." Buzz grinned, then looked back at Tom. "Long drive for you, I'll bet. Traffic must have been hell."

"It was all right." Tom glanced compulsively back to Tess before he answered, the surveys becoming a nervous tic. He couldn't stop watching her. That shimmering blade dangling over her bare toes made him nervous. What sort of person worked barefoot with sharp tools? And why should he care? He just wanted the damn keys already; he just wanted a shower, a bed, to be out of the car for more than ten minutes. He wanted to stop sweating. There was one thread of sweat in particular that was winding around his left shoulder blade and driving him insane.

". . . Mermaids."

"What?" Tom swerved his gaze back to Buzz, lost. Christ, how long had the man been talking?

"I said *everything*'s about mermaids this time of year,"

Buzz repeated pleasantly. "You're lucky, getting here just in time for the festival."

Tom saw Tess glance at him over her shoulder, her survey brief but pointed.

He cleared his throat, wondering what about any of this could be considered lucky.

"You know," he said, "I'd just really like to get those keys."

THE TWO MEN WALKED UP the driveway, through a maze of standing bird feeders, and into the red trailer.

"Excuse the mess."

Piles of folded linens covered almost every surface in the kitchen—the counter, the chairs. There was even a pile of washcloths on each of the four range tops.

"I'm never this disorganized," Buzz said, relocating a stack of bath towels to the dining table. "Usually I got all the cottages set up weeks in advance. But this year . . . I don't know. Losing Frank sort of took the wind out of my sails, I guess." Buzz pulled down a coffee tin from the windowsill above the sink, tilted it, and reached in. After a moment of fishing, he retrieved a loaded key chain and handed it to Tom.

"Now don't let all those keys freak you out," Buzz said. "Chances are half of them don't even go to anything anymore, but Frank figured you should have them all, just in case. I labeled the important ones—you'll see. The front door and the padlock for the lighthouse. Those old crows at the historical society might have gone and changed the lock—who knows? Maybe Frank warned you; they thought they were in line for the keeper's house too, so don't be surprised if they give you hell for a while over it."

Tom rolled the stack of keys in his palm, fanning them out with his thumb and seeing the tiny strips of masking tape on several. "They've already been in touch actually."

"Figures." Buzz glanced to the window, a thought sparking. "Your brother waiting in the car?"

Tom pocketed the collection of keys. "He's not here yet," he said, his voice unnecessarily firm, as if he were trying to reassure himself more than Buzz Patterson. "He'll be here soon."

"Well, in case you're wondering"—Buzz smoothed his beard—"I'm the only one in town who knows what happened. Why you're here, I mean. How Frank knew you."

"He didn't know us," Tom clarified sharply. "He didn't know anything about us."

"Of course not," Buzz said quietly with regret. "I didn't mean it that way. Hell, don't pay any attention to me, son. I say all the wrong things all the time. My sister, Joan, used to say that I was like a garbage disposal in reverse, that I spit all the crap back out. Frank always thought that was funny. He used to try to mend things between me and

Joannie. Didn't do much good. She and I never really saw eye to eye. Fought like cats and dogs from the time we were kids. You close to your brother, Tom?"

A loaded question if ever there was one, Tom thought, musing on his answer as he glanced to the window. "I try to be," he said.

Had to be, was more like it. Not a day went by that Tom didn't wish his younger brother could have been outfitted with one of those bracelets they put on criminals to monitor their whereabouts. What Tom wouldn't have given for such a device over the years when Dean would disappear for weeks at a time on one of his drinking binges, leaving Tom to scour the city for his whereabouts, only to have his younger brother, strung out and delirious, resurface without warning, promising not to vanish again.

"Frank said you're a teacher. High school."

"That's right," said Tom.

"Think you might try to find something around here?"

"That's my intention, yes."

"Wish you luck. It's been a bad few years. Cutbacks and all that. Might have to travel to find something."

"I'll do what I have to do."

When they were back outside, Tom tugged his cell phone out of his pocket, frowning down at the small screen.

"It's real hit-or-miss with those things around here," Buzz said. "And you might as well use it for a paperweight when you get down to the Point. You'd probably have more luck with a pair of cups and a string."

Tess emerged from the woodshop just then. Tom watched her cross the driveway, watched her skip up her steps, locking eyes with him for a deliberate moment before she slipped inside her cottage.

"Doesn't she make you nervous doing that?" Tom asked, staring at the watermelon door she'd closed behind her, a dried wreath tacked to it now crooked.

"Doing what?"

"Using those sharp tools without proper shoes. She could really hurt herself."

Buzz sighed. "It's not her toes I worry about," he said. "For the record, she doesn't know about you and your brother. I didn't see the point. You're here now, and I'll leave all that up to you. Who you want knowing, who you don't."

"My brother doesn't know," Tom said, "and I want it to stay that way."

"He doesn't know what? About me?"

"About any of it," Tom said evenly. "Dean doesn't know who Frank is, who he *was*. To *us*. My brother hates any kind of charity. He sees it as pity. He wouldn't have understood why I took the money at all, let alone as long as I did."

Buzz frowned. "This is a small place, son. If you didn't want him knowing, then maybe you should have stayed where you were."

"That wasn't possible. My brother has a hard time saying no to things that aren't good for him." Tom glanced around. "I'm hoping he could learn how to in a place like this."

"Frank said he struggles with alcohol."

"Frank had no idea what my brother struggles with. No idea whatsoever."

Tom began back to his car. Buzz followed.

"Now, you sure you don't want me to go down there with you?" Buzz asked. "CMP got your power on, but old houses can be finicky. Some are tough to warm up to. Old pipes, old wires. You never know what kind of dust you'll kick up when you flick a switch. It's been a while since anyone's really lived in that house, you know."

"Thank you, but I'll be fine, Mr. Patterson."

"Oh Jesus, call me Buzz. Everybody does."

Tom tugged open the driver's door and climbed in, yanked his seat belt across his chest, and snapped it locked.

Buzz glanced into the car's backseat, seeing only a duffel bag and a few boxes of books. "If you need anything," he said, "anything at all, you come right back, okay? Day or night. I promised Frank I'd look out for you."

Tom turned on the engine.

Buzz leaned down. "For what it's worth, he was sorry as hell for what happened, you know. He never forgave himself."

Unmoved, Tom considered Buzz with narrowed eyes, saying only, "Thank you for the keys," then pulling away.

TOM HAD ALMOST TOSSED FRANK'S first letter, not intentionally, of course (though he did often wonder later what might have transpired differently if he had). It was just

that there had been so many sympathy cards in the weeks
following the accident that Tom had had to pile them in a
milk crate at the bottom of the stairs. When Dean had
finally come home from the hospital and taken one look at
the teeming collection, Tom had whisked the whole cancelled lot into the hall closet.

It was only timing that had prevented Frank's letter
from landing in that milk crate graveyard. By the time the
tidy brown envelope had arrived among their mail, almost
four months had passed since that frozen winter night.
Even as Tom had opened the envelope, even as he'd unfolded
the stiff typed pages and the ten one-hundred-dollar bills
had spilled into his lap, so new and crisp he'd nearly cut
his thumbs counting them, he'd known it wasn't any ordin-
ary condolence note.

His first thought was that it had been a joke, someone's
sick attempt at humor, but that was too unimaginable.
Who would joke about being responsible for causing a car
to swerve off a snowy road and fleeing the scene, knowing
there were people injured—dying—inside? Who in his
right mind would find amusement in crafting such a horrible story of culpability—and punctuate it with a thousand dollars in cash?

The letter promised more monthly offerings of the
same amount, but Tom had doubted it. For that reason,
he'd put the money away and not so much as touched it for
almost a week, too unsure of what to do with it. After all,
there was no return address, no name, just an initial, *F*,

which might not have even been accurate, and gave no indication of gender. The debate within Tom was dizzying. His first thought had been to burn the bills, to waste them, to give them no purpose whatsoever, and by doing so, he would rob this murderous benefactor of his or her attempt at restitution.

But then Dean's pain pills had run dangerously low, and so Tom had untucked that envelope from his sock drawer and pulled out one of the stiff hundred-dollar bills. He'd taken the long way to the pharmacy, thinking that with the extra time he might still have a chance to change his mind, but he hadn't. Laying down that money had filled him with a clammy feeling that had spread across his skin like a chill. And there had been that suspicious look in the pharmacist's eyes as he'd rung up the prescription. Had Tom stolen the money? Was it counterfeit? How did an eighteen-year-old who'd previously paid for two months' worth of meds in dimes and quarters now arrive with a hundred-dollar bill?

When Tom pocketed the change and left with the package, he knew there would be no going back. Like a junkie who thought he could use once and not get hooked, so Tom would make himself and Dean addicts to this blood money—assuming more money came, which Tom remained certain wouldn't be the case. Until the following month, almost to the day, a second envelope, a second payment, arrived. And so the schedule began, and with it, the guilt. Dean could never know.

It would be several more months before their benefactor would identify himself as male, years before he'd sign his first name, which was Frank. And only in the year before his death would Frank resort to sending checks, and with them, the last name and address Tom had been denied for so long.

But of course, it had never been about blaming Frank Hammond. The truth was that for Tom there was a partnership in their guilt, his and Frank's, that in their own ways, they had both been to blame for the accident, so it had never been a question of guilt. What had angered Tom, what still did and probably always would, was that Frank had not served any penance for his crime, while Tom's life had been forever dismantled for his part. And worse, Tom's receipt and spending of Frank's blood money only served to further exonerate the man. But what choice had Tom had? Their parents, one a recently laid-off teacher, the other an out-of-work secretary, had fallen behind on their life insurance premiums in the months after their father's dismissal, leaving the boys with nothing but debt. Pills and physical therapists cost money, as did the cigarettes and alcohol Dean administered liberally when he decided the painkillers weren't working fast enough or lasting long enough.

But Frank had never known of Tom's complicity in that frigid evening's events, and that alone had, on many occasions, given Tom moments of great peace. Just to know that Frank Hammond believed himself solely responsible for the death of their parents, the death of Dean's Olympic dreams, sustained Tom on nights he would surely have stepped out on a busy street and been run over rather than face another night of looping if-onlys. *If only he'd never pushed Dean to take him to the party. If only their father had never answered the phone. If only Tom had asked Dean to look behind them.* Then maybe it would have been another car pushed off the side of the road, somebody else's parents thrown into an embankment, somebody else's lives shattered.

They were partners in crime, he and Frank, unwitting but bound forever.

And now Tom was here, in this empty house on an equally barren lot that resembled the deck of a great ship.

At least that was how it seemed to Tom as he rounded the last bend in the dirt road to the Point and the property came into view.

He pulled the Volvo in front of a vinyl-sided garage and climbed out to be greeted with a choppy breeze, sour with the tide. He was just glad to be on firm ground, to be there at last, even if it was like landing at the end of the world, he thought, looking gravely around the land. Still, he couldn't think of a more fitting place to see the end of his twisted partnership with Frank Hammond.

The keeper's house stood a ways beyond the edge of the driveway, settled in a sloping field, a modest clapboard building with a gambrel roof, its white paint aged to gray like old linen. Beyond it, far down the Point, he could see the shape of the lighthouse. Tom pushed through the wind and crossed the stretch of overgrown grass toward the house, climbed the front stairs to the narrow covered porch, and jiggled the key in the lock until the door gave way. A breeze followed him inside the house, stirring up the staleness of the damp room like a broom. There wasn't much to see—just a table with turned legs and two chairs in one corner; a doorway leading to a kitchen; white plaster walls, yellowed like old paper; bare wood floors rubbed dull in places; a few windows with views of the sea, framed by lace curtains heavy with dust.

You really went all out for us, didn't you, Frank?

Tom moved to the center of the room, taking it all in—the yawning cracks, the water stains like dripped coffee across the plaster ceiling. He crossed to the fireplace, dragged his fingers along the edge of the painted mantel, rolls of dust falling over the side. He made his way to the windows, parting the curtains to look through the milky glass, and there he saw the tower in full. It stood at the end of a weathered footbridge, rising up from its granite base to the top of the lantern room. It had to be thirty feet high, Tom guessed, though it looked smaller than he'd imagined it, or maybe it was simply dwarfed without a beam. Frank had written that the coast guard had decommissioned it in the thirties and built a new one up the road in Port Chester.

What a long walk it must have been for a keeper, Tom thought. The keeper would have trudged through that barren stretch of grass twice a day, sometimes more, the wind, or maybe snow, needling his skin. Tom had read of lighthouse keepers as a boy after visiting a tower on the banks of Lake Michigan. He'd been awed at the great weight of responsibility they undertook, their mission as both tenders and rescuers, seeing nature at her most treacherous and trying to intercede—and always under the sweep of that lamp.

What man didn't wish for a guiding light on the horizon of his life, a flash to signal danger or safety? Living next to a lighthouse that had no beam seemed ironic to him.

Tom let the curtain drop and turned for the stairs. The second floor was divided into four small rooms, each stifling with the warm smell of mildew and trapped tide. He moved to one window, pushed the curtains down their rusted pressure rod, and tugged up the sash, letting in a cool breeze that smelled of rain and seaweed. There wasn't much up here, either. Each room had only a single bed and a small dresser topped with a sturdy lamp, its pleated shade as yellowed as the walls.

Returning downstairs, he came into the kitchen and flipped a wall switch, bathing the stark room in a flat greenish light that flickered a moment, then stilled. It was just as bleak, with a range, a woodstove, an old refrigerator, countertops in speckled linoleum. The tap coughed and sputtered, running brown, then clear. Relief coursed through him.

He unpacked the car of his bag and his two boxes of treasured books. Then he opened a can of chicken soup and brought it to a gentle boil on the stove, drinking it from a mug at a table with a broken-off corner that he just knew he'd spend the next however many months catching his sleeve on.

He looked around at their new home, their new life.

Their one last chance after so many last chances.

1887

LYDIA HARRIS HAD ALWAYS BEEN terrified of the water. For as long as she could remember, the very smell of salt filled her with fear.

There was no logic to it. She'd never been close to drowning, never been tossed roughly into a wave and coughed and sputtered her way to the surface the way her sisters had. For one growing up on the Maine coast, not taking to the water was almost as blasphemous as loathing blueberries or fearing snow. Which was all the more reason why her acceptance of thirty-year-old sailor Linus Harris's marriage proposal had shocked everyone, especially her older sisters, Rachel and Pearl.

The truth was it had shocked Lydia a bit too, but that was how enormous her love was for him. She'd sooner live with her watery nightmares than live without him. And so she'd left her sisters in Kittery and followed Linus to Bridgeport, Connecticut, where he had secured work on a new fleet of fishing trawlers. He found them a sunny room in a boardinghouse near the wharf, though he promised to have them in a house of their own within the year, both of them certain she'd be pregnant with their first child by then. But after three years, none of their plans had come to fruition. Though Linus loved the work—as Lydia could plainly see each time her handsome husband returned through the door, stinking of salt, his face and hair burned by wind and sun—she couldn't conceive a child, and even worse, the nightmares she'd endured in their first year of marriage had not only persisted but strengthened in their terror: vivid, drawn-out visions of losing her husband to the blackness of the sea, dreams so dreadful that there was nothing Linus could say to erase them in those dark and terrifying moments after Lydia had woken, crying out, startled like an infant, and bursting into tears at once.

So when Linus returned home on a mild March afternoon with news of a keeper's post at a lighthouse in a small town in Maine called Cradle Harbor, Lydia nearly wept with relief.

"I take this to mean I should apply for the position?" Linus had teased, still holding Lydia after she'd buried herself in his arms in her joy.

She looked up at him, her wet eyes pooling with apprehension. "You wouldn't hate me?" she said, even as Linus carefully dried the streams of her tears with his thumbs.

"How could I ever hate you?" he asked.

"You love the water," she said.

"But I love you more."

And so it was settled. Rachel and Pearl, so happy to know their baby sister would be closer to them once again, made the long trip to Bridgeport days after learning the news, under the guise of helping Lydia to pack, though all the women knew it was a pale excuse since the young couple had been living in nothing but a single room and could fit the entirety of their worldly possessions into a handful of hatboxes.

"Linus says we'll have a house there," Lydia reported, settling herself between her sisters on the love seat, then rising soon afterward for more tea, too excited to stay still for long.

"As well you should," said Rachel, the eldest of the three sisters. "Now you can finally have those beautiful babies we've all been waiting for."

"Oh, you and your *babies*, Rachel." Lydia's sister Pearl had been blessed with milkweed blond curls that had not darkened even the slightest bit through the years, even as Lydia had watched her own pale hair turn an indecisive shade of brown at age thirteen. "Not every woman believes it's her calling to bear children, you know."

"We all know you certainly don't believe it," Rachel said.

"So be it." Pearl gave a mischievous smile over her teacup. "Maybe I just fancy my waist and my sleep far too much."

"You say that now," warned Rachel. "Just wait until Simon slips that ring on your finger and you find yourself awake at night, coming up with names for your children."

"First of all, dear sister," Pearl clarified, reaching for one of the iced tea cakes she and Rachel had brought, "Simon Wiggs will not be putting *anything* on my finger, least of all a ring, and if I should find myself in the unfortunate state of marriage someday, I suspect the only thing I will be lying awake over will be to think of ways to untangle myself from the situation."

Rachel just rolled her eyes. "You're incorrigible."

"That's what Simon said," replied Pearl, winking at Lydia.

Lydia laughed loudly, grateful more than anything to have the subject of motherhood turned away from her. Too embarrassed to admit their lack of success, she'd merely told her sisters that she and Linus had wished to wait for a more suitable living arrangement in which to bring their baby into the world.

When their giggles had subsided, Rachel said, "As thrilled as we are, I still think you're very brave, Lydieloo. It will be hard, hard work, this new job. This new life."

Hard? Lydia didn't think so. And Linus hadn't suggested that as he'd rattled off the list of his daily chores. Tending to the lamp and the fog bell, trimming the wick, washing the windows. Trekking up and down curved metal stairs, clock winding, checking the channel markers. It had seemed manageable enough. And he'd have help too, he'd told her. There was a neighbor just down the road from the lighthouse, a young man who'd assisted the last keeper.

Besides, Lydia thought as she poured her sisters more tea, there wasn't much chance of a man drowning in a lighthouse, was there? It wasn't as if a hand might reach up from the sea and pull him down from all the way up there.

"YOU'RE AWFUL YOUNG FOR A keeper."

Those were the very first words the man with the pointed chin said to Linus when they'd arrived at the Point three weeks later. Linus had smiled in his usual way, as if the man had been humoring him, when even Lydia could see the frosty tint of the old man's eyes.

"Our last keeper was retired," the man went on to say as he led them up the lawn to the keeper's house. "But then it's really a young man's job. All the up-and-down. Not to mention the walk just to get there."

Indeed, it was a long trip, Lydia thought, looking at the

path Linus had trudged through the hedges, the path she refused to follow, even as the old man had given her a wary look. This was as close as she planned to get to the lighthouse.

"It does seem far," she said to Linus later that afternoon as they watched the men unpack their things. "I thought you said the towers were always close. For emergencies."

"Some are," Linus answered. "It all depends."

On what? Lydia had wanted to ask. What could possibly have possessed the builders of this place to stand their lighthouse so far from the house? Not that she minded the siting. Hardly. If it meant she and their babies could sleep farther away from that crashing surf, she would be grateful.

Indeed, the house itself was lovely—lovelier than she had expected. There were built-ins and crown molding. Outside there was already a garden. The previous keeper's wife had started it, the pointed-chin man had said. She left tomato plants as high as sunflowers.

Lydia would see her plants twice as high in the fall. But it was only spring—*barely* spring, April, that quixotic month that enjoyed its tease. Just when the earth would finally begin to thaw and those tentative buds would poke their velvety heads through the softening soil, a nor'easter would blow through, blanketing a hopeful ground in two feet of snow for a week.

No, she would wait for May before she began to peel off the layers of their bedspreads, before she could throw up the sashes and keep them open. For all she knew, the coming week might find her carrying a child and dizzy with all the enviable symptoms of pregnancy.

Yes, she'd find her way out here on this rugged fingertip of earth. She'd steer clear of the rocks and the surf. There was a good deal of both grass and trees. If she stood right on a calm day, she might never even know she was so close to the water.

Still, the man with the pointed chin stopped in the parlor doorway and took Linus aside to whisper, "You think she can handle it out here, do you?"

"Of course she can," Linus answered, smiling at her. "My Lydie can handle anything."

LINUS LIKED THE WORK MORE than he expected; Lydia could see that at once, and it relieved her to no end. There was much to learn, which didn't bother him. He'd always loved new things and loved a challenge. Even his entries in the log book revealed his enthusiasm for his work. While he was required to just record his daily routines, Linus exceeded expectation and filled his journal with remarkable details, weather reports, wildlife sightings, birds that had landed on the gallery railings or nested in the eaves of the oil house. Each night, while they enjoyed tea, he would recite the passages to her, the habit quickly becoming routine. Lydia craved the readings, grateful for their intimacy, happy to know all her husband did and saw when she would look longingly down the walkway from their kitchen window, wondering what filled his hours away from her in a place she couldn't bear to see for herself.

It took only a few weeks for the town of Cradle Harbor to grow fond of the good-looking young couple who'd come to care for the lighthouse. They were that sort of people, warm at the outset, equally sociable, blessed with good humor and good hearts. Linus quickly made friends who told him at once that he was too gregarious to be a keeper. Since he was often in town to get supplies, sometimes he'd stop to chat with men along the wharf.

Lydia too made friends, most of whose husbands were fishermen.

"You must be anxious to start a family, dear."

"We're still settling in," Lydia had explained as politely as she could manage to the group of women in Annabeth Owen's kitchen a few weeks after they'd arrived. "There's no rush." But as she'd looked around at their expectant faces, Lydia could see that there was. Had none of them struggled to conceive? Surely she wasn't alone. Yet how would she know? To ask would have been unthinkable.

But that was to be in the past. Here Linus was relaxed. Certainly the post would have moments of danger, of anxiety. Just the other week a storm had lashed at the house and the tower with such intensity that Linus had spent the entire night in the lantern room, making sure the lamp stayed lit and watching the sea for ships in peril. And there was no question the work was constant and the hours long. But the chores never seemed to exhaust him the way work had on the sloop.

"You must be going out of your mind down there," said another woman whose name Lydia couldn't remember, though she was fairly certain it began with *T*. "I couldn't take it—I know that much."

"It'll be different when the babies come," Annabeth said, smiling. "You'll see. You'll never know quiet again."

It *would* be different, Lydia told herself, for the rest of the afternoon, and into the next week. And when her monthly came, as reliably and thickly as it had every month without fail since she was twelve, she told herself it was only a matter of time. She was only twenty-six. And besides, she still had so much to do. The garden she wished to expand. The rooms she wished to paper. The fruit she meant to can.

So she didn't worry.

"THIS IS ANGUS KEENE," Linus announced one day in early June, coming into the kitchen with a dark-haired man. "He's Miles's brother. He's the man I told you about. He'll be helping me. Helping *us*, really."

"Ma'am." The man tipped his cap to Lydia and smiled shyly. He was young, she thought, glancing quickly at his sturdy frame and the soft brown curls that crept out under his brim.

That night at dinner, Lydia served fish chowder and corn cakes.

"I met an interesting man in town today," Linus reported. "Eli Banks. He owns the cannery. A real character. You'd never know he was some big businessman. We got talking outside the post office. He asked me if I knew anything about sailboats."

"And of course you said . . ."

Linus grinned. "Not a damn thing."

Lydia smiled. "I'll bet."

"He's looking to buy one. He knows nothing about sailing. He has one in mind and wonders if I'd come by and give it a look, tell him what I think."

"Why? Is he going to buy it for you?"

"No," said Linus, "but he did say he'd invite me aboard for its maiden voyage."

"Sure he will." Lydia gave Linus a playfully suspicious glance. "More like invite you so that you could be his captain." Still, even as she said it, Lydia knew the suggestion of a day on a boat would have thrilled her husband. She knew how much Linus missed being out on the water.

"He seems young, doesn't he?" she asked, taking the seat across from her husband.

"Banks?"

"No, Angus."

"He's twenty-four," said Linus, then drew back in mock offense. "Are you saying I'm so *old*?"

"Hardly." Lydia laughed. At thirty-four, her husband was still as fit and youthful as he had been the day they'd met. Still, Linus reached across the table to tickle his wife for her teasing, getting in a good pinch to her side before she'd scooted out of reach, moving to the stove to refill his bowl.

"I still don't see why you need him here."

"An extra pair of hands is always wise," Linus said, pulling a corn cake from the basket. "Especially once you're with child. If you should need me, Angus can take over. He can man the lamp days at a time if necessary."

"But what of his own family?"

"He isn't married. He lives with Miles and Sarah down the hill. He has no ties to anyone here. He told me as much."

Lydia considered the information, thinking it curious. Angus was a good-looking man; surely there was someone who interested him in the village.

Linus wore a suspicious look when she returned with his bowl, wagging his butter knife at her. "I know what you're thinking, you know."

"What?" Lydia asked him.

"Don't you try to play matchmaker for that poor boy as you did with the Reynolds fellow. You leave him be."

"I did not," she defended, taking a corn cake and buttering it. "I merely suggested the Lewises' daughter was also fond of music."

"I need that young man here and paying attention," said Linus. "Work up there requires caution, Lydie. You find someone for him to fall in love with, and he'll become so stupid over her, he'll slip off the gallery."

"You're stupid over me, and you've yet to even trip over a loose brick," she said.

"That's because I'm remarkably steady."

"Yes, you are."

They smiled at each other, the smell of salted fish and creamy broth circling their bowls and filling the air between them with each sweep of their spoons.

ONE WEEK LATER, Eli Banks sent a carriage down to the Point.

"You could come too, you know," Linus said, Lydia walking beside him down the front steps of the house. It was a cool, crisp morning. A breeze carried the scent of new leaves.

"No, thank you." Lydia stayed on the grass while Linus settled into the buggy's upholstered seat, a faded plum that Lydia thought would make a lovely color for a nursery. "All this just to look at a silly boat," she marveled.

"Banks promises to have me back by lunch," Linus said.

"Good. I'm making ham and potato soup. You be sure and tell him it's inedible when it's cold and that I don't plan to leave it sitting forever on the stove." She blew her husband a kiss, and he grabbed the air to catch it.

BY TEN, the soup was made and fragrant in the kitchen, the smell of simmering ham detectable all the way upstairs as

Lydia cleaned their room and put away their clothes. By eleven, the morning clouds had finally cleared the sky, and the sun was strong enough to make yard work comfortable. She'd been meaning to start on the shallow stretches of earth that trimmed the base of the house, thinking how much she missed her rows of lavender and mint. She set down a folded cloth to protect her skirt and knelt at the end of the garden, turning the soil with her spade.

After a few moments, she saw movement out of the corner of her eye and spun around, startled. Angus Keene stood there, looking startled too.

"Sorry, ma'am," he said, moving toward her. "I didn't mean to scare you."

"No," she said, rising to her feet. "You didn't scare me. Linus told me you'd be here today. I just forgot, that's all."

"I had to get something from the oil house." Angus motioned to the red-roofed building at the top of the hill. "I meant to go around the other way, but I think the smell of whatever that is on your stove changed my mind." He smiled sheepishly. "I'll be cleaning the lamp for most of the afternoon if you need me for anything."

Lydia brushed the dirt from her hands, thinking she was wrong, that he didn't look quite so young standing there, squinting into the sun, with the shadow of a beard she hadn't noticed when she first met him. "You're welcome to some potato soup," she said, gesturing to the house. "It *is* practically lunch. I know I could eat."

"I didn't mean it that way," Angus said. "I wasn't sniff-ing for an invitation. . . ."

"I know you weren't. And it's not the best I've ever made, but it *is* hot. Biscuits too."

"I wouldn't feel right," he demurred. "Not with Mr. Harris not here."

"Oh, for goodness' sake," Lydia said. "Linus isn't that sort. And I have my suspicions you aren't, either. Besides"—she smiled at him—"I'm one of three children. Frankly, I don't know how to eat alone."

Angus chuckled at that. "All right then. Maybe a small bowl."

SHE SET A HEAPING SERVING in front of him a few minutes later, large enough to make him chuckle again.

"You're sure I'm not keeping you?" Angus asked, watch-ing Lydia as she joined him at the table.

"Not at all," she said. "If you must know—and don't you dare tell my husband—the truth is that I've been snooping most of the morning." She gave him a mischievous smile. "The previous keeper left quite a few things upstairs. Papers and books and such. Most of it was dreadfully boring, but I did find the most amusing book: *The Sea-farer's Wife's Handbook*, it was titled. You can't imagine it. It even contained instruction on how to hang chimes to quiet mermaid song, which is apparently very dangerous to sus-ceptible men's ears. Have you ever heard of such a thing?"

Angus bit back a small grin as he spooned his soup. "No, I can't say I have. I suspect that belonged to Captain Barton's wife. She was a bit off, I'm afraid."

"Linus said you were his assistant too?"

"That's right," Angus said. "I like the work. I like the quiet."

"It is that," Lydia said. "Although I imagine it's not quiet when Linus is there with you. My husband is one of the most talkative men I've ever known."

Angus nodded, then smiled. "He's good company. Captain Barton never said much. I don't mind either way."

"Oh, you'll make a wonderful husband with that attitude," she said.

He blushed as he wiped his mouth. "My sister-in-law hopes so. I think she's impatient to have me married so I'll move out."

Lydia smiled. "It will happen for you." There was a certain calm, a certain comfort in saying those words to someone else, having been the recipient of the same advice herself for so many years now.

"It's fine," Angus said. "I'm not in any rush."

They looked at each other for a moment then, long enough that Lydia looked away, feeling self-conscious. Angus must have sensed it too, because he was quick to suggest a new topic.

"You must like going up to the lighthouse."

"Oh no," Lydia said. "I don't go up there. I won't."

"You don't like heights—is that it?"

"I don't like the water."

Angus stared at her. Lydia shrugged, accustomed to the reaction now. "It makes no sense, I know," she said. "Married to a lighthouse keeper."

"Then you've never been up there?" he asked. "Not even once?"

Lydia shook her head.

"It's not so bad, you know. It's beautiful, really. I'd be happy to show it to you."

How many times had Linus offered the same? Lydia had lost count. And yet, Angus's simple suggestion left her with trepidation, the fluttering of possibility. So when they finished, she followed him back outside, taking one of Linus's coats just in case the wind was terrific, and they traveled the wooden walkway. She scanned the sea as she went. *It's calm as can be,* she told herself. *Not a whitecap in sight.*

Inside the tower, she felt a chill and pulled the sides of Linus's coat tighter around herself.

"You don't have to do it," Angus said, pausing a moment before beginning the curved metal steps that led to the lantern room. "I can walk you back if you've changed your mind."

"No," Lydia said firmly. "I haven't changed my mind."

Why she should go with him and not with Linus, Lydia wasn't sure. Maybe she wanted to boast of her courage to her husband, to surprise him. That was what she told herself as she followed Angus Keene upward, clutching her skirt high as she climbed the twisting stair. Her heart raced when they reached the trapdoor, thundered when she climbed up at last into the lantern room, grateful for Angus's hand when it reached down to close over hers and steady her final steps.

"Are you okay?" he asked.

"I think so," Lydia said, dizzy suddenly. Though several of the windows were covered with curtains to keep the sun off the lens, she could still see a sweeping view of the water. "Oh my," she gasped. "It is spectacular, isn't it?"

"Yes, it is."

"Do you ever go out there?" she asked, pointing to the gallery.

"Sometimes," Angus said. "But you don't want to go out there. It's not safe. The floor gets slick. And I've told Mr. Harris the railings are loose on one side."

"Oh, I wasn't asking to go out—don't worry." She glimpsed two small unmoving clumps of brown farther down the gallery, squinting to make them out. "What are those?" she asked.

"Birds," said Angus. "They get confused by the light and fly into the tower at night."

"The poor, tiny things," she whispered. "That's just awful."

"It is. Most mornings there are a few. We have to tend to them." Angus looked at Lydia. "Mr. Harris didn't tell you?"

"No," Lydia said. "Linus always spares me things like that."

Angus smiled gently. "As well he should."

Again, the air grew silent between them. Lydia felt foolish suddenly, being here with him, the way she'd so quickly accepted his invitation, only to find herself so nervous and afraid, she didn't know whether she could make it back down the stairs.

She touched her throat, then her temple. "I'm afraid I'm not as brave as I thought."

"It's all right," Angus said. "I'll go first, and I'll help you down."

"BANKS BOUGHT HER, JUST LIKE that!" Linus reported when he came into the house shortly before three.

Lydia was in the parlor, mending a pair of wool socks, fully recovered from her episode in the tower, her skin flushed with heat from the flames that crackled in the fireplace.

"So you think he's chosen well, then?" she asked.

"Oh, she's a beauty, Lydie."

Linus came beside her, dropping to one knee and taking her sewing from her hands. He tugged her down to the floor, sitting her between his legs in front of the fire. She pressed her hands around his. "Your fingers are like ice," she whispered.

"Then maybe I should put them somewhere warm."

There were benefits to living in a house far from neighbors, Lydia thought as she tucked Linus's hands under her skirts, closing her eyes as she felt his palms flatten on the insides of her thighs. It would have been easy enough to tell him of her adventure in his absence, of her time in the lantern room with Angus, of how she'd faced the view of that cold sea and not fainted, having come close, certainly, but having managed to survive. But she didn't. Instead, she took her husband's hand and led him up the stairs, thinking dinner could wait, everything could wait.

If ever there was a moment ripe for new life, this was it.

Two

THE CLOSED SIGN WAS ALREADY in the window by the time Tess arrived at Russell's Seafood Market at three and rushed up to the locked door. Pressing her face to the glass and squinting in, she saw Julie Russell behind the counter and rapped to get the young woman's attention over the din of oldies that Tess could hear through the glass.

Tess's oldest friend looked up and waved.

"You have no idea what I had to do to keep your scallops safe," Julie said as she opened the door, her short blond hair kept back with a red plastic headband. "Bitsy Pullman nearly wrestled me to the floor for them. And let me tell you, that woman's nails are *sharp*."

"Jules, you're a goddess!" Tess said, giving her friend a fierce hug as she stepped into the store. The chill of the room was a welcome contrast to the humidity outside; the wet, salty scent of seafood was always a comforting smell. When she was growing up, the Russells had been wonderful friends to her, their store and shingled cape just behind it a second home to Tess. Even now that Julie had a husband and a new baby of her own, she and Tess remained close, especially when festival season came around. Maybe it was because Julie knew how hard this time of year was on Tess, how her mother, Ruby, had savored the festival, had inhaled its magic like a fragrance till her lungs were full. When word spread that Ruby had drowned in the cove, it was Julie and her parents who'd come down with hot meals and warm hearts to comfort Buzz and Tess.

"Where is everyone?" Tess asked, glancing around.

"Where do you think?" Julie said as she returned behind the counter to gather Tess's order from the case. "Dan and Dad are working on the float with Timmy, and Pat and Mom are over at the restaurant stockpiling chowder as if it were the end of the world."

"It can't be," Tess said. "Tomorrow, fine. But let me have tonight."

Julie grinned, snapping the top on a dish of lobster meat. "Think Pete'll do the Dash with you this year?"

"He'd better," said Tess. "I evicted three generations of daddy longlegs from behind my bathroom sink for that man. I'm going to spider hell."

"You know, I heard that guy moved into the lighthouse this morning."

"Who told you?"

"Who do you think?" Julie gave Tess an even look over the top of the display case. "The phone tree went into effect two seconds after Libby Wallace saw him pull in for gas at Wiley's."

"Of course it did." Tess strolled over to the window, looking out at the green where festival workers were busy setting up booths and hanging lights in the branches of the oaks that lined the square. She knew better than any-one how fast news of a stranger in town traveled. "He came by for the keys."

"Then you met him?"

"Only for a minute."

Julie smiled. "Libby said he's sort of handsome."

Was he? Tess hadn't really noticed. She'd been too busy watching him fumble to defend himself when he'd been caught spying on her, at the way he'd pulled at his collar as if his tie were choking him. She grinned at the memory, feeling a small but fleeting spark of remorse for accusing him, sure even as she'd said it, that he hadn't meant to spy at all. Something about Tom Grace told her he didn't find humor in life the way she'd learned to. Teasing him had been too tempting. And she'd never been one to resist temptation.

"Here you are, m'lady."

Julie arrived at the counter with two brown bags. Tess rushed back, opened each one, and peered in, drawing in a deep breath of the fragrant shellfish. She closed the bags and glanced up to find her best friend's eyes pooling with concern.

"What?" Tess asked.

Julie shrugged. "Nothing. I just know how badly you want this to work out, that's all."

"I want a lot of things, Jules. I want a new muffler for the Bug. I want a dishwasher. I want my thighs not to rub together when it's hot."

They laughed at that, but they both knew her craving for Pete Hawthorne wasn't the same as any of those things—not even close.

Still, Julie's expression remained strained. "He's not the only man in the world, you know."

Tess rolled her eyes. "God, you're as bad as Buzz."

"We worry about you. So sue us."

"And lose all this free fish? No way." Tess leaned over and kissed her friend good-bye on both cheeks.

"Call me!" Julie shouted after Tess as she moved to the door, tugged it open, and rushed back out into the afternoon.

THE BANNER WAS CROOKED.

Edith Hawthorne had been vexed with the inarguable knowledge since that afternoon, when she'd driven her Buick into town, headed for the historical society's meeting, and nearly steered right off the road as she'd squinted up at the swath of powder blue vinyl that stretched from one side of Wharf Street to the other. Just to be certain, she'd driven around a second time, and sure enough, it was as crooked as Ida Purcell's bottom teeth.

It was no surprise to her. This was what came with laziness. Edith could remember the early days of the festival when a man would never dream of setting foot on the green in anything less than a collared shirt and shoes with socks. Women wore slacks or skirts, and if you so much as dropped a straw on the grass, someone would be on your heels to snatch it up.

Not anymore.

Nowadays you didn't dare look too long into the crowd for fear you might see some vulgar show of skin or read something crass on the back of a T-shirt. Now the green grew littered and trampled after just a few hours. By the time the festival was over on Sunday afternoon, the town would look like a bug-splattered windshield in need of a bottle of Windex.

"Okay, maybe it's a *little* off center," Vera Blake

consented wearily, tired of standing in front of the museum's picture window and taking her seat around the oak conference table instead.

"A little?" Edith looked back at the historical society's secretary as if she'd suggested the Tower of Pisa's lean was barely noticeable. "It's atrocious. It's like an airplane in a nosedive."

Mary Sturgis left her post too and took her seat. "I told Bill that Harold wasn't up to it this year, but you know Bill."

"Awful," said Edith. "I've got a good mind to get Denny to bring our ladder and fix it myself."

"There's still no word from Tom Grace," Mary said. "I checked the voice mail *and* the e-mail this morning. Nothing."

"He obviously means to shut us out," Edith said. "It's all well and good not to return phone calls a thousand miles away. I'd like to see him ignore our request when we're standing two feet in front of him."

"Did you look into the back taxes?" asked Vera. "You said you were going to the town office to check."

"I did," Edith said. "They're all paid up."

Mary frowned, stymied. "What about an inspection? Do we know it's livable in the condition it's in? We could always force him out that way."

"There's a brother too, remember," Vera added. "Don or Dan—"

"Dean," corrected Mary.

"I don't care what that will said; Frank would never have wanted this," declared Edith, folding her arms decidedly. "It doesn't make sense."

"We should leave word at the house," said Mary. "Drive down there this instant and leave a note on the door, so the minute that rude man arrives, he knows we don't plan to leave him be until he agrees with our terms. Don't let him get too comfortable."

Vera rolled her eyes to the ceiling.

Edith nodded, lifting a finger the color of uncooked shrimp. "We'll take my car."

TOM GRACE WAS STANDING IN THE BATHTUB, trying to understand why not a drop of water would come out of the showerhead, when he heard the rumble of tires. He came downstairs and walked out to the porch just in time to see three women climb out of a wood-paneled Buick and make their way across the lawn. The one in front with the tidy knot of white hair and green rubber boots fancied herself the leader, Tom could tell, but as was clear by the close proximity of the others to her heels, her authority was by no means unanimous.

He guessed at once who they were.

He would be civil, he assured himself as he approached them—civil but firm.

"Mr. Grace?" The woman in front stopped, and the others fanned around her like nervous chorus girls. "What a nice surprise. We thought you weren't due in for another day. I'm Edith Hawthorne, president of the Cradle Harbor Historical Society. We spoke on the phone." Edith extended her arms to make her introductions. "This is Mary Sturgis, our treasurer, and Vera Blake, our secretary."

"Welcome," said Mary. "I hope we haven't caught you at a bad time?"

"Well, actually, you have," Tom answered. "I was just in the middle of a plumbing repair and I—"

"Repair?" Edith leaned forward, latching onto the word. "Is there something wrong with the house?"

Tom looked between the women, reading their eager expressions.

Mary clasped her hands together. "We'd just like a few minutes of your time."

"I thought I made my position clear on the phone," Tom said.

"You did, indeed," said Edith, "but now that you're here, we thought you might see *our* position in a different light. Now you can understand why people would want to see where Linus and Lydia Harris lived, where the tragedy first took shape."

"Frank *did* explain the historical significance of this property, didn't he?" Vera asked.

"Oh, I do admire you, Tom." Mary glanced wistfully up at the house. "Most people wouldn't last a night in there. So bleak and drafty. And rumors of ghosts."

"That was why they had to decommission the tower, you know," said Vera. "The keepers kept abandoning their posts, saying they could hear Lydia's footsteps on the stairs. It just got to be too much."

"Fortunately I don't believe in ghosts," Tom said evenly.

"All the same," said Edith, "it must need a daunting amount of work. I assume Frank had it inspected for you? That wouldn't be much of a gift to leave you a house that wasn't up to code. The state's housing inspectors can be quite ruthless in their standards, you know."

"Now, Tom," said Mary, "if you aren't prepared to assume the responsibilities of this historic site, we can certainly make arrangements to relieve you of this burden."

"No one will be *relieving* me of this property," Tom said firmly.

"Then you won't mind if we recommend an inspection from the State Historic Preservation Office as soon as possible," said Edith. "This house is of great historical significance to this town, and we simply can't allow it to continue to fall into disrepair."

"It's not in disrepair."

"You just said there was a problem with the plumbing," Mary reminded him.

Tom frowned, feeling bamboozled. "I didn't say *problem*."

"No, you used the word *repair*," clarified Vera.

"What we're trying to say," continued Edith, "is that unless you intend to make the necessary corrections, we will have no choice but to alert the state to the conditions Frank left you and your brother to contend with."

Mary folded her hands over her purse. "The safety of our residents is our primary concern. You do understand?"

"I understand you're threatening me with eviction if I don't let you bring strangers through my house," said Tom.

Only Vera's face revealed a hint of remorse. Edith and Mary stood firm, not denying his accusation. The air between them fell silent but for the clanging of the loose garage door in the distance. After a long moment, Edith pointed to the car and said, "Come, ladies. Let's leave Mr. Grace to his repairs."

Tom watched them march across the grass and climb back into their car, watched the Buick catch the soft shoulder on its way out, fishtailing briefly, then righting itself to rumble out of view behind the pines.

TESS STOOD IN HER UNDERWEAR at the foot of her bed, considering her options.

She'd wear the violet top. She looked good in the violet. She *felt* good in the violet—sexy. It wasn't tight, and it didn't make anything look lumpy or strained. She knew Pete liked red, but her mother always said red was a fickle color—it was fine to wear in the daylight, when all it could attract were bees and butterflies, but after sunset, red was just asking for trouble. It was why she never drank red wine or ate red meat past six, and for the longest time, neither did Tess.

But then Ruby had all sorts of theories when it came to colors.

"What about green?" Tess had asked once when they'd been living in California. "Is green okay?"

She and Ruby had been sharing a corned beef sandwich on the roof of their apartment building, miles from the water but pretending they were on the deck of the *QE II*, their legs stretched out and growing pink, their toes, painted just that morning, already chipped. "Green is fine," her mother had answered, "so long as it isn't too yellow. Something closer to blue is really best."

Tess had frowned at that. "What's the matter with yellow?"

"Nothing. On its own, it's transporting. But you have to be careful when you blend colors. You really do."

"You mean when you're painting?"

"I mean all the time." Ruby had reached out then and wiped a streak of dressing off Tess's cheek.

"I like peach," Tess had announced, tearing into a package of broken saltines they'd taken from the salad bar, spraying crumbs into the air. "And I like olive green and copper and watermelon too."

"You can like any color you want," her mother had declared, wiping her hands on the towel they were sitting on.

Tess picked out the largest pieces. "Except white."

"Except white," her mother had concurred.

Dressed now, Tess moved to the kitchen, hearing the

chime of the oven done preheating. There wasn't much left to do, she decided, giving the room a look. She'd set the table hours ago, put out candles, turned on the stereo. She'd made the lasagna; now all that was left was to bake it. She pulled the pan out of the fridge, hearing a knock as she opened the oven door. She knew it was too early to be Pete when she called out, "Come in!"

Buzz stepped inside, holding a box of lightbulbs in one hand. "I noticed the shed's outside light wasn't lit. I brought you a new bulb, just in case you'd run out."

"Thanks." Tess watched him set the box down on the table, knowing he hadn't come by for a burned-out lightbulb.

Buzz stuffed his hands into his pockets and rolled back on his heels as he surveyed the interior, taking note of the table. "Expecting company, huh?"

She gave him a disapproving look as she bumped the oven door closed with her hip. "You know I am."

"Must be nice."

Tess reached into the fridge for the bottle of white she'd been chilling and set it down on the counter, refusing to take the bait, knowing that wouldn't stop him. Sure enough, he pressed on. "I mean, the guy sneaks out of here before dawn and then gets to sneak back after dark to a five-star meal. Hell of a deal if you ask me."

"I *didn't* ask you," Tess said, yanking the cork out of the bottle hard enough to cause a loud pop. "And he doesn't *sneak*. You make him sound like a criminal."

"Well, if the shoe fits . . ."

Tess rolled her eyes, refusing to let him squash her delight tonight. It was the same every time Pete came back into her life; she'd face the court of Buzz and plead her case, always to the same verdict, no matter the evidence.

"Just seems fast to me, that's all," he said. "Three days ago, he's living with her. Today, he's all done and making house with you."

"You moved me and Mom here in less time than that," Tess pointed out.

"Yeah, well." Buzz frowned, thwarted. "That was different," he said.

"How?"

"I wasn't a creep."

Tess turned back to the wine and waved at him over her shoulder, seeing there'd be no reasoning with him. "Good night, Buzz. Love you. Don't let the bedbugs bite."

"Yeah, yeah, yeah . . ." Buzz sighed and wandered back to the door. Reaching for the knob, he stopped and turned back. "He seems nice, doesn't he?"

"Who?"

"Tom Grace."

Tess drew down a wineglass from the cabinet. "Don't even," she warned.

"What?" Buzz shrugged innocently. "I just said he was nice; I'm not trying to play matchmaker."

Tess gave him a dubious look.

"I'm only saying he's new in town and maybe you

could, I don't know," Buzz stammered, "bring him a damn pie. Something neighborly."

"I don't have time to bake, Buzz."

The sweet and damning smell of pumpkin cheesecake was fragrant in the air, not to mention the cheesecake itself that sat prominently, cooling, in the center of the table. Buzz cocked his head toward it as he opened the door. "Yeah," he said on his way out, "I can see you don't."

Three

NIGHT FELL, creeping into the keeper's house like an indigo fog. Swollen banks of blue-gray clouds rolled across the sky, parting briefly to send flashes of sun through the milky windows, casting shadows up the yellowed walls, turning them butterscotch, then gold, shivering shafts of silver that rode the cupped seams of the floorboards.

Tom closed the bathroom door and sighed. He was done. Whatever term they used in boxing when a fighter wished to surrender to his opponent, Tom was calling it. No matter what he did, no matter what he twisted or flipped or tugged, he couldn't draw a single drop of water out of that tub. And worst of all, he was ten times sweatier and fouler than he had been when he'd started. He'd never wanted anything in his whole life as badly as he wanted a shower. It wasn't just the sweat; it was the tension. His whole body ached with it. He felt as if he'd been in a perpetual state of clenched muscles since he'd arrived, and being in this dark, empty house wasn't helping. He worried about Dean getting there; he worried more about him *not* getting there. What if Buzz Patterson had been right? What if Tom had made a terrible mistake bringing his brother here? What if Dean found out that Tom had taken charity from the man who'd stolen Dean's dream and lied about it for almost seventeen years?

Tom gripped the banister as he came down the stairs, dizzy with it all.

He needed air; he needed space.

He thought of Buzz Patterson, his bright red trailer on the hill, his stepdaughter walking barefoot through a sea of woodchips on that uneven floor.

Anything you need, Buzz had said. *Day or night*.

Tom looked at the clock, frowning at the late hour and hoping the man meant it.

WHEN THE TURN TO THE cottages was caught in the pale cone of the Volvo's headlights, Tom followed the road and parked at the bottom of the slope, relieved to see Buzz

Patterson's porch light on. He climbed up the path to the door, a change of clothes in a roll under his arm, and knocked several times on the metal door, waiting in the faint light while squinting and swatting at an onslaught of moths drawn to the bulb just as he had been. He pulled the collar of his sport coat up to his jaw and folded the corduroy lapels across his chest. It wasn't a cold wind, but it had a bite to it.

After several minutes, he gave up and walked back down to the car. He was reaching for the door handle when he heard a woman's voice behind him.

"He's at Pike's."

Startled, he turned and found Tess Patterson standing at the screen door of her porch. He wondered how long she'd been there and whether she'd watched him go to the trailer. Maybe she'd even seen him swinging at bugs like an idiot. Most likely she had.

"Buzz goes every Monday." She pushed open the door and stood on the top step, leaning against the screen to keep it ajar, a glass of wine in her hand. The faint smell of cream sauce floated toward him. "It's dollar-draft night," she said. "He never misses it." She gestured to the bundle under Tom's arm with her glass. "Moving out already?"

"No," he said, glancing down. "I was actually going to ask Buzz if I could use his shower. I can't get the one in the house to work, and I'm . . . well, I . . ."

"You stink."

"Right. That."

Tom met her eyes then, seeing a brief flash of softness there. She was drunk; he could tell at once. It wasn't just the wine in her hand—it was her voice. He had learned to recognize that faraway sound, the tone of someone who thought she might be in a dream, or maybe just hoped.

Above them, a set of wind chimes knocked together, filling the air with their music.

"Why so many of them?" Tom asked. "They're all over town."

"It's tradition. To honor Lydia." Tess rolled her wineglass under her lip, giving him a narrowed look. "You don't know much for someone living in the keeper's house, do you?"

"I guess not."

"Don't you care what happened there? Don't you want to know about the Mermaid Mutiny?"

"I don't have much interest in fairy tales."

"That explains that line down the middle of your forehead," she said, pointing with her glass. "You shouldn't worry so much."

Tom touched his brow reflexively. Easy for her to say, he thought. This woman who was so carefree, she worked with sharp blades over her bare feet.

He glanced to the trailer. "I can wait for Buzz in my car."

"He could be hours."

"I don't mind waiting."

"Or you could use mine."

"Yours?"

"I do have one, you know," Tess said, a teasing smile pulling at her lips. "I do bathe."

"I'm sure you do. I didn't mean . . ." What *did* he mean? Suddenly Tom was aware of the emptiness around them, the vastness of the night; he wasn't used to the blackness of the country. Then behind her, in the beckoning sliver of soft light where her cottage door had been left ajar, he caught the smallest glimpse of a warm cocoon just steps beyond where they stood. He wanted to come inside. Looking at her, a glance intended to be quick that caught and held instead, he thought, he *believed*, she wanted him to say yes.

"You're sure it's no trouble?" he asked.

"I wouldn't have offered if it was," Tess said. "I tell people when I don't want them in my house."

Tom thought it over a moment longer, but there seemed little point in waiting. He climbed the steps, and without a word, he followed her in.

THE SMELL OF CREAM SAUCE and garlic was much stronger once he stepped inside. He couldn't remember a time when anything had ever smelled as good. More evidence of her work filled the interior. There were several sculptures, a wood relief of an underwater scene, carefully carved crabs and scallop shells, a sandpiper and a heron. Tom's eyes drifted around the room, catching briefly on a blue and green painting of a girl at the edge of the shore.

Then he saw the table. It was neatly set, candles flanking an uncut pan of lasagna, an opened bottle of wine, and unmatched silverware on a lavender tablecloth.

He looked at her. "You're waiting for someone."

"I thought I was." Tess scooped up the bottle of wine and held it out to him. "Join me?"

"No, thanks."

"Suit yourself." She refilled her glass and drank deeply.

Inside now, under the light, Tom could see that she'd been crying; her eyes were slightly puffy, her lashes clumped and wet. He wondered what sort of man she'd been expecting and why that man had changed his mind.

Tess carried her wine to the table and took a seat, her toes curling over the chair rail. Tom felt out of place suddenly, this exposure of her heartbreak more revealing than seeing her breast that morning. He stepped toward the door, reached for the knob, then stopped. A warm rush of concern filling him, he turned back to her, suddenly not sure he should leave her this way.

"Will you be all right?" he asked.

"I don't think so." Her eyes filled. "You want to know the craziest part?" she asked. "The cheesecake didn't even crack. They always do, but this one didn't. It was perfect. Anyone would have said that was a sign. Wouldn't *you*?"

Tom nodded, not because he had any idea what she was talking about but because he felt it was the kind thing to do. She seemed so fragile to him now, the indignant woman outside her woodshop that morning nowhere in sight.

He couldn't help himself. "He's a fool not to come. You're beautiful."

Tess looked up at him, her moist eyes bright and wide. He'd startled her, Tom thought. Or maybe she didn't believe him. He couldn't quite believe himself that he'd said it, even as the words had sailed out of him. It wasn't like him. It was nothing like him.

He forced his gaze to the bathroom door. A shower, he thought. He needed a cold shower. But the room was so comfortable, full of smells he never got to enjoy. There was so much color—and the music. He rarely had music playing anymore, and he missed it. Life with Dean never afforded him the luxury of those pleasures.

"Maybe a quick shower," he said. "I'd be grateful."

And as he moved to the bathroom door, as he opened it and stepped in, he heard her whisper behind him, "Me too."

IT WAS A TINY SHOWER, so small Tom could barely turn around in it, but he didn't care. He groaned the minute the hot water hit his scalp, closed his eyes, and let the stream pour down his forehead, his nose, his shoulders. A collection of nearly empty shampoo and conditioner bottles sat crowded and dented in a plastic basket that hung from the showerhead. He didn't want to smell like anise or cinnamon or pears, so he scrubbed his hair with the bar of soap he'd brought with him, the lather meager but enough.

Done, he took a towel from the wicker shelf and looked around as he dried off, marveling at all the decoration in the tiny space, the dried roses that wreathed the mirror, the mirror itself painted silver and covered in stenciled purple stars.

And mermaids. Christ, there were mermaids *everywhere*. While he shaved, he stared at a tiny figurine perched in her soap dish. A painting of one, no bigger than a postcard, hung on the back of the door. Another mermaid, this one ceramic and no doubt a Christmas ornament he decided by its telltale hanger, swung from the arm of the room's only light. In the hollow of the toothbrush holder sat a plastic cup with a mermaid decal on it.

So this was how it was to live in Cradle Harbor, he thought. It meant growing up in a world of fantasy. Indeed, she'd acted as if the town's legend were fact and not folklore. But no wonder she had such delusions, surrounded by all these trimmings, this soft blanket of magic. Tom envied her just a bit. What he wouldn't have given for one night of fantasy, to surrender to the unexpected.

When he stepped out of the bathroom, he found her asleep, one leg dangling over the side of her bed. He approached her slowly, not wanting to startle her a second time in one day if she woke up, but it was clear from her breathing, her mouth open and releasing a whistling snore, that there was little chance of that.

Gently he lifted her legs onto the bed, but when he moved to pull the quilt over her, Tess stirred and reached for him, catching his tie, her tug just enough to unbalance him. There was a moment when her eyes fluttered open, an instant when Tom was certain she saw him, saw who he was, and who he *wasn't*, but still she found his lips.

It was a warm kiss, tasting of wine and gingersnaps, but when Tom tried to right himself, Tess's arms circled his shoulders, her hands linking, locked, and then he was dragged down on top of her, the movement so swift that he didn't have time to shift before she'd spooned against him, pulling his arms around her.

He froze, staring at the crown of her head, seeing the uneven part of her auburn hair. He could smell the pear shampoo he'd seen in the shower and couldn't help taking in deep, sweet breaths of it.

When he moved to slip away, she gripped his hands. He stilled.

"Hold me," she said. "Hold me tight."

So he did, wrapping his arms around her, feeling the fullness of her breasts push against his forearms, her breath hot against the insides of his wrists.

It made no sense to stay. He'd only come for a shower. He didn't know her, and what he did know of her, he didn't understand. But still he remained, his palms curved over the swells of her breasts where she'd set them.

Just a few minutes, he told himself, until she was asleep, deep enough that he could untangle her from his arms, until he could gently unlace her fingers from his. Over the top of her head, he watched the clock on her cluttered nightstand, her glass of wine precarious atop a pile of magazines. Five minutes passed, then ten.

It was almost thirty minutes before Tom finally tried again to move away from her, and when he did, he did so carefully, like a lover not quite ready to leave.

Tom knew it would have been best to flee, to head for the door before Tess woke up, but he couldn't. Instead, he took her glass of wine off its dangerous post on the nightstand and carried it to the kitchen counter. He covered her perfect cheesecake and the pan of lasagna and returned them both to the fridge. On his way past the table, he blew out the weeping candles. Only then did he finally go, closing the door quietly behind him as he finally stepped back outside into the crisp night that no longer seemed so vast, the ceiling of stars above remarkably bright.

Text sent 9:14pm to 312-555-1614:

hey, tommy. just left cleveland.
how's the lighthouse?
seen any mermaids yet?
c u soon. dean

The old mattress released a breath of warm, mildewed air when Tom dropped onto it; the sheets, cool and worn, smelled faintly of mothballs. He'd seen a clothesline on the side of the house. He'd hang everything from it tomorrow.

It was stifling under the eaves. He rose and pulled up the window sash, a gust of damp air blowing in and cooling his warm skin. He could see the tower in the distance. Moonlight painted its ivory shell a shade of periwinkle, just pale enough to contrast its tapered shape against the blue-black expanse of the sea, the lantern room and its iron gallery glinting faintly at its top.

He lay back down on the bed and rested an arm under his head. He didn't know what to do with himself when Dean wasn't around, when he didn't have to constantly keep on top of his brother to make sure he wasn't drinking too much or eating too little, when he wasn't driving Dean's one-night stands home because Dean'd had too much to drink the night before and couldn't be roused from sleep. For the last one, a stripper named Burgundy, Tom had even made breakfast, scrambled eggs and wheat toast, while she'd regaled him with stories of five-hundred-dollar lap dances. When he'd dropped her off at her apartment, she'd tried to give him money for gas, fistfuls of crumpled singles; he'd declined.

Now Tom closed his eyes, demanding sleep, but instead, warm thoughts of Tess Patterson tore through him like sore muscles each time he turned on the mattress. He remembered the way she had fit her body against his, the smell of her skin, the view of her nightstand interrupted by her hair, pear-scented and tinted copper, the mole behind her ear, the lobe dotted with three holes.

He opened his eyes and stared at the sloped ceiling, trying to focus on the tiny cracks in the plaster.

He was tired. Lonely. And Tess Patterson was beautiful. It was natural he'd be aroused. Not that he could ever be interested in a woman like her, a woman that unpredictable, that uncontrolled. God, no.

Tom kicked the sheets free at the end of the bed and let his feet hang over the edge.

There, he thought. Much better. He closed his eyes, seeing the shape of the tower behind his lids, black against a pewter sky. He'd sleep now.

And soon, he did. But several times in the night, he dreamed he heard the phone. Once he even rushed from bed to answer it. But every time, the cell sat dark, and eventually he slept through.

Tuesday

Three Days before the
Mermaid Festival

BANKS'S WIFE, A PRICKLY WOMAN named Millicent, told her husband that he had no business buying a boat he couldn't steer, so Banks assured her he knew a man who could: a lighthouse keeper just a few months into his post, a sailor who missed his time on the water. Linus Harris was his name, and he had assured Banks that he could manage a modest boat with ease, and certainly take leave of his duties at the tower for a short sail.

—*The Mermaid Mutiny and More:*
A Complete History of Cradle Harbor

Four

BEVERLY PARTRIDGE DREW DOWN HER sunglasses and surveyed the village of Cradle Harbor from the front seat of
her rented sedan.

She hadn't expected it to be so busy, so colorful. When
Frank had spoken of his hometown—which he'd done so
few times over the years—he'd called it quiet, sleepy. He'd
talked of thick banks of morning fog rolling across the
sea, of hearing nothing but the faraway clanging of moor-
ings on the water, gulls squawking at one another on an

empty pebble beach—except during the festival, he'd admitted once. Frank had said that the first weekend of August turned the town and all its inhabitants on its ear, like a sudden breeze overturning a picnic.

Beverly had waited for so long for him to reveal his home to her, to share these pieces of himself, but he'd refused. In the beginning, she'd told herself it was his right to keep secrets. After all, the reason a man had a mistress was to forget himself, not be reminded. But as the years had passed, three then five, her patience had waned. By ten years into their affair, her curiosity had turned to craving. When his wife, Joan, had died, Beverly had pleaded with Frank to let her come and be with him after the funeral. He'd told her it wasn't possible, wasn't right, and so she'd stayed away, sure that with Joan's passing, his tight grip on his other life would loosen and Beverly would finally be granted access to the part of him he'd kept hidden from her. But in the months that followed Joan's death, instead of turning to Beverly as he'd done for nearly fifteen years, Frank began to turn away. His calls came less frequently; his visits too. Where once she'd have looked forward to handwritten letters at least every other week, now only a few postcards came. They were nothing but loose, rambling sentences, useless observations about the weather and the loss of sunlight as fall approached. Beverly had scoured them like the map to a great treasure, sure there were hidden pledges of love somewhere in the few lines.

It was his death that was the final straw. No wonder

he hadn't told her how ill he had become. Even to the very end Frank had wanted to keep her from finding out. Surely he'd known if he confessed how close he was to dying, she would have rushed to his side, making the pilgrimage despite his orders that she not come. And now she knew why he had never told her. It seemed she wasn't his only secret.

It would never have occurred to Beverly to search the Internet for information about her lover. At fifty-eight, she had little patience for computers, but when her older son, Daniel, had grown weary of her constant grief over not knowing more about her beloved's death, he'd suggested she do an online search. He'd offered to do it for her, but Beverly had been too afraid of what her son would certainly find in an obituary.

But it was she who was shocked at what she found.

It was like unwrapping something fragile. With each click of the mouse, Beverly couldn't believe the layers she peeled away, and with each one, a startling discovery; the man she thought she knew she hadn't known at all. And clearly, based on the outrage and shock of the town residents, they hadn't known him, either.

Frank had bequeathed property to a pair of young men named Grace. The news had shocked her breathless, and so Beverly had searched on, stopping only when she came across an article from a local paper that quoted a resident—the head of the town's historical society, in fact—who boldly suggested that the young men might be Frank's illegitimate sons. The mere suggestion had filled Beverly with such a sense of betrayal, she'd nearly collapsed with it. But instead, she'd stayed glued to the computer for the rest of the night, searching for everything she could find on Frank Hammond and the brothers to whom he'd bequeathed the town's precious lightkeeper's house.

Frank had stopped her from finding out the truth when Joan had died; he'd stopped her before his own death. But he couldn't stop her now. By that next morning, her eyes blurry but her thoughts crystal clear, Beverly had decided she would go to Cradle Harbor, the epicenter of her lover's life and lies. After all, she was as entitled to answers as any of them.

He won't leave his wife; they never do. How many times had Beverly heard that wisdom imparted to other women she'd known over the years? But she hadn't wanted Frank all to herself—at least not in the beginning. By the time she and Frank had met, her husband, Clark, had been dead almost two years and Beverly had come to enjoy her independence. She wasn't looking to marry again, wasn't looking to have more children. She knew she was a pretty woman, the sort that men looked twice at, looked long at, even when they knew you saw them watching. Not that it was all luck. She knew better than to be so smug. She'd taken care of herself over the years—her figure, her skin—and it showed. Even pregnant, she'd kept her weight gain low, and she'd made sure to get back into shape quickly after each delivery. It had been important to her to keep her body intact. It was still.

Not that the transition was an easy one. No matter how quickly she regained her figure, Beverly had found herself struggling to resume her normal intimacy with Clark. This was not because she didn't love her husband, but because she never understood how a woman could be both mother and lover. Once Daniel was born, she had felt a strange distancing from Clark, an alteration that she was all too aware of; yet there was no stopping it. When Frank had appeared, there was no confliction. He knew her only as a woman, and Beverly embraced his vision entirely, soaking up his attention like parched soil.

She'd been sure of so many things. Then she'd learned about Tom and Dean Grace.

Winding her way into town, Beverly had tried to imagine Frank driving these roads, maybe Joan beside him. Each car she'd passed, she had wondered if Frank had known the driver, and how well. She was especially nervous to meet this Buzz Patterson. Frank had spoken highly of his brother-in-law over the years, the only relative he'd ever revealed anything about. Buzz Patterson owned seaside cottages and rented them out, which was perfect, really, since she'd need a place to stay. She was confident that Frank had never revealed their affair to his brother-in-law, so there would be no risk of exposure should she try to draw information. And why wouldn't she try? She hadn't come all this way to make friends. She'd come for answers, and as harsh as it sounded, she'd played nice long enough. She'd soothed the ache of Frank's loveless marriage, usually without any hope that he might untangle himself. She'd made him a priority while he'd made her a footnote. Who could blame her for feeling so betrayed?

The town's center was small, just a handful of streets spilling into a green, a short stretch of public beach nestled between the fingers of several old piers. Now Beverly turned away from the water to face the storefronts that lined the wharf, their windows dressed with banners and decorations. Which one to go into for directions? she wondered. It was like looking at gifts under a Christmas tree, not being sure which to open first. Now that she was here, opportunity was everywhere. Every encounter was a chance to get closer to the truth, a chance to snoop, to peek inside the sealed package of Frank's life.

She decided on a gift shop with an amusing underwater display and stepped inside, the air fragrant with the sticky sweet smell of scented candles. A pair of old men stood behind the register, matching white-haired heads bowed over opened boxes.

The thinner of the two held up a tangerine coffee mug, the mug's handle in the shape of a mermaid, and he cursed. "Dammit, Wall. They sent the wrong mugs again."

The other man looked up over the tops of his reading glasses, seeing Beverly, and offered her an apologetic smile. "The orange don't sell well," he explained.

"I can imagine." Beverly looked around the store, seeing shelves of green and blue wigs, rows of Cradle Harbor T-shirts and baseball caps. She'd never seen so much mermaid merchandise in all her life—mermaid pot holders, mermaid shot glasses, even mermaid nail clippers. How absurd.

She stepped up to the counter. At her elbow, a rack of cast mermaid key chains dangled from their hooks, tinkling softly.

Wallace Mooney wiped his hands on his pants and tugged down his glasses. "Looking for something in particular?" he asked.

"Yes," said Beverly. "I'm looking for directions to Buzz Patterson's cottages."

"Oh sure." Wallace fished a pencil out of a standing tin, tugged a piece of scrap paper from a stack, and began to sketch a map. "Hope you've got a reservation," he said.

"I certainly do. One of the last, he told me when we spoke on the phone."

"Good for you. His cottages have some of the best views in town. Real pretty spot."

Beverly smiled politely. "So I've heard."

SHE WASN'T EVEN SUPPOSED TO be at the perfume counter that day. Normally she worked the makeup counter—she had for nearly six years—but one of the new girls had fallen sick in the middle of her shift and Beverly had agreed to cover for her. After all, it had been the start of the holiday season, and the lunchtime rush at Marshall Fields was impossible to manage alone.

She'd noticed the man with the tidy salt-and-pepper hair

at the end of the display long before he made his way toward the register to ask her for a sample. He'd noticed her too, because he'd moved deftly around the other salesgirl who'd approached him first and walked straight to Beverly instead.

"It's for my wife," he'd said as she'd sprayed the tester slip, letting the scent settle before handing it to him. He'd taken a quick sniff and nodded.

"It won't smell like that on her, you know," Beverly had said. "It's an entirely different smell on the skin."

The man had looked at her then, wearing a tentative smile.

"I can spray some on myself and let you see," Beverly had offered.

"If you wouldn't mind."

She'd spritzed the inside of her wrist and held it out. The man had leaned in, close enough that Beverly could see the flecks of gray in his eyes, long enough that he could see her see them. He smiled, and she wasn't sure what pleased him—the perfume or something else.

"I'll take that," he said, reaching for his wallet.

"Good."

Lots of married men came through the store during the holidays, some even to her counter. It had upset Clark, thinking that other men came on to her, thinking that she was kind to them, maybe even a bit of a flirt. But she wasn't. Until that day, until Frank Hammond, Beverly hadn't ever taken a man's number or let a man buy her a late lunch.

Maybe it was because Frank hadn't tried to hide the fact that he was married, and maybe it was that honesty that made him all the more attractive to her. They sat with coffees in the restaurant. He'd bought her a pastry, which she hadn't touched and probably wouldn't, even though he had pushed it gently toward her as they talked. Beverly had told him she was a widow and that she had two teenage boys. Frank had explained that he owned a business in Maine and that he was in Chicago for a conference. When the check came, he insisted on paying, though Beverly wouldn't allow it. But when the taxi arrived, she let him help her inside and let him close the door for her; while she shuffled across the seat and waited for him to climb into his side, she kept her eyes forward. But after a while, as the driver steered them wordlessly down Michigan Avenue, she felt his eyes on her and she turned to meet them.

And as she sat there, she'd thought, *This is how these things happen. Like this. This quickly, this innocently. After years of walking past a smiling stranger, you decide one day at forty-three years old you'll stop and talk to him. You'll tell him things you wouldn't have told most strangers. You'll let him tell you the same. And then it begins.*

This.

BUZZ SAW THE WHITE SEDAN just as he was coming out of the trailer with an armload of newly laundered blankets. The woman driving didn't see him, not at first. When she climbed out of the car, dressed all in white, she looked in the other direction, down at the stretch of cabins he had been airing out since morning, as soon as the fog had cleared and the sun burned hot enough to bake out months of lingering tides.

It wasn't as if they *never* had guests outside of festival season. Sure, it wasn't a regular thing—not like it was for Donny and Brenda up at the Heron House Inn, or the Pollards' B and B. It used to be, when Buzz first opened the cottages twenty years ago, he could expect a dozen or so visitors every month. Lots of times it was old friends who had been passing through; enough guests to keep him busy with laundry and cleaning. But in the last ten years, he and Tess weren't seeing much in the way of visitors— except for festival season, of course. But that wasn't exactly a measure of their reputation or service. God knew people would pay big bucks to sleep in someone's lobster pot if it came to that.

This time of year, though, Buzz worked up a hell of a sweat. It didn't help, of course, that he'd put on weight in the years since Ruby had drowned. He'd let himself go— wasn't that the ugly phrase people loved to throw around about other people? Not that he could be too sanctimonious. Many a morning he'd look in the mirror, certain Ruby wouldn't even recognize the man who scowled back at him. Once he'd been so fit, so strapping, she'd called him "Buzz the Red," her Viking. Now he huffed as he made the march down the path to meet the woman in white, feeling the beads of perspiration clump under his ponytail, under his arms, in the lines of his palms.

Somehow she looked as fresh as a new roll of toilet paper. She was tall, too. And quite pretty in that fussy, fixed sort of way. Her skin was as pale and unblemished as apple flesh. She was lost; that was his first thought. She had to be. Women like that didn't want cottages with torn screen doors and drawers that stuck. They wanted suites, rooms filled with antiques and canopy beds with no fewer than ten pillows on them.

"I'm looking for Buzz Patterson," she said, even before he'd reached her, her voice crisp like someone used to speaking in front of a class, or someone just used to being listened to.

"I'm Buzz." He could see himself in her lenses, a funhouse view, his head like an eggplant, his graying red moustache pointing down to his chin. But mostly he could see sweat. His forehead was one glistening scarlet parking lot of perspiration. He was grateful when she took them off.

Her eyes were a stunning lavender-blue, the lines around them remarkably faint.

"I'm Beverly Partridge," she said. "I have a reservation."

Buzz frowned at her. There had to be some mistake. He didn't have anyone coming in today, and he didn't remember a Beverly Partridge on the list.

"I think you must have the wrong place," he said. "I don't have a reservation under that name."

The woman blinked at him, her polite smile dropping. "You must," she said firmly. "We spoke on the phone. You said I was getting the last one you had available."

He did? Buzz bit at his lip, trying to recall. Jesus, he couldn't keep track of anything anymore.

"I sent you a check last week," she continued. "You said you'd hold it until I arrived. I've come from Chicago."

Chicago. He swallowed, feeling the sweat bubble again along his neck.

"I'll go look," he said, "but I'm telling you, I don't remember."

Still a knot turned in his stomach as he walked back up the hill, twisting tighter when he got to his desk and began rummaging through the impossible piles of papers he'd meant for months to file.

Halfway down the stack, there was her check.

Pale pink, and edged with tiny white roses.

"*Shit.*" Buzz hung his head, blowing out a deep sigh.

Defeated and distraught, he walked back to the kitchen and looked out the window to see Beverly Partridge still standing by her car, fanning herself impatiently with a brochure. What a mess, he thought. There was no way she'd find a place this close to the festival.

His gaze drifted past her, down the line of cottages. He did have *one* option. It would cause him a hell of a lot of anguish, but it would also save his neck.

He debated the idea a few more agonizing minutes, his

eyes fixing on the cottage at the end, pink and navy blue, before he resigned himself to his fate.

TESS HATED THIS PART. The plastic rings always pinched her fingers, and her arms always ached from reaching up so high. Not that she cared today. After waking up with a hangover, she was just glad to be feeling something other than a piercing headache. But changing out a vinyl shower curtain in cottage three and listening to Rosanne Cash weren't going to clear her tangled brain—any more than wine had been the only reason for her fuzzy head. She couldn't shake the memories of the night before: thoughts of disappointment, hurt, Pete not showing up, Tom Grace arriving instead.

Tom Grace.

What had she been thinking? She'd pulled him into her bed, put his hands on her . . . Oh God, she'd been so drunk. Or had she? She hadn't been so drunk that she didn't remember how much she'd wanted him to lie beside her in that moment, how good he'd felt behind her, the smell of old books on his sleeve, the smell of mint soap on his knuckles.

She'd woken to find that he'd put away her food, blown out her candles. He'd *cleaned*.

Why would he do that?

Tess only hoped he didn't think she'd made some sort of promise to him last night, that some kind of deal had been sealed between them just because she'd kissed him. Not that she hadn't been guilty of doing the same once. Barely six hours after Pete had first taken her down to the beach and kissed her under the pier, holding his hand over her mouth when they'd heard voices above them and she'd giggled madly, she'd biked to his house that next morning before the sun was even up to leave him a carving she'd done of a scallop shell. It was a rough little thing—she'd been carving only a few months—but she'd wanted him to have a piece of her, something no one else could give to him. She'd set it carefully on the hood of his Mustang, grateful that his sour mother wasn't anywhere around, only hoping Edith wouldn't spy it first and remove it. For the rest of that day Tess had waited for him to come by the cove and declare his love. But he'd stayed away almost a week. When he'd finally arrived, she'd had to remind him about the shell, and he'd stared at her a full ten seconds before any sort of recognition had crossed his face, then saying only, "Yeah. That was cool. Thanks." She'd told herself it hadn't mattered if he remembered or not; she'd told herself what *did* matter was that he'd come at all. How could she have known at sixteen that she'd allow him so many chances to be her everything?

"I'm opening Pink."

Tess looked up, startled to find Buzz standing in the bathroom doorway; she hadn't heard him come in over the music. She reached over to turn down the volume.

"Pink," he said again. "I'm putting someone in Pink."

Tess nearly slipped off the lip of the shower stall. She blinked at him. "What?"

"You heard me," Buzz said, nodding to the door. "I have to. I double-booked. Lady's out there right now—came all the way from Chicago."

Tess released the curtain and let the loose end sail down. "We don't rent Pink," she said firmly. "We never rent it."

"I don't have a choice. I can't turn her away—everywhere else is full."

"So give her my place and I'll stay with you."

"You will not," he said. "That's just dumb."

"It's not dumb," she defended, panicked now. "You said yourself Mom's studio isn't set up for guests."

"It can be," Buzz said, as determined now to open it as she was to see it stay closed, Tess could tell. "All it needs is some clean sheets, a wipe-down, a few minutes of a good breeze. A half hour and it's ready to go."

"What about Mom's paintings?"

"What about them?"

"You can't just leave them up there," Tess said. "What if this lady tries to take them or knocks them off the wall and tears them or something?"

"Oh, for Pete's sake, Tessie. Listen to yourself. She's a person, not a puppy."

"I don't want you renting it."

"Now, look." Buzz stepped toward her. "I'm not asking your permission. I screwed up, and I need to make things right. I just wanted to let you know, that's all."

Out he went, leaving Tess standing in the shower stall with a mouthful of excuses he wasn't going to let her get out, a hundred more reasons why he couldn't break his promise and open her mother's studio to a stranger. If this was his way of punishing her for not listening to him about Pete, he could go right ahead, she decided, batting the shower curtain out of her way. The day wasn't over, and as far as she was concerned, regardless of Buzz's exit, neither was this conversation.

"I REALLY *AM* SORRY ABOUT THE MIX-UP," Buzz said as he took Beverly up the four cupped treads to the porch and led her into Ruby's shingled studio. The sour scent of old oil paints was apparent but not as choking as Buzz had feared. Even the few minutes he'd had to leave the screen door open and throw open the windows had done wonders. Now the sweet smell of newly mowed grass blew in.

"It belonged to my late wife," Buzz said, looking over to see Beverly surveying the room with a narrowed gaze. "She was an artist."

Beverly touched her throat. "I can see that."

"Just so you know, there's no charge for it," said Buzz. "I'll give you back your check."

She looked at him. "Don't be silly. I don't expect you to do that."

"I know you don't, but I wouldn't feel right charging you."

Beverly considered this, clearly uncomfortable with the offer. "No," she said firmly. "I want to pay you. I'll take a reduced rate, but I won't take it for free."

"All right," he agreed. "How about half price?"

"Fine," she said, moving around him to continue her tour of the small space. Buzz watched her as she strolled past the wall of Ruby's paintings.

"I'm not usually this disorganized," he said. "It's been kind of a bad year. I just lost someone close to me, and I guess I'm still kind of trying to wrap my head around it."

Beverly turned to Buzz, looking almost startled, he thought, though he couldn't imagine why.

"I gave you a microwave," Buzz said, pointing to the counter, "so at least you'll have something to heat up your food. I'll bring you some restaurant menus. Got a few places in town, more up the road in Port Chester. No phone in here, but I usually let renters get calls up at my place if it's an emergency. Same thing with local calls."

"I won't need that," Beverly said. "I have a cell phone."

"They don't always work out here. There's coffee on my porch every morning. It's not that fancy stuff, but it gets the motor going. Doughnuts too. Fifty cents apiece. Honor system—I keep a kitty on the railing. Tips are always accepted and appreciated."

"I don't drink coffee," Beverly said curtly, frowning at a nude painted in shades of orange and blue.

Buzz smiled cheerfully. "That's fine too," he said, moving to the door. "Oh, and just so you know, the yellow one across the driveway belongs to my daughter, Tess. You'll see her around. She's got a sign-carving business, but she helps me out too."

For a moment, paused on the threshold, Buzz thought he might warn her of Tess's mood, feeling oddly sorry for this woman. But he didn't.

The truth was that for the first year after Ruby's death, Buzz had wanted to leave the place untouched as much as Tess did. His grief had been so great, so bottomless; he'd tried to keep everything Ruby had ever touched intact. But coastal buildings didn't do well left to their own devices in the middle of winter. Paintings could survive being ignored, but not plumbing. Buzz could still remember Tess's pleas that he not reopen the studio that following spring; the grudge she'd held (nearly a week!) when he'd started to put away some of her mother's paints and supplies. Finally, tired of the fight, he'd promised to leave all of Ruby's canvases on the walls and not to rent it out, not even during the festival, and the bargain had appeased Tess. No wonder she'd looked at him today with such panicked confusion, then such contention. Buzz would bet ten bucks that right now she was storming around the cottage he'd found her in, wiping down countertops and windows with a vengeance.

He bet she thought he'd done this to hurt her, and the theory made his stomach knot with pain. Climbing the steps to break the news, he'd hoped she was old enough to see both sides of things. But maybe kids never quite grew up when it came to grudges against their parents.

ALONE AT LAST.

Beverly walked to the day bed and sat down, trying to slow her racing heart.

She'd done it. She was here, really here. Fifteen years of loving someone and she'd finally stepped into his world.

But, oh, what a world it was, she thought, looking around the sunlit room, the gaudy paintings on the walls. She hadn't expected the cottages to be so . . . *rustic*. Not to mention her host. Frank had never mentioned Buzz was an old hippie; he certainly had never mentioned anything about Buzz's wife. Knowing Frank—or at least, the Frank she'd *thought* she knew—Beverly couldn't imagine two more different men. And if this man was Joan's brother, what did that say about Joan?

How Beverly had wondered about that woman. At first, there had been little point to such musings. When she and Frank had parted after that first afternoon, Beverly had never imagined she'd hear from him again. After all, he had only come into town for business, and she was a widow with teenage sons—what future was there in that?

Then the flowers had arrived—fat, fragrant yellow blooms. (Had she mentioned that yellow was her favorite color? Had he been so attentive that he'd remembered?)

When Frank returned to Chicago for more business two months later, Beverly agreed to see him again. They walked along the lakefront for a while, wandered through the Botanic Garden, and when they returned to his hotel at one, his need startled her. Clark had never been so brazen, so craving. It left her frightened; it left her exhilarated. Even as she rode the train back to her car, hopelessly aware of a smile that refused to be drawn down no matter who looked her way, Beverly was certain she'd been given a drug she would have no hope of flushing from her system. Soon she came to believe Frank carried a terrible pain and that she alone could relieve him of it—the pain of a bad marriage.

She wouldn't believe that was a lie too.

Beverly glanced down at the colorful quilt beneath her. Running her fingers over the frayed seams where blocks of garish fabrics clung to one another, she caught the faint but sour scent of mildew. She needed a plan, of course. It wouldn't do to skulk around. She wasn't a private detective. She had no idea how one did this sort of thing, how one snooped without snooping. But she'd figure out a way.

Because it was all here; she was certain of it. Somewhere in this small town, maybe just up the hill, existed the answers she feared knowing, but feared never knowing far more. And she wasn't going back to Chicago without them.

Five

TESS PRESSED HER BENT GOUGE into the wood and hit it with
her mallet, pushing out a deep groove and drawing in the
faintly sweet smell of the fresh basswood. She worked her
gouge and mallet up and down the sides of the mermaid's
torso, but still her eyes drifted to the window, to the view
of the cottages where for the last hour a woman in white
had been walking in and out, neatening the wicker chairs
on the porch and shaking out rugs, as if she might be moving in forever.

Had Buzz at least removed her mother's journals? What if this woman flipped through them, thinking they were there for her pleasure? What if she spilled coffee all over the pages or got them sticky with food? This woman wouldn't understand the globs of dried paint on the wall beside the window. She wouldn't know anything about the night they'd been put there. She wouldn't see constellations carefully replicated from the sky; she'd see random droplets of paint.

Tess's mother had tried three other cottages before settling on the one at the end and painting it a blinding pink. It was primer, Buzz had tried to explain to her, not meant to be used as a final coat, but Ruby had refused to cover it and couldn't understand why anyone would. Buzz had just smiled at her, as if she were the cleverest woman in the world for thinking so.

"Of course it would *have* to be this one," Ruby had proclaimed brightly to Tess several weeks later when Buzz had gladly filled her shelves with every art supply she'd requested, never minding the price. "It's the strongest of the cottages. You can tell by the windows. See how clear the glass is? The salt won't stick to it. It can't." Tess had nodded agreeably, eagerly, though she could swear the panes were as foggy with grime as the ones in the other cottages.

Those early years were flawless, long stretches of days peppered with Buzz's unflagging adoration for her mother. She remembered dinners on the beach, eating fish cakes gritty with sand, and Sundays spent wandering flea markets, then filling the back of the truck with a tangle of old wicker and wrought iron—*These silver platters will be perfect for mixing paints!* She recalled hanging lights at Halloween just in case they were too busy at Christmas. There had been the carob brownies that Ruby sent for Tess's school holiday party, decorated with red-hots and frozen peas (*Like red and green Christmas balls, see?*) that no one would eat, so Tess emptied them on her way home, not wanting to hurt her mother's feelings. She remembered making sand castles in the middle of winter, gathering wood for bonfires on the Fourth of July, outrunning deerflies and making rose hip tea. There had been grilled corn on the cob and fresh blueberry custard straight from the tub. Through it all, her mother had been effervescent, and Buzz had worn the perpetual flush of a man in love.

Tess had truly believed it could last.

"Damn."

She looked down, horrified to see how deep she'd been making her cuts while her mind had drifted. It was no good, she thought. At this rate, she'd carve her poor mermaid down to a toothpick, she was so undone.

She just needed to see Pete. She deserved an explanation, didn't she? She deserved to be told to her face why he hadn't come. She should have demanded one hours ago. Instead, she was hiding in her woodshop, as if she were the one who'd done something wrong. She'd been so sure this time, so certain he was finally ready to make a commitment to her, that promise for which she'd waited so long.

So why hadn't he? He was free now; there were no excuses, no other women to consider, no complications—at least, none she knew of.

Screw it. She set down her tools, brushed off her hands, and stuck her feet into her sneakers, her heart racing. Fine. If he wouldn't come to her for dinner, then she'd bring dinner to him and show him just how much work she'd gone to for him.

Confident of her plan, Tess packed up the pans and loaded them into her VW Bug. She was snapping her seat belt into place when she saw the woman in white had returned to the porch, this time with one of her mother's quilts, which she was draping over the railing in full sun. The outrage, already bubbling, flared up in full, bursting and hot. Tess climbed out of the car and marched across the driveway.

Hearing her approach, Beverly glanced up. "Oh, hello. You must be Te—"

"You can't leave that in the sun," Tess said firmly. "It'll fade the colors."

Beverly frowned, startled. "I wasn't going to leave it outside long. I just noticed it had a strange smell, and I thought I'd let it air out a bit, that's all."

Tess drew down the spread, bundling it carefully in her arms. "If you think it stinks so badly, then Buzz can find you another one."

"There's no need to be rude. All I meant to say was that it—"

But Tess had already turned and walked off, taking the quilt with her into the car and piling it on top of her pans, determined to get the whole lot as far from that woman as she could.

IT HAD TAKEN HIM MORE THAN AN HOUR, but Tom had managed to lay out all four mattresses, the cushions on the home's only sofa, ten towels and five bedspreads on the back lawn of the house. All that remained were the sheets Tom had balled up into enormous piles at the top of the rise.

He stood and surveyed the sea of linens. Now that they were in the sun, he could see just how badly yellowed the old mattresses were, the unfortunate and unidentifiable stains so stark against the grass. Lumpy and grim, they were pathetic. The bedspreads were not much better, their scalloped edges frayed and torn.

All morning he'd watched the tiny screen of his phone, compulsively checking the signal bars that fluctuated madly up and down every time he crossed a room or a doorstep. Finally, he'd climbed into the car and driven to the edge of the road where he'd been relieved to find a signal and soon after, a text message from Dean, telling him he was close, not more than a day away; Dean was confident of it. After reading it, Tom had put in a call but got voice mail and left a message, telling Dean that service was spotty on the Point but to *please* try anyway.

The night before, Tom had had a savage nightmare of

Dean taking a turn too fast and plummeting off a rocky cliff. In his sleeping panic, Tom had rolled off the bed, landing on the smooth wood floors. When he lay back down, he heard mice in the walls. After that, his dreams had been cluttered with visions of Tess Patterson, brief but potent glimpses that seemed only to strengthen his recollections. After waking, as he'd made coffee from a jar of instant he'd bought in desperation at a gas station, he'd recalled the strange encounter in her cottage. Had he really been only an hour in her company? It seemed so much longer. Even now Tom felt as if he'd known her for some time, as if he could recall every inch of her room from memory, the colors of her bedspread (peach and pumpkin flecked with gold); the color of her cabinets (mauve with pearled knobs). He even swore he could still smell her shampoo on his skin when he woke, and he continued to take compulsive whiffs of his sleeve just to be sure.

But why wouldn't he ruminate on her? It had been a very long time since he'd been that close to a woman—two years, to be exact. Nancy Martin, the English teacher from the middle school had been going through a divorce, and Tom had given her a ride home from a conference. They'd gone out to dinner four times and made love after their second date. Then Dean had gone off on one of his disappearing acts, so Tom had cancelled their fifth date at the last minute, promising to reschedule, but by the time

Dean had resurfaced as he always did weeks later, unwashed and practically undead from his binge, Tom had
forgotten his promise. The truth was he was thankful for
the excuse. He couldn't care for Dean and care for a woman at the same time. It didn't work that way; it couldn't.
What woman could understand that? Not that he hadn't
enjoyed Nancy, and not that he hadn't found himself
grateful (just the word filled him with guilt) to be free of
Dean in those impossible days of his brother's absence, but
no matter the fleeting moments of relief when Tom felt he
could actually breathe for once, no matter those, Tom
knew he could never choose them over Dean.

Still, he'd made valiant efforts at dating over the years
since the accident, thinking from time to time that sex
might be a reasonable way to cope with it all. He'd started
running, mostly at night because he couldn't sleep. He
tore through parks like a man being chased and wouldn't
stop until he couldn't breathe, until he was certain his
heart would bounce straight up his throat and land on the
sidewalk, done with him; some nights he truly hoped it
would. One night he ran all the way to Oak Park, another
night to the lakefront. By the middle of that first summer
after their parents had died, most of their friends had
drifted away—*faded* was the word that Tom used—paling
from their company like steam under a defroster, and he
hadn't blamed them. They'd been mostly Dean's friends,
mostly other swimmers, but there had been one girl from

his class who'd come to check in on him several times in August, on her way to Williams. She'd sent Tom postcards until Christmas, but he never wrote back. Once Dean was home from the hospital and still not able to walk, there was just too much to do.

In his mid-twenties, once he began teaching in earnest, Tom tried again, but he often felt like an old car left sitting too long. Everything worked well enough, but he felt sluggish. The few times he had enjoyed a woman, Dean would stumble into some kind of trouble, and Tom would have to wash his hands of the romance. In secret, he'd always thought of himself as one of those men who might excel at sex if all the stars aligned, who could find himself remarkably agile in the moment, surprisingly so, thrilling his lover, who had never expected such prowess, such exuberance from such a serious person. But whatever chance he had for those moments of startling glory was left in that snow, buried in that embankment.

But it had been nice with Tess Patterson, nice to hold her, to squeeze into her shower, nice even to put away her food. Maybe it was the brevity of it, the surprise of her that had aroused him, that kept him thinking of her still. Maybe it was just being alone. He could have started running again as well, but where was there to run in this place? With so much darkness, a person could run right off a cliff if he wasn't careful.

No, he couldn't run. So if Tess Patterson wanted to see him again, if she wanted him near her again, he would enjoy that. Until Dean arrived, he might just enjoy a lot of things.

RICKY BOGGS WAS DRAGGING BOXES of roofing tiles from the back of his pickup when Tess pulled up to the site. She knew Pete had been helping out at the Marshall job when Ricky found himself low on help, which always happened during festival season. Workers, even the most dependable men, took full advantage of the season's short-lived whimsy, committing transgressions that were usually forgiven a few days after the celebration ended. Tess didn't see Pete's truck anywhere, but that didn't mean anything; he might have loaned it out, or he might have walked over from his dad's office in town.

"He's not here, Tess," the contractor called out to her before she even reached him, his voice as wary as his expression.

"And you're not going to tell me where he is, are you?" she said.

"Tess . . ."

"I just want to talk to him, Rick. I'm not going to set anything on fire."

"Go home, hon." He shoved the tailgate closed and clapped his hands clean. "Don't do this to yourself."

Tess glanced around the job site, seeing the familiar faces of men she'd grown up with and gone to school with; they were looking at her as if she were a lunatic. Her cheeks burned. She wanted to crawl under her front seat; she wanted the earth to crack open and swallow her up — anything to avoid their pitying stares. But what did she expect? They all knew her history with Pete Hawthorne. They knew how he'd broken her heart when he'd left her for Angela, knew how she'd waited and how she'd pined. She stepped back to let a group of men come for the boxes Ricky had just piled on the grass. What the hell was she doing? She wasn't the crazy one. She wasn't the one who had something to be ashamed of. She wasn't the liar, the jerk.

She was just the fool.

She walked back to the VW, climbed in, and pulled out, too angry to cry, but too determined to just go home. So he wasn't at the job site; so what? She'd just keep driving, just cruise around until she saw his truck. What did she care if it took all morning, she decided as she steered through town. Her day was shot.

WHEN SHE REACHED THE SEAFOOD MARKET, she swung her car into the parking lot. Julie, Tess thought. The only person in town who wouldn't judge her, who wouldn't say, "I told you so" any more than Julie had ever said it over the years that Tess had been wrong about Pete Hawthorne. But when she pushed through the front door of the store, Tess didn't see her friend anywhere.

"She had to go home and help Sue with the chowder

orders, hon," white-haired Bert Russell shouted above the crescent of customers that had curved around the counter, calling out requests. "She'll probably be back in an hour or so if you want to wait for her."

But Tess couldn't wait. The tears she'd been too angry to let loose were finally pushing their way up her throat and nearing the edges of her lids. She felt herself jostled by a new rush of customers, locals who wanted to get their fish before the flood of tourists descended on the town and cleaned out every case, every muffin tin, every chowder bowl.

She turned and pushed through them, determined to get back to her car where she could fall apart in private. She managed, barely, drying her eyes with paper napkins as she raced down Route 9, seeing nothing but the road, then suddenly, a break in the pines up ahead, the telltale white marker on the tree; her breath caught. It was the road to the Point.

Good, she thought, her rage returning, hot and fierce again. If she couldn't clear things up with Pete, she'd clear things up with Tom Grace and stop anything before it started. Not that she imagined he would expect something. If anything, he might be more embarrassed than she was. After all, he didn't seem the sort to end up in a stranger's bed. Just seeing that flash of her bare skin had clearly undone him, leaving him fidgeting like a horse stuck in a stall with a tireless fly.

She took the pocked road all the way to the end, to

where the keeper's house sat, stark and quiet, just the top of the tower visible beyond it. The Volvo was there; Tom was home. Uncertainty fluttered through her.

She needed this, Tess told herself. She needed this one piece of closure today; otherwise it was all too much. She couldn't make Buzz keep Pink safe from a stranger; she couldn't find Pete and make him explain, make him want her back. But if she could make herself clear to this teacher, if she could close the door with him—the door that hadn't been opened, merely cracked, the slightest, thinnest peek of a crack at that—if she closed it firmly, then that would be something at least.

Coming up to the porch, Tess pulled back the screen door and prepared to knock, then stopped, hearing movement, thumping sounds, at the back of the house. She came carefully around the side and stared, awed. The lawn was nearly covered in mattresses and cushions, and there, same white shirt, sleeves rolled up now, was Tom Grace, spreading out quilts and blankets, securing their corners with stones, as if he were planning a mass picnic.

She folded her arms. "It won't help, you know."

Tom looked up at the sound of her voice. He rose, then wiped sweat off his forehead with his arm. "How's that?"

"Laying them out like this," Tess said. "They'll still smell like salt. Everything in Cradle Harbor smells like salt."

"It's not the salt," he said. "It's the mildew."

They stared at each other, uncertain. He looked a whole lot better this way, she thought. He was rumpled, his hair slightly scattered, his shirttails popping out a bit over his belt.

Just tell him, she thought. *Tell him and get it over with. He's looking at you as if he's going to ask you something, as if he wants something. Tell him.*

"I have coffee," Tom said. "It's really terrible stuff, and I don't have any milk—"

"I can't."

"Oh."

He looked disappointed, Tess thought. Or maybe not.

"I just came because I wanted to be clear about what happened last night," she said. "I wasn't feeling like myself. I was confused."

She watched his eyes narrow skeptically. He didn't believe her; she could tell. Maybe he remembered it differently. And maybe it wasn't the entire truth. Maybe she had known full well who he was and she'd wanted to kiss him anyway, but that didn't matter now. She'd been drunk, loose, hurting. Surely he could understand that. Men used that same excuse all the time. Not that it was an excuse.

"I just didn't want you thinking there was something to us now," she said, "because there isn't."

Tom didn't reply, just moved down the row of mattresses, snapping the edges to try to flatten the lumps that still resembled mountain ranges.

Staring at him as he worked, Tess grew frustrated by his silence.

"You're mad, aren't you?" she said.

He shrugged. "Not at all. Actually, I'm fairly accustomed to people who drink too much and then think they don't have to be responsible for their actions."

"That's a rotten thing to say. You don't know anything about me."

"I know you should take responsibility for the things you do. I know you kissed me. Among other things."

"Because I didn't know what I was doing."

"So you keep saying."

Tess felt the skin of her ears warm, certain the lobes were a bright scarlet. "You don't believe me—is that it?"

"It doesn't matter what I believe. Excuse me." Tom reached down to scoop up one of the piles of sheets he'd brought outside and moved past her, headed for the empty clothesline that stood on crooked poles a few feet down the lawn.

Tess followed him, reaching him as he flung a fitted sheet over the clothesline, the rope stiff with age and dried salt.

"I don't sleep around," she said firmly. "I'm sure that's what you heard, but I don't. They said the same thing about my mother, and it wasn't true about her, either. I have to be in love with someone to sleep with him. And it just so happens that I *am* in love with someone. Someone *else*."

Her heart racing, she stared at his profile, waiting for him to call her bluff, to be cruel and point out that he knew damn well the man she claimed to be in love with had stood her up. But he didn't. He simply kept his eyes firmly on his task, drawing up another sheet and laying it over the line, saying only, "Then I guess we're clear."

"Good." Tess gripped her bare arms, feeling suddenly chilled even though the breeze had thinned noticeably since she'd arrived and the sun was unfettered by a single cloud. She'd made her case, and now she could go.

So why hadn't she?

The last sheet hung, Tom turned to her, clearly wondering the same thing.

Tess swerved her gaze to the lighthouse, a safe thing to look at, she thought.

"I haven't been up there yet," Tom said, seeing where she looked. "Would you like to go with me?"

Tess turned back to him, their gazes holding.

"Why would I want to do that?" she asked.

"I don't know that you do. That's why I asked."

She didn't have time for this. She had plenty to do, so much it made her head spin.

But his dark eyes were a warm brown. She didn't remember their being so warm.

"Maybe just for a minute," she said.

THEY WALKED THROUGH A BRISK wind down the twisting path to the tower, flanked by hedges and saying little. They took turns glancing at the horizon where the sun was dropping gently behind lavender clouds. Tom freed the padlock and wrenched the heavy metal door open. Tess stepped in first, and he followed. With the door ajar, there was enough daylight to illuminate the interior, the brick walls, the twisting metal staircase.

"You first," he said, giving her room, and she took it.

The climb to the top was harder than he imagined, the sharp curve of the metal stairs and the view to the bottom making him dizzy. He gripped the railing and followed her up, through the trapdoor and into the lantern room. Once he was inside at last, out of the dark and into full light, the panorama revealed itself, the view of the sea endless in nearly every direction. A pedestal stood in the middle where the beam would have perched; it now carried only the weight of a simple plaque: CRADLE HARBOR LIGHT: BUILT IN 1854.

Tess walked to the windows; Tom followed her, certain he heard the unmistakable clatter of wind chimes. Sure enough, he saw a set tied from the railing, banging in the harsh wind.

"Seems like a strange place to hang chimes," he said.

"Lydia didn't think so." Tess spread her hands against the curved glass. "She had to be sure they never came back."

Tom frowned, confused. "The men?"

Tess smiled. "I thought you weren't interested in fairy tales."

She had him and she knew it, Tom thought, seeing that same curious flash of warmth flicker across her face, tilt her lips briefly, then slip away. All right, he'd admit it. He was slightly intrigued. Or maybe he just wanted an excuse to keep their conversation going.

"Did it work?" he asked.

"If it did, Lydia never knew it," said Tess. "She was so heartbroken she jumped from the gallery right after she hung them. A neighbor found her body washed up on the rocks."

Tom shifted his gaze away from her to the view of the gallery, thinking how cold and desolate it looked on that metal walkway.

Tess considered him in the quiet. "So why you?"

"Why me what?"

"Why did Frank give the house to you?"

Tom shrugged, driving his hands into his pockets. "I was just as surprised as everyone else," he said. "I barely knew him."

"But you *did* know him? I mean, no one gives away a building to a total stranger." She traced lazy circles on the glass. "Buzz won't tell me anything."

"What makes you think there's something to tell?" Tom asked.

"There's always something to tell. Everyone has a story. Everyone has secrets."

Tess turned to face him fully then, the air filling suddenly with the scent of her, familiar to him now. He wondered why she had lied to him. She hadn't been that drunk. Twice he'd seen her eyes flutter open as she'd urged him down beside her, both times flashing with recognition. And she knew he knew; Tom was certain of it. Still, she'd made her claim.

"Do you ever go out there?" he asked her.

"You mean the gallery?"

"No, the water. Do you swim?"

"Sometimes," she said. "If it gets hot enough. Do you?"

"Never." Tom looked out at the sea, the pewter blanket white-tipped and rippling. "Dean, my brother, is the swimmer. Not me."

"Then he'll love the Mutiny Dash," Tess said.

"What's that?"

"The opening night of the festival, everyone gathers on the town beach at dusk, links hands, and rushes into the water. Just like Linus and the others did."

"Sounds unpleasant," said Tom.

Tess smiled. "It's not when you run in. You barely feel the cold."

"I'll take your word for it."

"What about your brother?" Tess asked. "Is he a teacher too?"

"No. No, he's not a teacher."

"What does he do, then?"

"As little as possible."

Tess frowned at him. "I don't understand."

"Dean's not much for working. He never has been."

"Maybe he's just never found the right job."

She was defending him, Tom thought. She was defending someone she didn't even know. But then she'd probably adore Dean. Most women did. He was like a bonfire in the middle of a cold room. Everyone wanted to get close

126

and warm their hands on his heat. But it was easy to throw caution to the wind when you knew someone would always be there to chase it down. Their parents had done so for the first seventeen years of Dean's life; Tom had merely picked up where they had left off.

"I don't think that's his problem," Tom said. "Dean's like a child who'll dump out a whole box of cereal to get to the prize. He lacks any kind of self-control. He always has."

He turned to find Tess studying him. In the silence, the space around them grew thick. Outside, the sea looked frigid to him, but inside the lantern room, he was burning up.

This was his chance, Tom thought. It was his opportunity to smooth things out between them, though why he felt compelled to do so he hadn't yet decided. He knew only that he wanted to.

"I'm not like that, either, you know," he said carefully. "I really did just come over last night for a shower. And I meant what I said. You are beautiful."

Tess glanced to the trapdoor, as if she'd heard movement. "It's getting late," she said. "I should go."

Dean was right, Tom thought. He was awful at this.

He stepped back to let her pass, giving up. "Then we'll go."

THE WALK BACK WAS AS quiet as the one there, past the graveyard of mattresses and the sheets snapping madly on the line. Reaching the porch, they turned to each other.

Tom nodded toward her car. "I'll let you get back t—"

"I'll have coffee."

Tom blinked at her, startled by her suggestion, but he could see she'd startled herself more. "All right."

Tess followed him inside the old house and sat at the kitchen table while he fixed them two lukewarm mugs, the coffee watery and the color of tea.

"I warned you," he said, seeing her expression as she stared down at hers.

Tess looked up, realizing she hadn't really wanted coffee. She didn't know what she wanted. She'd only come here to tell him something. She wanted to find Pete; she wanted him to explain why he'd changed his mind, why he'd forgotten his promise, all of his promises, ten years of them. But instead she was here with this strange man in a house that she hadn't set foot in since she was seventeen, a house that smelled of old books and old plaster, with walls so white, so bare, a person could lose her way, snow blind.

"I should go," she announced.

"Then go," Tom said, his expression, once patient, now frustrated.

But when Tess stood up, her feet felt heavy, stuck. Suddenly, all she could think about was walking to those stairs, the corners of which she could see from where she had been sitting, setting her hand over that worn banister, and following those ancient treads that had been used so many times, their wood was rippled like wind over water.

Their eyes met and held.

"I don't know what I'm doing here," she said. "I can't even drink coffee without cream."

"That's not a crime, you know."

Her feet came loose then. The moment she felt her freedom, she went to him, rearing up and pressing her lips to his mouth just as she had done the night before. Only this time her eyes were open, wide open, so there could be no confusion.

And this time, Tom Grace kissed her back. He took her face in his hands and steered her mouth under his, his own eyes blinking just to be sure. But he *was* sure. As little sense as it made—and it made *none*—Tom was as certain about wanting to kiss her as he had been about moving Dean and himself to this damp and lonely house at the end of the world.

"The mattresses . . ." Tom pulled back the tiniest bit from her mouth. "They're all outside. Everything soft is outside."

"I don't care," Tess whispered.

Neither did he. In that moment, and for the first time in a very long time, Tom didn't care about anything but sliding over this woman, sliding into her. He didn't care about police calls or cell phone signals or empty liquor bottles rolling around the back of Dean's car. He didn't care about secrets or guilt or regrets.

It was the sea air, Tom told himself as he lowered Tess carefully to the floor. He was drunk on salt, overtired, maybe even a little lost. Here, without Dean, he wasn't sure who he was, but he liked this person he was becoming. This person who after a single day, not even twenty-four hours, craved someone he didn't know, who thought obsessively about a split second of breast, a stash of empty shampoo bottles in a cluttered bathroom, the sweet smell of fresh wood curls pooling on the floor of a crooked shed.

Beneath him, Tess closed her eyes.

TOM FOUND THEM A BLANKET, a cheaply made thing that, even almost threadbare from wear and wash, was still scratchy and stiff. They hadn't undressed, only unzipped, though his hands had sought out her breasts and managed to free them from her bra. Now they lay there, considering the ceiling.

When Tess rose without a word, Tom expected she meant to leave, to flee without saying good-bye, regretting what they'd done, but then he heard the creak of the refrigerator door, the thud of several cabinets opened and shut, and a few minutes later, the padding of her bare feet returning across the floor.

She sat back down on the blanket, across from him, considering him.

"Do you know that you have absolutely nothing to eat in this whole house?" she said.

"I know." Tom rose up on his elbows. "I'm working on it."

Then she remembered. "I have lasagna. And cheesecake. They're in the car." Tess saw his eyes narrow quizzically and she said, "Don't ask."

"I won't." Tom smiled. "Maybe you should go get them."

"Maybe I should." Tess smiled back at him. It was a remarkable expression, he thought. Her whole face seemed to light up.

Tess reached out to the crease between his brows, the groove so severe in the shadows of dusk, like a scar. She rubbed the line gently with her fingertip.

"You should really do something about that," she said.

Then she was gone.

1887

"I DON'T HAVE TO GO, Lydie."

Lydia licked mustard from her fingers, the thick slices of baked ham she'd cut for her husband's lunch tucked neatly between two pieces of bread. It was nearly seven. Banks's carriage was due to arrive by eight so the men could set sail by ten.

"Of course you have to go," she said, as calmly as she could, even as her heart thundered to imagine him on the water again.

"It's not as if I haven't been out recently," Linus had patiently reminded her in the weeks leading up to this day. "I go out on the boat to take soundings all the time." It was true; he did. Yet somehow those regular trips to check the channel markers in the inlet never worried her. But this would be different. This was a sailboat, and he'd be the only one on it who knew what to do if conditions grew rough. And it had been months since he'd sailed.

But as anxious as it made her, Lydia knew her husband needed the distraction. It was now their fourth month in their new home, and it seemed the fresh landscape had done nothing to further their plans to start a family. Once she'd suggested they meet with a specialist in Boston, someone who might advise them, but Linus had bristled so terribly at the idea that she'd dropped it at once, the look of perceived failure on his face so crushing, Lydia had wanted to cry.

She wrapped his sandwich in paper, trying to focus her nerves on the crisp edges, setting it inside a basket with a tin of Indian pudding, shortbread, and several wedges of hard cheese. "I'll be fine here," she said. "After all, it's only a day."

Linus crossed the room to her, his coat not yet buttoned all the way. "Trying to be my brave girl, I see."

"I don't have to try," Lydia said proudly.

"I know you don't." He glanced through the kitchen window to the tower, something he did compulsively as of late she noticed, as if a chance existed that it might not be there. He pulled her into his arms. "It's not even one day. I bet we're back before three."

"You'd better not be," she teased. "I didn't go to the trouble to wash this old thing for a half-day show."

"Fine, I'll wear it to bed tonight," he whispered. "How does that sound?"

"Itchy."

Linus laughed loudly at that and kissed her, tasting the blueberries she'd scattered in their pancakes that morning.

DESPITE HER JESTING, despite the flawless ceiling of blue that hung over the Point, Lydia felt a keen sense of fear the moment Linus left. It wasn't as if she didn't have things to do. There were her gardens to weed, bread to bake, beans to soak, two pairs of trousers that needed repairing, wash that needed hanging. Yet she couldn't manage to finish any of it. The house seemed stifling to her, but when she dropped to the ground to weed her gardens, she couldn't get through a single row before she climbed to her feet again and looked around the property. She knew Angus had arrived—she'd seen him cross the walkway to the lighthouse a few minutes after Linus had left. When the young man emerged again just before lunch, Lydia waved to him from the clothesline where she struggled to hang sheets in a fierce wind. When one escaped the line before she could pin it and tumbled across the yard, Angus raced for it, catching it after a short chase. He returned, winded but smiling.

"Slippery things, aren't they?" Lydia teased, taking the sheet from him. "Thank you."

Angus glanced up at the sky. "Perfect day for a sail. I'm sure Mr. Harris is enjoying Mr. Banks's new boat."

"I'm sure he is. Do you like to sail?"

"Oh, I wish. The only time I'm on the water is to help my brother fish for herring."

"I'm sure your nephews help too?"

"The older one does," Angus said. "He's practically a fish himself."

"My husband can't have children."

Lydia didn't know what made her say it, what made her give up this terrible truth to a total stranger so abruptly when she couldn't summon the words to her sisters in three years. She knew only that it felt good, so incredibly freeing, to have said them.

She turned slowly to Angus, wondering what he could be thinking. His expression was not as she expected. She'd been so sure he'd shake off her words; that he'd look to the horizon, mention the sun or the clouds, anything to bury her impossible confession. Instead, he looked upon her with such compassion, such sadness, that she cried at once.

DUSK CAME AND WENT.

Lydia could see the glow of the lantern in the tower

room from her post at the kitchen window, growing brighter as the sky darkened. Surely Angus couldn't stay there all night.

She tried to busy herself with dinner, but her hands shook so badly while she poured the cornmeal that more fell over the side of her bowl than went in. With every crackle or crunch that she heard outside, her eyes flew to the door, sure as she was that it was Linus returned home.

At eight thirty, Angus came by. He stood in the doorway, his hands in the pockets of his canvas jacket. She had wanted to appear calm, as if she hadn't given much thought at all to Linus's lateness, to the blackening of the sky, the quickening of the wind off the water. But Angus had only to look at her face before he offered, "I can stay on, ma'am. I've no one at home waiting."

Linus would want him to, Lydia told herself. After all, she couldn't possibly resurrect the flame on her own if the lamp went out.

"You don't mind?" she asked, her voice thin with fear.

"Not at all. I can sleep in the tower. I've done it before."

"Don't be silly. You'll stay here, in the house."

Angus shook his head firmly. "No. I couldn't."

"That's nonsense. Why should you sleep on a cold floor when there's an extra bedroom?"

Lydia knew why, of course, and she could see he wouldn't be swayed. He agreed to wait while she brought him a pillow and a stack of quilts.

"One'll do," Angus said, taking only the top quilt. "It stays plenty warm up there."

Lydia walked him outside. "If you need anything," she said. "Anything at all."

"They probably just pulled in somewhere for the night. Maybe they needed a repair. I'm sure Mr. Harris'll be back first thing."

She smiled gratefully, forcing her smile to remain until she'd closed the door behind him and collapsed against it.

WHEN SHE WOKE, Angus was in the yard, chopping wood, already with an impressive pile behind him. She pulled on one of Linus's coats, bracing herself for the early-morning chill. Angus heard her approach and lowered his axe, tipping his cap.

"I noticed you didn't have much kindling in the shed," he said.

"Shouldn't you go back?" she asked, squinting against the bitter air. "Your brother must be worried."

"It's all right. He knows I'm here. He knows . . ."

That Linus is missing, Lydia thought. The whole of the Harbor knew. They were all missing—Linus and Eli Banks and two other men whose names she didn't even know. It seemed outrageous to her now, this lack of knowledge.

"I should go into town, find out what news there is," she said, looking around, thinking the blades of grass looked so stiff and cold, as if they would surely snap off like icicles if touched.

"Let me go," said Angus. "If I take the boat, I can be across the bay in a half hour. Save you hitching up the horses."

No, she thought. She couldn't bear to be here alone with this knot in her stomach, this weight against her temples, this racing heart.

Nothing could be worse than this fear, she decided.

"I'll go with you," she said.

Angus frowned at her. "Then you want me to hitch up the buggy?"

"No," Lydia said, seeing his eyes fix on her with confusion. "I'll go with you in the boat."

SHE SAID NOTHING AS HE rowed them across the bay. She wasn't even sure she could have made a sound come out if he had requested one. She'd lost feeling in her hands—not from the cold, though it was brisk on the water—but from the terrible way she'd crushed them between the folds of her skirt and kept them there, as if doing so might contain her panic at being so close to the ocean. It helped some to keep her eyes down, to focus on the puddles of seawater that rocked back and forth at their feet. Angus had set a log under her shoes to protect them. The leather of his boots glistened wet, the toes a dark brown.

"If it helps," he said, "you can look at me."

Lydia studied the lines of his face, the shape of his nose, trying to decide if his hair was chestnut or just a very deep chocolate. If he minded her study, he didn't let on. Occasionally he glanced at her as he rowed, his smile slight but steady.

THERE WAS A GREAT DEAL of activity on the wharf when they arrived, so much that their small boat was steered to the side, though as soon as someone recognized Lydia, their passage was reinstated.

Two men helped Lydia out and led her up the landing while Angus stayed behind with the boat. The scene on the street was chaotic and loud. The town manager was there. Though she'd met him only once during their first week at the Point, when he'd come by with his wife to welcome them with a pie, Lydia recognized him right away. She didn't, however, recognize the woman beside him, dressed in a fitted jacket of burgundy patterned velvet and standing stiffly with her gloved hands at her sides as if bracing herself for a terrible gust of wind.

She had to be Mrs. Banks, Lydia thought. She'd called all of the men in town to find her husband. She might not even know that Linus was missing too. And where were the wives of the other men? Before Lydia could seek them out, she felt a hand on her arm.

"Lydia." She looked up to meet the worried features of

Annabeth Owen's husband, Merrill. "I was on my way to the Point. Did Linus say anything to you about changing course?"

"Nothing," she said. "Why would he?"

"I don't know."

"That's Banks's wife, isn't it?" Lydia asked.

"Yes. Come on. I'll get you to her."

A few moments later, the woman in burgundy turned her attention to Lydia. "You are?"

"Lydia Harris. My husband, Linus, sailed with your husband yesterday."

"Oh." The woman's face drained of its color. She reached for Lydia's hands, clasping them in hers and giving them a firm shake. "Don't you worry for him, dear. They're all fine, I'm sure. My husband is wicked and often extends his trips this way. I'm not worried. Really, I'm not."

If she wasn't worried, then why all the commotion? wondered Lydia. Why the news of a search party that had already been dispatched?

"We'll let you know as soon as we hear anything," a man in a coast guard uniform told Lydia. "In the meantime, we'll send an officer to tend to the lighthouse."

"That's not necessary," she said. "My husband left someone in charge."

This news seemed to startle the man. "Why did he do that? Did he expect to be away longer than just a day?"

"No," Lydia said quickly, feeling suddenly as if she

were guilty of something, as if she'd said something wrong. "It's just that I can't manage the lamp when he's gone. I'm afraid of the water, you see."

But he didn't see; Lydia could sense that well enough. The man frowned at her a moment, then nodded for Merrill to escort her away from the crowd.

"You really should let them send someone down," Merrill Owen said, stepping so close, Lydia could smell the sandalwood of his shaving soap.

"No," she answered dully, searching past his shoulder for a glimpse of Angus. "It's fine. Angus knows what he's doing."

Behind her, men mumbled in a crowd.

"It doesn't make sense," she heard one say. "There's just not that many places they could go."

"And the weather," said another. "It's been nothing but calm."

Lydia wanted to clap her hands over her ears. She couldn't bear the cacophony of theories, or bewilderment. Finally, like something shining, Angus appeared. She pushed past Merrill, pressing through a crowd that was curved around the dock, and reached him at the edge of the landing.

"I can't be here," she said. "Please take me back."

SHE COULDN'T EAT.

She sat at the table, staring at the bowl of soup she'd

ladled. She'd served one for herself and one for Angus who had insisted on taking his dinner to the lantern room, sure he would catch a glimpse of Banks's boat before the sun dropped completely. Nothing seemed real. She picked up her spoon and turned it in her fingers as if to hope this moment, this nightmare, wasn't flesh and bone. But the utensil felt heavy and cold in her hand, and she set it back in her bowl, letting it sink into the thick, milky broth.

When Angus appeared, she knew she couldn't bear another night alone in the house. She decided she would beg him if she had to, but there was no need. Maybe he saw the terror in her eyes when she met him at the door; maybe he saw something else. Whatever the reason, Angus agreed to make a bed for himself in front of the hearth.

Lydia stared at the linens she'd given him, tinted gold from the fire. "I'm not entirely sure I can live without him," she whispered.

"They'll find your husband," Angus said. "Mark my words. They'll find him safe and sound."

Try as she did to believe him, Lydia couldn't sleep. Her mind tumbled with the certainty of something ending, something closing up. And it was in those moments of panic that she rose from her bed and padded down the stairs. She could hear Angus's breathing in the darkness, and she paused a moment in the doorway, the last embers of the fire just enough to outline his shape. If he shunned her, she would pretend to have been walking in her sleep. But when she came beside him, when she nudged the

143

quilts open enough to slide in, he didn't hesitate to draw her against him. When she slipped her hand through the gap in his trousers, he didn't stop her.

She told herself this would bring Linus back. If she carried a child, he would know it. Wherever he was, her beloved husband would gather his strength, and he would return to her. And she would make things right the only way she could now. There was no one else she wanted to raise a child with, no other man she wished to spend the rest of her life with, but she could not live without a child. If they waited too long, all could be lost. Never again would she have this chance.

The light from the cooling embers was faint, growing fainter—so faint, Lydia might have thought it was Linus's hands on her, Linus's body coming over hers.

But this man smelled different, like woodsmoke and damp leaves.

She could feel Angus's breath near; she knew he would kiss her.

"Do you love someone?" she whispered.

"Yes," he said, reaching her mouth. "Very much."

THEY FELL QUICKLY INTO A routine. But what else was there to do? Four more days passed, three more search parties being dispatched and returning without news. She and Angus spoke little during the day, sharing polite conversation at meals, glancing at each other when their paths crossed, then coming together in the darkness, unmoving until dawn. Still, try as they did to keep their distance, Lydia feared the rumors had begun, a suspicion that was confirmed when Miles Keene came by one afternoon.

"I'm looking for Angus," he said quietly when Lydia arrived at the door to greet him. She stepped back to offer Angus's brother entrance as she always did, but Miles wouldn't move, no matter that rain fell. He stood just outside the doorway, as if afraid to get too close. It wasn't like Miles, this distance, this quick tone, these lowered eyes, but Lydia knew well enough what had come over him.

"He's in the tower," she said with a small smile that did nothing to change Miles's fraught expression, but she hadn't expected it would.

Miles nodded and left. Lydia watched him make his way down the path.

HE KNEW NO ONE WOULD believe him, but the truth was that Angus hadn't meant to fall in love with her. As he stood in the lantern room, working the rag over the lens, his mind thumbed through memories like the pages of a book, catching on passages. Had he known that first day, standing in the keeper's house, meeting her eyes for the first time? Had he known then that he might care for her this way? He frowned, his circles on the glass growing smaller, slower as he considered it. No, he thought. And if he had, surely he had dismissed such feelings. He knew better than to feel something for someone he couldn't have. But then, to blame it on circumstance would have been false too. Taking her hand that day and helping her up into this very room he stood in now, standing beside her as she'd faced the vista of the sea, Angus had been stirred by her, deeply so, and the feeling had seemed almost binding, so intimate and startling that he'd wanted to reach into the air for it and store that fleeting sensation in his pocket like a souvenir, to keep and hold for the future. He and Lydia could have been the only two people in the world at that moment, and he wouldn't have minded it. Confessing that, even in the quiet of his mind, filled him with culpability, yet he refused to accept any guilt. After all, he had done nothing wrong. He had only comforted someone who was hurting, doing what any compassionate person would do. That he loved her, that he even believed he could make her happy outside this fortress of white and light and salt didn't change that.

Now as he looked out onto the lawn and saw his brother sweeping through the hedges, Angus knew his reasoning would mean nothing to anyone else. The truth he knew in his heart would be as firm as a handful of sand to anyone else who tried to hold it.

When Miles finally emerged from the opening in the lantern room floor, he said nothing, simply moving to the windows and looking out a long moment before he turned to Angus, his voice thick. "I was wondering how much longer you plan to go on this way."

Angus kept his eyes on his task. "As long as it takes," he said. "She can't manage all this by herself. She can't even bear to climb the stairs."

"You know that's not what I mean." Miles dragged a chapped hand down his eyes, his cheeks, as if trying to rub the expression of dread from his face. He moved to the lens, his voice dropping. "People are talking, Angus."

Angus worked the rag harder against the glass. "I care for her. It's no one's business."

"Don't be dim. You know how it is. It's not right, your being here. Day and night."

"He's not coming back."

"No, he's likely not," agreed Miles, his expression still strained. "But it doesn't change that she's a married woman and the two of you are . . ."

Angus's eyes darted to Miles then, waiting for him to finish his thought and knowing what Miles meant to say but couldn't bring himself to, the flush of color on his brother's full cheeks explanation enough.

Miles sighed. "I know you care for her, Angus. Anyone can see that."

Angus moved around the lens, eyes down, jaw set. Here it was, he thought, the moment where it would all change for him, the moment he couldn't turn back from—grains of sand, feathers caught in the wind. Only he could grasp what was real now. "Tell Sarah I cut down that frame she wanted," he said. "I left it against the house. It should fit now."

Miles stared at his younger brother. Angus could feel his gaze, knowing without looking that Miles hoped for some sign that he might relent, and as much as Angus could never mean to cause his brother grief, he could no sooner relent now than he could fly over the water like a gull.

IT WAS MERRILL OWEN WHO came charging up the road just before noon on Friday, his long face splotchy with excitement. He was so winded when Lydia arrived at the door, he couldn't speak for several seconds, but of course he didn't need to. Lydia knew at once.

"They've been found," she said, breathless.

"Yes," Merrill managed, wincing when he swallowed. "They're alive. Thank God, they're alive."

Six

THERE WERE DAYS IN THE beginning, lots of them, when Buzz never really believed his luck. It wasn't that he hadn't been wanted by women before, but Ruby was by far the most dazzling woman he'd ever laid eyes on, and that she'd agreed to sleep with him even once would have been amazing enough.

One minute he'd been a mopey divorcé who'd taken the invitation of some old friends to meet at a folk festival in New Hampshire; the next minute he'd found himself rendered speechless by a woman with frizzy blond hair and an enormous smile who had set up a table selling her paintings on the back of old license plates. Buzz had already decided he'd buy one, but then a little girl—her daughter, he suspected—had swooped in with her sales pitch, delivered between bites of brownie and a fierce stare over the top of her oversized sunglasses. Buzz had left their booth with five pieces. But he'd also left with the woman's name ("Ruby—like the slippers") and the plan to come back later that afternoon to see her again. She was thirty-five, she told him. And she'd just come out of a bad marriage. So had he, but he didn't have any kids. She'd asked whether he liked kids, and Buzz had answered that he did, though when Ruby had asked him why he never had any of his own, he'd shrugged. It hadn't been for lack of wanting; he had always enjoyed kids and had always liked being around them. But Beth had never seemed comfortable with the idea, and he'd let the subject fall away over the years.

"Sounds like you and she weren't a good match. It's not your fault," Ruby had said then, her eyes so bright that Buzz had felt as if she'd lifted a weight off him with those simple words, as if she'd granted him some kind of absolution.

Later, they'd carried plates of barbecued chicken and coleslaw to one of the bonfires that would rage long into the night. She'd explained that they'd come from California, having always wanted to see the East Coast. (He would learn later that they'd been kicked out of their apartment after Ruby had spray-painted the car of their salacious landlord and he'd threatened criminal charges.) He'd told them he had always wanted to see California but that he'd gotten only as far as Nevada and that he lived in a small town by the water.

And that was when Buzz had mentioned the mermaids.

"No way!" Tess's green eyes had grown enormous on her small face. The night air was cold enough for a blanket—Buzz had found Tess and Ruby one. Ruby's eyes looked like beads of amber in the firelight; he could have stared into them all night.

"Are the mermaids still there?" Tess asked, bursting.

"Maybe." Buzz grinned. "You'll just have to come visit me sometime and find out."

"We could come back with you right now," Ruby said, her expression so serious, Buzz had been speechless for a moment. Could they really do that? Surely Ruby had a job somewhere. Surely Tess had school to get back to—third grade, maybe fourth; he wasn't sure how old she was. But when Buzz saw the pile of garbage bags that Ruby picked through that next morning to find them fresh clothes, he knew at once she and Tess hadn't anywhere to get back to, and the desire to offer them a home, a safe place, was instantaneous—utterly irrational but fierce. He knew how it would look to bring them back to the Harbor, and he knew his sister would have a fit over it. What would he say? The truth was that even as he packed them into his truck two days later, he didn't know himself what had come over him. But was that so wrong? All he knew was that in the last forty-eight hours, he'd found someone who never once asked him if he ever planned to cut his hair or if he was sorry he'd gotten that tattoo of a raven on his right forearm. He had found someone who made him laugh, someone who made him want to make love again, someone who made the world seem kind and warm for a man who had spent a good portion of his forty-four years on it feeling anything but.

"It snows there, doesn't it?" Tess had asked on their way up Interstate 95. Ruby had fallen asleep just outside of Portsmouth, minutes after they'd crossed the Piscataqua River Bridge into Kittery. But Tess had barely taken a breath since they'd left the festival. Buzz didn't know kids could talk so much or so long without stopping.

"It snows," he'd answered. "Some winters more than others."

"It doesn't snow in California."

"Sure it does. In some parts, it snows a whole lot."

"I thought you said you'd never been to California," Tess had said.

"I haven't. I still know it snows there."

"So where does it snow?"

"The mountains."

"Maybe," she'd consented, but only after staring at him long enough that Buzz had looked away from the road to meet her leveled gaze. He'd had no choice but to chuckle then, startled to see how someone so tiny could be so damn stubborn.

"What were you thinking, Buzzie?"

His sister, Joan, was the first to make her concern known several weeks later, after he'd settled Ruby and Tess into the trailer. Truth be told, Buzz had marveled at her restraint. His sister wasn't one to wait to speak her mind when it came to his life choices. The three of them—he, Joan, and Frank—had come together to ask Buzz's opinion on a new television, but Buzz knew it was only a ruse to get him alone.

And sure enough, as soon as he was delivered his coffee, as soon as he'd drizzled cream over the top and stirred it to beige, Joan had started in.

"I mean, really, Buzzie," she said. "You bring this woman home, this woman who has a child—a *child*—and you think you'll set up house? Just like that? For goodness' sake, you don't know anything about this woman. You met her at a music festival. Was she even sober? Were *you*?"

"Joan," Frank interjected disapprovingly. Buzz's sister lowered her eyes, brushing lint from her skirt.

"Sometimes things just happen," Buzz defended, his gaze moving to Frank. "Things you don't expect."

"Are you prepared to put this child in school?" Joan asked. "She has to be in school."

"I'm registering her tomorrow, as a matter of fact," Buzz said.

Joan glanced at Frank.

"It's just so soon after Beth," she said softly. "I just don't want to see you get hurt again, that's all."

"It's been a year, Joan," Frank argued. "He's divorced; not widowed."

Buzz had smiled gratefully at his brother-in-law for that.

Later, after the conversation had finally veered onto a more pleasant road and they'd enjoyed a second cup of coffee, Frank walked Buzz back to his truck.

"Joan worries for you," Frank said gently. "You know that's all it is."

"She worries, all right. She worries I'll embarrass the hell out of her."

"We both know I'm the one who could do that."

Buzz nodded, looking down as he always did when Frank spoke of the accident. If people wondered why they were so close for being such different men, they need only have known of the confession Frank had revealed to Buzz just a few months earlier.

Frank had never intended his secret shame to be anyone else's burden, but as he'd already learned for himself, people could find themselves in the wrong place at the wrong time. Looking for a pen, Buzz had come upon newspaper clippings of a car accident outside of Chicago that had claimed the lives of two people and seriously injured another, articles about a high school student named Dean Grace who was a rising star in the world of competitive swimming.

When Buzz had confronted him about the discovery, Frank might have lied, of course. He could surely have brushed off the clippings, claimed they had belonged to someone else, claimed the boy had been a relative, a friend's son, anything. But the truth was that Frank had been secretly wishing for a chance to relieve himself of the burden of his crime—and he knew there was no one he could trust more than his brother-in-law.

"I ran a family off the road, Buzz."

"You what?"

"I wasn't drunk. Nothing like that. I was reaching for the map and I *drifted*. . . ."

Buzz had stared a long while at Frank, his thoughts straining to put this information together. "What are you saying?"

"There were boys in the car too. Teenage boys. One was a champion swimmer. He was going to the Olympics. That was what all those articles said, anyway."

"Oh Jesus, Frank."

"I meant to stop right away; I really did. I drove back into town to go to the police, to get help, but I—I panicked. I thought of Joan, I thought of everything. . . ." Frank looked toward the window, where Joan and a neighbor were laughing over a stretch of rugosa bushes that separated their properties. "I got as far as Toledo before I pulled over at a phone—I couldn't take it. They connected me to the area dispatch, and I told the officer that I'd seen a car in trouble. Crashed. He said they were already on the scene, that there were fatalities, so I just hung up. I was in shock," he admitted. "I've been sending the boys money every month. The older one knows everything. I send him money and he takes it. I'd give them everything I have if I could. It wouldn't be enough, but I would."

"Wait, you're saying this boy knows? How do you know he won't go to the police, Frank?"

"He doesn't know my name, and even if he did, I don't think he would risk it. I don't think he can be without the money now." Frank looked to the window again, his gaze falling this time on the lilac bush that hugged the side of the garage. "I'm going out there in a few weeks. It's a conference—I don't really have any business going, but I've told Joan I need to. Really, I just want to see them."

"See them? Frank, you can't do that."

"I don't mean face-to-face," said Frank. "Just . . . I don't know . . . drive by their house. Just see if they're all right." He turned back to Buzz, his eyes filled with tears. "I just have to see them for myself."

"But this young man has proof," Buzz pressed. "He has your confession. He could take all that to the cops, for Christ's sake."

But he never did. Buzz would remind himself of that fact over the years. Tom Grace had said nothing, and neither had Buzz. And now the young man was an adult, and that adult was here in Cradle Harbor. Tom Grace was here, and Frank was gone.

God, Buzz missed him. This mess he'd made with Tess, the days it seemed he couldn't do right by her—which were more than the days he *could*—Frank could always seem to set things right between them. It was the salesman in him, Frank would say, always brushing off any admiration Buzz would send his way. But it was more than that. Frank could talk a pack of wolves off a found fawn. He made people see what they were missing, see what a waste of time being angry was, that life was too short for grudges; that they might not get a second chance to do the right thing, to say they loved someone, to say they were sorry. Frank had been that way before the accident. Afterward, it was his religion, and Buzz alone knew the reason for his total conversion.

Now Buzz looked out from the trailer window, hoping to see Tess's VW returned but finding the space in front of the woodshop empty. He did, however, see Beverly Partridge's white sedan.

Curiosity gnawed at him. It wasn't like him to check up on guests; far from it, his manner being the seen-not-heard school of hosting, but he did feel particularly responsible for this guest. He'd chastised Tess for her concerns over the safety of her mother's things; the last thing he wanted was to have to eat his words.

The cottage porch was quiet. Buzz took the steps carefully, hoping he wasn't disturbing her. He knocked just once, stepping back from the door in case she wanted to peek out. A few moments later, Beverly arrived.

"If this is about the quilt . . . ," she began stiffly.

Buzz frowned, confused. "What quilt?" he asked.

"She didn't tell you?"

"Who?"

Beverly folded her arms. "Your daughter. She threw quite a tantrum earlier."

"Oh hell." Buzz sighed, then rubbed at his beard. "I'm sorry. I probably should have mentioned to you that she might be a little chilly about your staying in here."

"Chilly? She was positively hostile."

"I'll speak to her," said Buzz, glancing back to the woodshop.

"Don't bother," Beverly said. "The last thing I need is another earful from her. I will, however, need a new quilt for my bed. She took the one that was here because I had the *nerve* to air it out over the railing for a few minutes."

So that was it, Buzz thought. *Ruby's favorite quilt.*

Beverly frowned at him. "Why *are* you here, then?" she asked pointedly.

"I just wanted to make sure you were comfortable."

"Aside from the *un*welcoming committee," Beverly said, "yes, I'm managing."

Buzz smiled gratefully. *The* un*welcoming committee.* Well, at least the woman had a sense of humor about it all, which was more than he could say for Tess.

"I'll bring you down a replacement right away," he said.

Beverly nodded tightly. "And a few extra towels, please."

"All right."

He could do that. He could do more than that; somehow Buzz felt as if he should. He'd balled up her reservation, and now Tess had given her hell for innocently hanging out a quilt. He was damn lucky Beverly Partridge hadn't reported him to the Better Business Bureau.

"If there's nothing else then," Beverly began suggestively, her hand on the door, her smile polite but clear.

"No," Buzz said, stepping back. "I'll get you that quilt and those towels."

"If I'm not here, you can leave them on the porch," she told him. "I'll be going into town in a bit and I turn in early, so I'd appreciate it if you could get them here before seven."

"Not a problem," Buzz said cheerfully, barely getting the words out before she'd closed the door on him.

WHILE TOM WARMED THE PAN, Tess set the table: two unmatched plates, two glasses, a plastic pitcher of water, candles she'd found in the pantry.

They moved about the kitchen together, shifting quietly around each other like passengers on a subway switching seats—passengers who'd shared looks of interest, quick ones, then longer ones, until it was clear that something romantic was at stake.

At the table, Tess cut into the lasagna, feeling Tom watching her as she dragged the knife back and forth.

"You sure he won't mind that I'm eating his dinner?"

She shrugged. "It's not his anymore." She served them each a fat square, the stringy cheese sticking to her fingers. "He had his chance."

"I don't have to worry about him coming over here in the middle of the night and challenging me to a duel or something over it, do I?" Tom asked. "Because I've never hit anyone in my whole life. I wouldn't even know where to aim."

Tess grinned, thinking Libby Wallace was right. He *was* handsome. "No," she said. "You don't have to worry about that."

They ate, the sky growing dark outside, so dark that the scalloped-edged noodles on their unmatched plates looked blue, even with the candlelight, but she had asked him not to turn on the overhead.

"I hate those lights," Tess said, glaring up at the old fixture. "They make every room look like an empty pool." Which had, of course, made Tom think briefly of Dean, but as was becoming common around her, thoughts of Dean were easily swept away. The smell of dinner was working its magic on the room, on the whole house. For the first time since he'd arrived, the house felt to Tom as if someone might live there. With the scents of life—food and company and the sounds of their conversation—suddenly the walls didn't seem so bare, the floors so cold.

She'd taken off her sneakers. He kicked one by accident under the table, startled at first.

"Where did you learn to carve like that?" he asked.

"Here and there. I'm self-taught, mostly. I wanted to paint like my mom, but I couldn't quite work the colors the way I wanted to, so she suggested I try something else. 'Something without colors,' were her exact words. Buzz knew a sculptor, and he showed me a few things to get me started. After that, I couldn't stop, really."

"You're very talented."

She smiled at him across the table. It had been a long time since someone had told her that, since she'd been asked about her work. She liked talking about it, liked thinking about it. For Buzz, for Pete, everyone who knew her, those stories of how and when were second nature. It was strange to think this man didn't know anything about her life. Tom Grace knew nothing about her mother, about the world they'd built together, about the years after she'd gone. But then, she knew nothing about him, either.

"I don't have an artistic bone in my body," Tom said, sawing at a stubborn rope of mozzarella. "I'm one of those people whose drawing of a person looks exactly the same way at thirty-five as it did when I was five. But I can draw a mean hangman if you ever want to play."

Tess laughed at that, tucking one foot under herself. "Well, I can't spell my way out of a paper bag, so you'll win for sure."

He was ravenous; Tom couldn't remember ever being this hungry before and couldn't recall food ever tasting this good, this fresh, this rich. When he'd scraped up the last swirl of sauce and ricotta, Tess looked at her own empty plate and said, "It's late. I don't like to drive in the dark. I'm terrified of hitting a deer or a raccoon."

"You could stay," he suggested, then added quickly, "I don't mean *with me*. I'll bring in the mattresses. I should anyway. You could have your own room. There's plenty of them upstairs."

But she didn't want her own room. Wasn't it too early for bed? Then why was she so tired, so ready to collapse? She glanced to the window, seeing the silhouette of the hedges shiver in the breeze.

"Don't bring the beds in," she said. "Leave them out there."

"What for?"

She got up from the table and moved to the door, beckoning Tom to follow. "You'll see."

OUTSIDE, THE AIR WAS ALREADY crisp with night's chill, the wind stronger when they rounded the house to the lawn. Only one of the spreads had broken free from its stone weights and been blown a few feet away. Tom swept it up and carried it to where Tess stood beside the least lumpy of the mattresses. She dropped down and looked up at him, waiting for him to join her. He did, tentatively, and they lay shoulder to shoulder, looking up.

The canopy of stars was endless.

"Do you know the constellations?" she asked.

Tom didn't. He'd grown up in the city, where it was rare to see the stars. He reached up, connecting the dots of Orion's belt, the only one he knew, the one everyone knew.

Tess liked the way his body felt next to her, the crispness of his shirtsleeves against her as she lifted her arm to point. "Okay, let's see who else is out tonight. . . . I see Lyra. And can you see those stars that make a cross? That's Cygnus, the Swan. . . ."

This was something Dean would do, Tom thought suddenly, watching Tess's face, caught in the path of the parlor light he'd left on, her fingers tracing the air. He wasn't thinking of just this moment, but all of it—stumbling upon a woman half dressed, making love to her soon after, lying under the stars in a sea of mattresses. These sorts of things happened to Dean, not to him. But Dean wasn't here. For now, for once, Tom could breathe.

"It's cold," he said. "Aren't you cold?"

"Freezing," she confessed. He shook the spread out over her. Tess gripped it gladly, pulling it around her shoulders and thinking at once she was wrong. The smell of the salt had gone; now there was only sunshine and cold grass.

She turned to Tom, considering him a long moment before she asked, "So, what are you?"

"What do you mean?"

"Your sign."

"Oh God, I have no idea. . . ."

She rose up on her elbow, frowning disapprovingly at him. "How can you not know your sign?"

Tom shrugged. "Because it doesn't matter."

"Of course it matters," Tess said, indignant now. "It explains who you are."

"An astrological sign doesn't explain who I am. . . ."

"Want to bet?" She narrowed her eyes in challenge. "When's your birthday?"

Tom stretched out his legs, crossing his feet at the ankles. "Oh, come on. I don't believe in all that."

"I didn't ask if you did. I asked you your birthday."

Tom gave her a weary look and surrendered. "January sixth."

"Capricorn," she said.

"So does it?" he asked. "Does it *explain me*?"

"Maybe." She grinned. "Capricorns are earth signs. They're grounded and responsible and very, very serious."

Tom frowned, too enchanted to be sore or even defensive. "Coincidence," he said.

"What about your brother?"

"Don't you want to quit while you're ahead?"

She smiled. "I can't lose. The signs are always right."

"Fine," he agreed. "December second."

"Sagittarius. I know all about them. My mother was one. Everyone wants to be near a Sagittarius. They're irresistible."

That was Dean, all right, Tom thought as Tess dropped down beside him again. He turned his head to her as she settled back under the blanket, wanting very much in that moment to corral the hair that blew around her face, to guide those auburn waves behind her ear, that ear with all the empty holes.

The desire to know things about her—anything, *everything*—consumed him suddenly. Try as she had to raise a wall to him that morning, her emotions had won out. He knew if he pulled even gently on a seam, the whole of her heart might open up for him. It was a possibility that should have terrified him, but in that moment, lost under the stars, Tom didn't care.

He reached out, gathered a few strands of her hair, and tethered them. Tess closed her eyes, as if she'd slipped into a warm bath.

"It can be hard to be around people like that," Tom said.

Tess's eyes opened. She twisted her body to face him, perplexed. "What do you mean?"

She didn't agree; Tom could see that at once. "They can wear you out, that's all," he said.

Her expression remained dubious. "Only if you try to control them," she said firmly. "Only if you try to change them. And I know that's true, because that's exactly what Buzz did with my mother."

Tom studied her as she traced the edge of his collar.

She looked up, meeting his eyes. "Not so much in the beginning." Her face softened again, as if she'd caught a sweet scent that reminded her of something. "At first they were so crazy about each other that my mother would have believed the sun was made of orange Jell-O if Buzz had told her to believe it. But then she started having her white days again, and he decided everything had to change."

Tom frowned. "White days?"

Tess smiled sadly. "That was what she used to call them. They weren't blue days, she'd say, because she never thought of blue as sad; blue was the color of water, and the water made her happy. But white was the absence of everything—the saddest, loneliest color she could imagine." Tom ran his knuckles along her cheek; again she closed her eyes, pressing into his hand like a cat.

"That must have been hard on you," he said.

"I was used to it. Those days never lasted long. We always got through them. But Buzz didn't understand that. He pushed her to see someone, to take medication, which she couldn't bear. He pushed and pushed. . . ." Tess hesitated, her eyes staying closed, squeezed shut for a moment; then they opened, slightly misted. "You can't push a Sagittarius," she said. "They won't change for anyone."

Tess rolled toward him, and this time she didn't need to ask for his embrace. Tom settled her against him as the wind lifted the edges of their blanket, brushing at the grass above their heads. Astrology, he thought, with its signs and legends. All the certainty she placed in things that were so uncertain—did she really believe it was all so clear-cut, so predictable? Was that why she lived her life without rules or constraints, because she thought the universe would simply keep order *for* her? And what of her mother? he wondered. She spoke of her mother's episodes like a child would, using romantic anecdotes to gloss over what any adult could surely see were bouts of deep depression, which Buzz had obviously detected and tried to remedy. Surely Tess couldn't resent the man for his concern?

"Oh!" Tess sat up suddenly, her eyes round with alarm.

Tom rose too, startled. "What's wrong?"

"We didn't eat the cheesecake," she gasped.

He chuckled.

"What?" she asked.

"By the look on your face, I thought it was something serious," he said.

She gave him a gentle push, sending him down on his elbows. "That *is* serious, Tom Grace," she said, coming over him. "That's desperately serious."

Tom scanned her face in the watery dark, fiercely attracted to her. He wondered what it would feel like to make love to her in this tangy breeze; to wake up under this sky, clothes and skin and hair damp with dew. "I could go get it," he said.

She smiled. "And two forks."

"Two forks, right," he repeated as he climbed to his feet, leaving her to watch him cut through the grass and up the hill.

It was at that moment that Beverly, full from a passable dinner of shepherd's pie, pulled her sedan to the side of the road. She had finally found a vacant stretch of coastline where the pines thinned, and she could see at last the great tower in the distance, but, more important, she could see the outline of the keeper's house above it. And then, there he was, stepping up to the door, slipping briefly under the yellow wash of the porch light, revealed.

It was hard to be certain from so far, but at this distance, he didn't resemble Frank in any striking way. He was certainly taller than Frank, leaner, though his hair was dark—rust colored. Beverly squinted, as if it would matter, wondering if he meant to come back out and thinking it wouldn't hurt anything to wait and see.

Wednesday

**Two Days before the
Mermaid Festival**

ACCORDING TO THE SURVIVORS, THEY could recall
only that something had pierced the hull of their
sailboat shortly after one on that fateful afternoon,
making a gash so deep as to flood it at once and sink
it within minutes. When the authorities asked the
exact location of the wreck, the men collectively insisted that they could not recall, nor could they recall how they came to find refuge on an island so far
off their charted course. In a statement given weeks
later to the police, one of the men, a banker named
Timothy Orchard, claimed, "It was as if we had been
gone only the few hours we intended, or merely in
a deep sleep."

*—The Mermaid Mutiny and More:
A Complete History of Cradle Harbor*

Seven

TESS AND TOM HAD WATCHED the stars until midnight, maybe a little later—Tess hadn't been sure; they'd fallen asleep at some point and Tom had woken first, shivering, the spread slightly damp, so he'd gently roused her and they'd gone inside, Tom dragging a mattress with him and Tess carrying an armful of sheets and spreads she'd collected on the way. They'd managed to navigate their way upstairs and flopped the mattress onto the empty frame, resuming their embrace on the narrow bed.

Now the silver light of dawn was everywhere, and with it, the crisp cool of morning in an old house. Where had Tom gone? Downstairs, no doubt. On her way past the window, Tess looked out onto the back lawn, thinking maybe she'd see him there among the field of mattresses, but she didn't.

"Tom?"

She passed the bathroom, walking through a veil of misty air, still fragrant with the warm smell of soap. He'd managed to get the shower to work—just how long had he been awake?

The house was silent. She came downstairs, peering down the hallway and then hearing movement on the back porch. Tess knew as soon as she caught the faint sweetness of cigarette smoke that it wasn't Tom, but she pushed the screen open anyway. The man sitting on the steps with his back to her was lean and broad shouldered. His hair was the color of cherrywood, short and spiky, looking like a buzz cut growing out.

The screen released an announcing creak. The man swiveled on the step to face her, his blue eyes magnificent, almost silver. "Well fuck me," he said, grinning. "Now I know why my brother was in such a hurry to get here."

Tess let the screen shut behind her. She knew at once who he was.

"You're Dean, aren't you?"

"And you're Tess."

"How did you know my name?"

"I'm psychic." Dean winked, handing her a piece of paper with a few tidy lines written on it.

Tess,

Wanted to let you sleep. I'll be back with breakfast. I hope you'll stay.

Tom

"I hope you will too," Dean said.

Tess crossed her arms, trying to cover herself; she felt underdressed and unprepared. "I didn't hear you come in," she said. "I didn't hear anything."

"I know; I watched you sleep for almost an hour. . . ." Dean paused, seeing Tess's eyes round with concern before he leaned forward and roared, "I'm kidding! You should see your face right now."

She nodded over her shoulder. "I should really go. Tom doesn't even know you're here. He'll be back any minute."

"And that's exactly why you're staying. I want to see the look on Tommy's face when he sees I found you first." Dean patted the space beside him. "Come on—I won't bite. Not unless you want me to."

Tess dropped down beside him, studying his profile as he dragged deeply on his cigarette, expelling the smoke away from her. He looked nothing like Tom, she thought, but he was handsome in his own way—strikingly so. She noted his straight white teeth, remarkably white for a smoker, and his eyes, which looked right through a person.

He held out the pack. "Smoke?"

"No, thanks."

"Health nut, huh?"

"Hardly."

"Thank Christ for that." Dean snapped the pack closed, then turned to her, surveying her again. "Man, you're way too beautiful for my brother. You know that, don't you?"

Tess smiled. "Tom warned me about you."

"As well he should have." Dean leaned back on his elbows. "He didn't warn me about you, though."

"I don't see how he could have. We just met."

Dean pointed to the lawn. "So, what's with the mattresses?"

"Tom wanted to air them out."

"Ah." Dean snuffed out his cigarette on the bottom of his sneaker, dropped the butt on the porch, clapped his hands clean, and turned to her. "Let's get going, then."

"Where?"

He rose. "Where do you think? The beach."

Tess looked up at him, tenting her hand over her eyes. "Shouldn't we wait for Tom?"

"What for? He won't swim with us."

"Who's swimming?" she asked, incredulous. "You don't even have a suit."

Dean grinned as he extended his hand. "Who said anything about a suit?"

———

TOM WAS RIGHT. WATCHING DEAN cut through the white-tipped surf beyond her post on the empty stretch of pebble beach, Tess could see he loved to swim.

Several times he rose up out of the water and waved to her; Tess waved back, trying to imagine Tom and him as boys. They were like night and day.

When Dean emerged, she watched him make his way up the beach. He limped. She'd seen the hiccup in his gait on the way down and assumed it was just a sore muscle, too many hours in a car. Clearly, it wasn't.

Dean stopped in front of her, then shook his hair over her like a wet dog.

"Stop!" she cried, trying vainly to cover herself.

He dropped down beside her, smelling cold. Water glistened on the end of his nose.

"I'm on to you, lady," he murmured, leaning close.

"Oh you are, huh?" Tess said.

"Yup." He narrowed his eyes on her. "I know why you won't come in the water with me."

"And why is that?"

"You're one of these mermaids I saw advertised all over town, and you don't want me to see your tail."

"That would make me a *half* mermaid," Tess corrected.

"Then I'm right?"

She shrugged playfully, scooping up a handful of pebbles and letting them slide through her fingers. "I'll never tell. Besides, you're the one swimming like a fish. For all I know, you're a merman."

"Come back in with me and find out."

"Maybe some other time."

Dean lay down on the pebbly sand, folded his hands under his head, and closed his eyes, drawing in a deep breath of sea air.

"What did you do to your leg?" she asked.

His eyes remained closed. "I was rock climbing. Fell almost thirty feet."

Tess gasped. "Oh God, that's awful."

"It was touch and go for a while. I was in the hospital for a long time. They weren't sure I'd ever walk again, believe it or not."

"When?"

"A few years ago." Dean squinted open one eye at her. "He's too old for you too, you know."

She laughed. "You don't quit, do you?"

"He's thirty-five, for Christ's sake. He's *ancient*. You need a younger man like me."

"Is that right?" Tess smiled. "And how old are you?"

"A mere thirty-four."

"A baby," she teased.

"It's true," said Dean, rising up on one elbow. "Ask anyone; I'm completely infantile."

"I'll bet."

"So, what do you do in this place?" he asked.

"I'm a sculptor. Wood-carver, mostly."

"An artist. That's fantastic. Maybe if I stick around, I could model for you."

Tess frowned, confused. "I thought Tom said you were moving here."

"That's what he likes to think." Dean hurled a pebble into the water. "I told him I'd give it a shot; I didn't make any promises. Tommy hears what he wants to hear."

"Then you're not staying?"

"I haven't decided yet." Dean grinned at her. "Why? Are you saying I have a chance?"

"I'm saying we should go back," she answered, blushing. "I think I heard a car."

TOM FELT THE CHANGE THE minute he stepped into the house.

It was a charge, an electricity in the air, as if someone had ripped off the door, filled the downstairs with helium, and nailed it back up. Dean did that to a space. He sucked the air out of it, leaving everyone around him gasping for oxygen. Even now as Tom searched the first floor, he could feel his lungs tighten.

"Dean?"

No answer, but there were two cars in the driveway, Dean's and Tess's, the sight of which had filled Tom with dread when he'd pulled through the trees. Relief had been his first reaction, relief to see Dean's beat-up Jeep, relief to know his brother had finally arrived, alive. But it was a fleeting reprieve. He had wanted to get there first, wanted a chance to step between Dean and the people of this small town, especially Tess. His brother was like a hot liquid you needed to temper, adding a small drop to eggs because if you added him too quickly, the whole world would cook right before your eyes.

Tom was on his way upstairs when he saw them. He caught a glimpse of the backyard through a window, and there they were, his brother and the woman Tom had just made love to, walking up through the hedges and laughing like old friends.

Tom might have known.

He walked out to the back porch and down the stairs to meet them.

"Tommy!" Seeing his older brother, Dean threw up his arms like an athlete who'd made a winning goal.

But Tom wasn't yet ready to dole out hugs. Glad as he was to see Dean, frustration won out. "I must have called you a hundred times," he chastised. "Why didn't you call me back?"

"Look at his face!" Dean exclaimed undaunted, swinging an arm around his brother's neck and cuffing him close. "What did I say, huh? I told you he'd panic. You're terrified I stole your girlfriend, aren't you, old man?"

"Okay, okay, okay . . ." Tom gently untangled himself from Dean's grip, offering Tess an apologetic smile.

"So, do you want to tell him, or should I?" Dean came behind Tess, grabbing her around the waist. He pressed his face to her ear, looking at Tom as he whispered loudly, "She's crazy about me, Tommy. She told me so."

Tom held up the bag in his hand and shook it, like someone looking to distract a ferocious dog with a steak. "I bought muffins."

"Great—I'm starved." Dean snatched the bag and rummaged through it, pulling out a fat blueberry muffin. He tore off a bite, spraying crumbs as he said, "Tell me there's coffee somewhere."

"In the kitchen," Tom said, then added quickly, "I only got two. I wasn't expecting . . ."

"So we'll share," Dean decided cheerfully, thumping Tom on the back as he thrust the bag back at him. He stepped between Tess and Tom, throwing an arm over each of them. "So, what's the plan, kids? What are we doing today?"

"What do you think?" Tom said, growing annoyed as he always did when Dean blew into a situation, insistent as a puppy. "We've only just moved in, Dean. Calm down."

"I'm gonna ask Tess and see if I like her answer better." Dean turned to her, grinning.

Tess offered him a smile, helpless again to his infectious energy. "I should go back and work," she said. "I'm finishing a sculpture for the library."

"What a couple of deadbeats!" Dean cried. "What kind of welcome party is this?"

"It's not a party, Dean," Tom said firmly, removing his brother's arm.

"It is *too* a party," said Dean, walking backward now to face them. "I just got here, and I'm saying we need to celebrate. And don't even think about trying to take her out to dinner, Tommy," Dean warned, pointing between Tom and Tess. "I want to keep an eye on you two kids. I say, let's do dinner here. Tonight. I'll make us a five-star meal. Tess, baby, how do you feel about lobster?"

Tom rolled his eyes. "We're not buying lobster, Dean. . . ."

"I love it," Tess said, throwing a playful look at Tom.

Dean clapped his hands decidedly. "Then lobster it is. Tell you what, Tess. You bring the wine, and we'll cover the rest."

"I can do that," she agreed. "Red or white?"

"Better bring both. Wouldn't want any wine's feelings getting hurt, now would we?"

Tom sighed. "Dean, she just said she has to work."

"Oh, fuck all that. Work is for when you're dead—am I right?" Dean pointed over his shoulder. "Now, if you'll excuse me, I have to piss like a racehorse. See you tonight, fair lady." He swept up Tess's hand and delivered it a quick kiss. "And thanks for coming swimming with me," he said as he started back to the house. "Let's do it again sometime."

Tom watched Dean climb the hill. "He's already been in the water?" Tom turned to Tess, looking panicked. "Christ, how long has he been here? I wasn't gone more than an hour."

Tess smiled up at him. "It's okay," she said. "We had fun. I like him."

"I can see that."

"You're jealous."

"Not at all. Dean's a great guy. You'd be hard-pressed to find someone who wouldn't agree with you."

"Is he always like this?" she asked.

"Except when he's not." Tom glanced at the house, hearing the back door thump closed. "He's up and down. You never know."

They walked up the lawn to the driveway. When they reached her car, Tess said, "He told me about the rock-climbing accident. You must have been so scared for him."

Tom frowned. Rock climbing—so that was Dean's newest story.

"I'm sorry I wasn't here, but I didn't want to wake you," he said. "I wanted you to sleep. I thought we could have a nice breakfast and . . ."

Tess rose on her tiptoes and quieted him with a kiss, soft at first, then deepening when his hand came up to cradle her face. He tasted cold, she thought, like fall.

"He's wrong, you know," she whispered.

Tom leaned back, searching her upturned face. "About what?"

"You're not too old for me."

He chuckled. "Oh great, is that what he told you?"

"Among other things." Tess slipped free of his embrace and slid into the VW.

Tom drove his hands into his pockets and leaned down to speak to her through the window. "I'd really rather you didn't bring wine. He can't handle it, and frankly, neither can I."

"There's that line again," Tess said, pointing to his forehead.

"Yeah, well. You'll see it a lot when Dean's around."

But I'm here now too, she wanted to say, but didn't.

Tom waited until Tess had rounded the wall of pines before he started back across the lawn to the house, aware of the small but insistent smile that came with him. For too long he'd seen life as a series of accidents waiting to happen, tragedies waiting to unfold. Just when did he decide all things unplanned brought chaos and grief? He'd steeled himself against the bad for so long that he'd also avoided any chance at the good.

Well, no more.

It was going to be different here. No more would he let his guilt get in the way. No more excuses. Dean would manage well in Cradle Harbor. It was a small town, a pretty town, a kind town—save a few crotchety old women. Maybe he wouldn't have to watch over Dean here, not as he had before. There was only one bar, and people looked out for their neighbors; that was clear.

Yes, it was going to be different, and now that Dean was here, Tom would tell him so. He'd explain it all as best he could. It wouldn't make sense at first—it barely did to Tom himself; yet he would try to explain how he came to be falling for a woman he barely knew, how he came to have this sensation of freedom and promise coursing through him—not in strange bursts, but as a constant, driving stream. He would try to explain how he came to see hope in the smallest things, how vegetables tasted different, how sour sea air smelled sweet. Like pears.

BUZZ WAS IN THE DRIVEWAY, knocking signs into the shoulder, when Tess pulled down to the cove. She made her way to the woodshop, knowing he'd be over to check in. Sure enough, ten minutes later she heard his heavy steps crunching over the gravel.

"I was getting worried," he said. "I wasn't sure I was going to see you today."

Tess glanced up, seeing him studying her, sure he feared she'd been with Pete. As she turned back to her work, her gaze stopped at her mother's studio, where the white sedan was still parked beside the cottage.

Buzz saw where she looked and frowned. "I heard you made quite an introduction yesterday."

"She was hanging Mom's quilt off the railing like an old bath mat."

"You could have just asked her to put it back instead of making a scene."

"Is that what she told you? That I made a scene?"

"She didn't have to tell me. I took a wild guess."

Tess returned to her sculpture, making her guideline

fatter than she needed to, sure she was angry enough to break the tip of the pencil right off.

"The woman didn't know, Tessie. She didn't mean any harm."

"I never said she did."

"Well, don't. It's not her you're mad at, so don't take it out on her," Buzz said. "Besides, you're the one who insisted I leave that goddamn quilt on the bed in there all this time."

Tess spun to face him again. "Because you promised no one would ever use it!"

They glared at each other. The room fell silent.

Tess glanced again at the cottage, thinking that as frustrated as she was, her anger seemed far less raw than it had the day before. Yesterday she'd left the cove, ready to see someone under her wheels. Now all she wanted to do was drive to the Point and climb back into that lumpy bed with Tom Grace.

Buzz turned to go. Tess called to him.

"I was at the keeper's house."

He stopped, then looked back at her.

"Last night," she said. "In case you were wondering."

"You were?"

Tess met his quizzical gaze, a small smile pressing at her lips, try as she did to subdue it.

"You told me to be neighborly, so I was being neighborly."

"You bring him a pie?" Buzz asked.

"A cheesecake, actually."

Buzz grinned. "Cheesecake's good."

"Don't look at me like that," she said, but not harshly. "I've only just met him, really."

"Well," Buzz replied with a smile, turning back to the door, "you have to start somewhere, don't you?"

"MISTER DON *FUCKING* JUAN!"

Tom had made Dean soup and stuck a hunk of bread on the edge of the bowl. Now he sat across from his brother as he ate, watching him tear the bread in two, dunking one end and chewing it eagerly.

"Just eat your soup, will you," Tom said, "before it gets cold."

"Seriously, Tommy. You don't go to bed with a woman for two years, and then you're here one day—"

"Two," Tom corrected. "Two days."

"Well, good," Dean said between slurps, "because it's about time you got laid."

Tom sighed. "Why do you have to say it like that?"

"Oh, forgive me, dear brother." Dean chuckled as he clapped a hand over his heart, bending his head in phony reverence. "I mean, it's about time you made *sweet, tender love* to your soul mate after *two whole days*." Dean picked up his napkin and chucked it playfully at Tom.

Tom caught it, folded it neatly, and set it back on the table. "So, how was the drive?"

Dean shrugged. "Shitty. Long."

"I still don't understand why you couldn't have just come with me when I left."

"Because we needed two cars."

"What does that have to do with anything? We still could have left together."

"I'm here now, aren't I?"

Dean pushed his soup away, leaned back, and fished his cigarettes from his pocket. Tom cleared his brother's bowl, carried it to the counter, and drew down a chipped saucer from the cabinet, seeing for the first time a bottle of scotch on the counter.

"I thought you were trying to quit those," Tom said quietly, crossing back to the table and setting the saucer in front of Dean to use as an ashtray.

"I was." Dean dragged deeply, tossing his lighter onto the table. "Now I'm not."

There was the challenge; Tom recognized it well—the thump of a closed door, the flat but fierce look that warned Tom to leave it alone, whatever grievance he'd been stewing over.

But Tom wasn't backing down this time. He returned to his seat, arms folded. "There's an outpatient clinic in Port Chester," he began, carefully but firmly. "They said you could come in for a consultation as soon as you got here. I explained the situation with the DUIs—"

"You what?"

"It's not rehab, Dean. It's nothing like that. I just thought you could talk to someone." Tom gave Dean a weary look. "You said you'd see someone when we got here."

"I said I'd *think* about it."

"No, you said you'd *do* it."

Dean crushed out his cigarette in the ashtray.

Tom lowered his gaze. "Why did you tell her it was a rock-climbing accident?"

Dean pocketed his lighter. "Because I got bored with the scuba-diving-off-the-Great-Barrier-Reef story."

"Well, I haven't told her anything yet," Tom said.

"Good, so don't. Now you can cover for me."

"I'm not covering for you, Dean. Not anymore."

Dean frowned at his brother. "What is that supposed to mean?"

"It's not supposed to mean anything. I'm just saying I think things need to be different here. I'm saying I *want* them to be."

Dean got up and crossed to the fridge, tugging open the door as if he hadn't heard a word. "So, what exactly *am* I making us for dinner?" he said. "You haven't got shit in here except— Hey!" He reached for the springform pan. "What's this?"

"Cheesecake," Tom said without looking. "Pumpkin cheesecake."

"Oh baby. Come to Papa." Dean pulled out the pan, whipping off the tinfoil and staring longingly at what remained. "Don't tell me you made this."

"I didn't. Tess did."

"Oh, you lucky prick. That beautiful woman made you a cheesecake?"

"She didn't make it for *me*," Tom said, standing up and moving to the sink.

He could feel Dean's study as he emptied the ashtray; he could predict the look of suspicion narrowing his brother's pale eyes.

"She's married, isn't she?"

"No, she's not married," said Tom. "There *was* somebody else. . . ."

"Oh shit, here we go again." Dean pulled a fork out of the silver drawer, closed it with his hip, and carried the pan back to the table, dropping carefully back into his seat and digging in.

Tom said nothing to defend himself, just watched his brother inhale the last of Tess's cheesecake, not stopping until he'd scraped the sides clean. Tom knew there was no point in arguing his brother's wounding comparison. With the reminder, the damage had been done. That was all that mattered, all that *ever* mattered when it came to that night, the one that had changed everything.

LIZ ARANSON WAS GOING TO be at the party. It was the only reason Tom had wanted to go.

Most of the time, *all* of the time really, he hated high school parties. And why wouldn't he? Standing in the

shadow of dynamic Dean was hardly his idea of a celebration, and Tom had never been able to hold alcohol.

So when Dean had declined, Tom had been indignant.
"Since when don't you want to go to one of Nathan Fielding's parties?"

"Since when do *you*?" was Dean's response, and it had
quieted Tom long enough for Dean to get to the fridge and
snap a soda off its plastic collar.

"I just felt like getting out, that's all."

"It's Liz Aranson, isn't it?"

"No, it's not."

Dean snorted behind the lip of the can. "You are such a
shitty liar. She's back with Fielding, Tommy. Move on."

Tom knew this already. He'd heard the news just that
week, but it hadn't deterred him from wanting to go to this
party. Quite the opposite, it only left him more resigned to
getting there.

"We'll just go for a few minutes," Tom said.

"So go if you want to go," said Dean, pushing past him
for the hall. "You're a big boy."

Tom followed his brother into the living room. "I can't
go without you—you know that. They didn't invite me;
they invited you."

"Fielding doesn't give a shit. He barely even knows
who comes and goes."

"Come on, Dean. I promise we'll be back by ten."

"I have a meet tomorrow, Tommy."

"I know. Which is why we won't stay long."

"Fine," Dean said, relenting at last. "But you're driving."

THE SNOW HADN'T YET STARTED when they climbed into their father's Datsun, though the air was close and tinged pink with an impending storm.

Liz Aranson had been a fluke, really. Girls like Liz didn't fool around with guys like him; Tom knew that as surely as he knew his own birthday. Maybe they did when they were drunk or bored, but Liz Aranson had been neither when she and Tom had fallen together that night at her parents' house. Not that it had been entirely without luck. He'd been assigned to give her his biology notes after her two-week absence with mono, and when he'd delivered them, she'd taken one look at the pages and burst into tears. He'd offered then and there to take her through them, line by line. "You should be a teacher," she said, sniffling. "You really should." He'd smiled. He'd never thought about that. Medical school was his plan. He'd been accepted early admission to Case Western, and all that was left was to wait.

"You'll never get laid in med school," Dean had warned when the letter had arrived. "You *do* know that, right?"

"Guys have girlfriends in medical school."

"I'm not talking about having girlfriends, Tommy. I'm talking about *getting laid*."

Then Liz Aranson contracted mono and Tom found

himself sitting across from her in her parents' living room, looking at her mother's collection of Hummel figurines on the shelf above the couch while Liz, her beautiful blond head bent, had agonized over the Krebs cycle.

Tom knew he never should have told Dean what happened, how Liz had leaned over the third night he'd gone to her house, this time her parents out at a board meeting and her little brother upstairs playing video games. How her hair had smelled of cherries and her breath had smelled of orange soda and how he was fairly certain he could still taste her kiss and that soda for days afterward. Tom never should have confessed that Liz Aranson told him she'd always wondered things about him, always secretly hoped they'd be assigned as lab partners, how disappointed she'd been to get Avery Judd instead. But most of all, Tom wished he'd never told Dean about what had come next—the rushing, the fumbling, heavy breathing, hearts racing, promises, plans.

"You do know it was all bullshit, right, Tommy? You do know that?"

Tom flexed his hands on the Datsun's steering wheel, refusing to answer. He just stared out at the road, wondering if they were close.

"The dude gave her mono, and now she's back with him," said Dean. "What does that tell you?"

"Left or right?" Tom asked when they reached the Stop sign.

———

THE DRIVEWAY AT NATHAN FIELDING's house wasn't nearly as crowded as Tom had expected, and neither was the inside of the brick house when they'd climbed the wide front steps and walked in. There were so few people that Tom found Liz and Nathan right away. They got beers from the kitchen where Dean was at once the center of attention, garnering backslaps and high fives from a group of class-mates. Tom pretended to take interest in a painting above the table, swigging his beer and draining it more quickly than he'd planned.

Liz and Nathan had moved outside. Tom could see them on the deck. He could also see the faint haze of smoke around them, hanging in the air longer than the steam of their breath. They were smoking pot, he thought. He could do that, couldn't he? What could they say if he walked out there? They'd have to offer him a puff—a hit? What did they call it?

"Hey, where's Dean?" That was as close to a greeting as Tom got when he stepped out. Prickly and still, the air was crisp with cold. Tom shoved his hands into his pock-ets, glad he'd kept his coat on, even if it was more of a Windbreaker. He looked at Liz, but she kept her eyes down, her soft blond hair falling conveniently over one eye. Nathan swung his arm over her shoulder. She had to be freezing, Tom thought. And there Nathan stood in his sweater, nice and toasty while his girlfriend shivered in a short-sleeved top, trying to look relaxed, comfortable. Tom drained his beer, hoping the rush of alcohol would make him reckless, bold.

It did.

He set down the empty can and shrugged out of his jacket.

"Here." He took a step toward Liz, holding it out. "You should put this on. You're turning blue."

For a moment, no one said anything. Liz just stared at him, her eyes pooling pleadingly. She made no move to take the jacket, and after a moment of bewildered frowning, Nathan finally said to him, "What the fuck are you doing, Grace?"

Tom looked at him. "She's cold. I'm giving her my jacket."

"She doesn't need your jacket." Nathan stepped up to Tom, steering Liz behind him. The whites of his eyes were tinted pink, his breath hot with the smell of beer. "If she needs a jacket, I'll give her my jacket, okay? Who the fuck do you think you are?"

"Hey, hey . . ." Pip Corson stepped in and placed a hand on Nathan's shoulder. "Easy, man. It's cool."

The French doors swung open. Dean burst out with the kitchen crew, his attention moving at once to the standoff. Nathan reared up and shouted, "Hey, Grace, your brother's a dick—you know that?"

Dean came over, drunk now too, his accusing eyes already on Tom who was still determined to glean some kind of acknowledgment from Liz. *Just one word*, Tom thought. *Just a smile to prove it wasn't a lie.* He heard muffled voices. He was aware of Dean and Nathan exchanging words, aware of people shifting around him, aware of his fingers growing numb with cold, the tip of his nose and his forehead icing over.

In the next instant he was in front of Liz Aranson, kissing her on the mouth, and he swore for the first few seconds, she kissed him back.

"Hey!"

Someone shoved him backward, hard enough that he hit the railing. Suddenly Nathan Fielding was in his face, screaming at him, demanding an apology, and then there was Dean, inserting himself between them.

"Get him out of here, Dean!" Nathan ordered, rushing at Tom even as two seniors forced him back. "Get your brother out of here before I kick his ass!"

They left the deck, the crowd parting eagerly for them.

"You *are* a dick—you know that?" Dean said when they reached the car, the snow falling hard enough to stick to the windshield. "Give me the keys."

"I'm fine," Tom managed, coming around Dean for the driver's door.

"You are so far from fine, it's scary," Dean said. "Now give me the fucking keys."

But still Tom refused. He snapped open the door and fell into the driver's seat, his head spinning. He just wanted to get away. He turned on the car, hard enough to make the Datsun squeal.

Dean gave up, sliding into the passenger seat and slamming the door. "What the hell were you thinking?"

Tom didn't answer. He knew there was a culvert on either side of the driveway, but he didn't want to ask Dean to help him see, so he just sent the car backward into the dark.

"Slow the fuck down," Dean ordered, swerving in his seat. "You can't even see where you're going."

Sure enough, the back end of the Datsun slipped over the side of the culvert with enough speed that Dean and Tom were snapped forward in their seats.

"Shit!" said Dean.

Tom pushed the pedal to the floor, but the wheels stuck.

Dean stormed out of the car to survey the damage, even as Tom continued in vain to free them.

"Forget it," Dean said, returning to the car. "It's in too deep."

He marched off toward the house; Tom climbed out. "Where are you going?"

"Where do you think?" Dean said. "I have to call Dad to come pick us up. I'm not waiting out in the freezing cold for a tow when I have a meet in six hours."

Tom didn't argue, knowing Dean was right. Frozen hands shoved in his armpits, he climbed back into the front seat, watching his breath swirl over the view of the house. He was not so drunk that he couldn't decide that if this was what wanting someone did, made a person lose control this way, then he wanted no part of it. He'd leave all that business to Dean, who was so much better at it anyway.

Eight

THOUGH THE STREETS OF THE village were quiet, there was still plenty of activity on the wharf and on the water: lobstermen bringing in their catch, or repairing their traps; delivery trucks thumping through the town's narrow streets; decoration crews continuing their work, stringing lights and hanging flags. Beverly surveyed it all with a pervasive sense of detachment. She hated how out of place she felt here. She never expected to feel so out of place. Of course, her accommodations, a disaster from the start, didn't help matters, not to mention her host, who seemed entirely ill-equipped to manage a handful of cottages, and his daughter, who had the manners of a feral cat. It was a wonder he'd managed to stay in business. She still couldn't fathom how Frank had associated with them, let alone been related by marriage. No wonder he'd kept them such a secret.

But she hadn't come here to make friends, Beverly reminded herself as she scanned the village green until she saw the squat, shingled building to the right of the square bearing its carved wooden sign: THE CRADLE HARBOR HISTORICAL SOCIETY AND MUSEUM. Beverly climbed out of the car, clutching her purse against her side, needing something to hold on to as she walked across the street to the museum. She couldn't remember the last time she'd been so nervous.

No, she could. It had been the first time Frank had come to the house. It had been a hot, windless May day, and she'd assembled the boys in the living room, having lured them inside from their incessant pounding of the basketball hoop in the driveway. She had explained to them as they stared at her, rubbing off sweat with the hems of their T-shirts, that this visit was important to her and that she wanted them to be polite. It was hardly a well-rooted romance, but she was determined to hold on to it. At fourteen and twelve, surely her sons were old enough to see that. Surely they wanted her to be happy.

But it hadn't been as easy as she'd hoped. Michael, her younger son, pouted outright from the start, while her elder boy, Daniel, chose the route of chilly indifference, no matter the tactics Frank had tried to employ. He arrived with gifts—sports equipment, video games, expensive items that, had they come from anyone else, the boys would have snatched up with joy. He took them to dinner, then to a movie of the boys' choosing—an insufferable action picture, the only saving grace of which was its length and excessive volume, which masked Beverly's and Frank's frequent whispers, and darkness that allowed their hands to drift together. When it came time to end their evening, Frank made his way to the door, having reserved a hotel room nearby, but Beverly insisted he stay at the house.

"The boys," he said, nodding toward the stairs. "What will they think when they wake up and find me here?"

Let them find you here, Beverly thought in a fit of childish petulance, leading Frank up to her room. It had been hard not to be angry with her sons, to not be certain they meant to sabotage her budding love, but Frank was quick to defend them.

"I have to earn their trust," he whispered as they lay in the quiet after making love, the boys asleep down the hall. "I understand that."

Beverly ran her fingers through his hair, thinking how good it felt to be with him, to be wanted this way, savored this way.

"So long as *you* trust me," he said, taking her cheek in his palm.

Beverly curled up against him. As foolish as it may have sounded, how could she not trust him? After all, most women with a married lover didn't learn the truth for years, if ever. She'd known it all along. Looking back now, Beverly saw that it was a mistake she'd made, presuming one confidence would secure all the others.

But it would be many more visits before the boys' chill would thaw, even if their doubts never truly melted away.

"Why don't we ever see *his* house?" Michael asked a few years into the affair.

"Because he lives in Maine," Beverly said evenly. "I've explained that to you both."

"So why doesn't he move here if he likes us so much?"

"He can't. His business is there."

"Then why don't we move there?"

"Because your school is here."

"They have schools in Maine too," Daniel chimed in from the other side of the table. The statement, a clear challenge to her, Beverly diverted with an offer of more chicken, more peas.

How could she explain to them that Frank needed her as much as she needed him? How could teenage boys understand what it was like to exist in a strained marriage, to live day in and day out with someone who never made you feel whole, as Joan had done to Frank, as Clark had done to her?

Of course, it grew easier once the boys were in college—easier for Frank, certainly; easier for her, not always. Without the boys to tend to daily, without the distraction of their constant needs, it was harder in the moments of increasing quiet to explain to herself why Frank had to stay with Joan if his wife was so difficult. Whenever Beverly suggested her nagging doubts, Frank would find a way to come to Chicago, or whisk her to a rendezvous in Boston or New York, decadent weekends that would always calm her cravings, reaffirm her commitment to him, enough so that when Daniel and Michael returned for holidays, Beverly never hesitated to appear upbeat when the subject turned to Frank.

Pull it together, she chastised herself as she mounted the steps to the museum. What did she have to be so anxious about anyway? After all, here she would surely find allies in her quest for answers. In all the interviews she'd read online, no residents were more outraged, more demanding of truths than the women who ran the historical society.

The door to the museum opened with the faint sound of a bell. Inside, two women stood around a reception desk, the warm, dry smell of old paper thick in the still room.

"Welcome." Edith was first to arrive, Mary on her heels. "Feel free to look around. The museum is free; however, there is a recommended donation of five dollars. It's up to you." Edith pointed to the desk where a slotted wooden box sat, clearly labeled DONATIONS.

Beverly offered a polite but short smile. "Certainly." She removed her wallet, sliding past the two women, and she pushed a folded bill through the slot.

Paid in full, she began to browse the exhibit cases, the

displays inside looking as worn and weary as the seasiders' faces who lined the walls in old photographs. She paused a moment at a photograph of a bright-eyed lightkeeper, or so the nameplate under him said.

"Handsome, wasn't he?"

Beverly turned to find Vera Blake beside her.

"Lydia was bonkers for him," Vera continued. "Truly crazy. No sane woman with a newborn throws herself off a lighthouse gallery. I don't care how much she misses her husband. Besides which, Linus was hardly well himself when he disappeared. All that mercury, you know. They used to float the lenses for the beam in the awful stuff. Lots of keepers went quite mad from it eventually."

Beverly considered the photograph again, recalling the story she'd come upon in all her Internet searches on the town, the Harbor's prized legend of four residents who walked into the ocean to be reunited with their mermaid lovers. "But there were others who left too, men who weren't lightkeepers," Beverly pointed out. "Mercury doesn't explain why *they* did it."

"Now you see why it's a legend," said Vera, winking. "Wouldn't be much fun if we knew all the answers, would it?"

Wouldn't it? Beverly had come here specifically for answers, so what was this nonsense about looking the other way? She glanced around the room, seeing the other two women still conferring at the desk. Beverly recognized the thin one from an article she'd downloaded, the one who'd been so outraged by Frank's broken promise. Surely that woman could understand Beverly's impatience, her hunger for answers.

"What can you tell me about the keeper's house?" Beverly asked.

From across the room, Edith Hawthorne's head rose up, her eyes looking their way.

"What is it you'd like to know?" Vera asked.

"Can I see it?" asked Beverly.

"Unfortunately, no." Edith approached, snapping her glasses closed and letting them hang from their chain. "You can see the lighthouse, though. There'll be plenty of opportunities this weekend. I assume you're here for the festival?"

"I really would like to see the keeper's house." Beverly could hear the urgency in her voice now.

"So would we," added Mary, stepping into their circle.

"It's not open to the public," Vera said. "Not yet, anyway."

Beverly looked between the women, seeing her opportunity and seizing it. "And why is that?"

Edith answered before the others could. "There's somewhat of a disagreement currently on the status of the property," she said. "It really should have been turned over to the historical society—"

"That was always the intention," Mary added.

"But for some reason it wasn't made official in time for the previous owner's passing," Edith finished.

Beverly nodded, trying to keep her expression light and calm. This could be it, she thought, the explanation she'd been seeking. Her heart raced, try as she did to slow it when she finally asked, "So who *does* it belong to?"

Edith shrugged. "Frankly, we don't really know."

"I mean, we *know*," clarified Mary. "We know their names, but we don't know how the gentlemen came to—"

"It's really not something we can discuss at this time," Edith said curtly. "It's a legal matter. You understand."

"I do hope you'll visit the lighthouse, however," added Mary. "The tower will be open all weekend. There's a schedule of festival events at the reception desk if you've not taken one yet. You'll want to get there early on Saturday. It can get quite crowded."

Beverly slid one of the pamphlets free from the stand beside the donation box, skimming it quickly while the women resumed their conversation.

Stepping back into the sun, she felt a rush of panic. She'd been so sure she'd arrive here to find a townspeople united in their need for answers, a townspeople as indignant as she was about being kept in the dark. But two days after her arrival, she had no more clues, no more answers. And the one place she'd been so certain would share her outrage was instead as even-tempered as a church social.

Then fine, Beverly thought. She'd not come here to stir up trouble, but if the women in the museum meant to keep a stiff—and sealed—upper lip, then Beverly would have no choice but to go straight to the source. She'd simply visit the keeper's house herself, come straight out and ask those men who they were and who they were to Frank. Certainly it would be awkward, and there was the chance they would refuse her an answer. After all, they didn't know her from a hole in the wall. They didn't owe her an explanation, but if they *should* grant her one, as painful as it might be, she had to know: Were they, or were they not, Frank Hammond's sons? Knowing that would mean case closed, end of story. Then she could climb back into her car and drive away from this place, get on with her life, put an end to this anger and hurt once and for all.

Back in the car, rolling down her window to draw a breeze, she steered through town, hoping she could find the Point without much effort. Sure enough, a half mile down the road, the white sign appeared, and she turned in, her heart crashing against her ribs with each frost heave. But it was for nothing. The driveway was empty, the house deserted. She could wait, she thought, and just be there when the men returned. But the longer she sat staring out at the house, the quicker her conviction sank, until finally she left. She'd go back to the cottage, she decided, pulling back onto the road. She'd gather her frazzled wits, make herself a cup of tea, and return in an hour or two. Surely they'd be back by then.

She had just glimpsed the steeple of the Baptist church over the top of the pines when she heard the telltale clunk of the tire, then seconds later the tugging and shudder of the wheel.

"Oh, for God's sake," she muttered, letting up off the gas and steering the car to the shoulder. She had only to open the driver's door and lean out to see the tire was flat. She found her phone and sighed. No signal.

She tented a hand over her eyes and scanned the road, sure with the growing traffic someone would stop. Walking was out of the question. No, she'd simply wait.

SOMETIMES, SAY, WHEN HE WAS driving a familiar route as he was doing now, Buzz would try to pinpoint the first time he knew Ruby wasn't the woman he'd believed her to be.

It was a natural investigation for a man mourning a lost love, though with each period of contemplation, the answer seemed different. Some days he was certain it was as early as their wedding, a casual ceremony they'd organized down at the cove almost a year after she and Tess had moved in with him, a five-minute exchange crowded with old friends who'd come to witness and celebrate, pitching tents on the lawn, or cramming into the cottages, some with as many as a dozen guests inside.

It was no wonder Joan had refused to attend. Aside from her deep-seated objection to the romance, Buzz's sister had never had much tolerance for his "hippie-dippy" friends, as she'd called them.

Frank, however, had enjoyed himself immensely. At one point he'd even joined the wedding party in an impromptu swim, drying off on the sand with the rest of them, swigging cheap beer and tapping his fingers to the bluegrass music they'd all taken turns playing with a pile of guitars. Much later, well into the middle of the night, when a bonfire was still glowing and popping on the beach, Buzz had found Ruby crying in the bathroom. She'd tried to deny it, but he'd heard the sounds even before he'd seen her moist eyes. For a moment, brief but terrifying, he'd wondered whether she'd regretted marrying him, whether the desire he'd watched bloom in her eyes in the months before had been false, but he'd pushed the fear away before it could grow, and they'd returned to the circle of their friends together, hand in hand, and toasted to their union under the electric pink threads of dawn.

Other days, when he was feeling more optimistic about life, Buzz was certain the warning signs came much later, when Ruby started to spend days in her studio without emerging for meals and refused any visitors except for Tess. She hadn't even cared that Tess would gladly skip school to keep her mother company in her time of need, a trend Buzz eventually put a stop to, much to his stepdaughter's outrage.

"You don't understand anything," Tess had said. She had missed the bus intentionally, and Buzz had had to drive her to school. "I have to stay with her. She needs me."

The fierceness in her expression and the look of panic crushed him. It wasn't right, he thought, a child being a parent to her mother. Never mind the hurt it caused him to think that Ruby might not have seen his love as sufficient emotional support.

"She's sick right now, kiddo," he'd said as gently as he could. "She needs medicine to get well."

"No," Tess had said, her eyes welling up. "You don't understand anything. The medicine only makes it worse. It goes away eventually. I just stay with her until it does."

Buzz had stared at Tess then, nearly steering them into the shoulder.

"You mean you've been through this before?" he'd asked. "Missed school before?"

"Sure I have," said Tess, without apology. "Plenty of times. I don't care. I know it's just school. It's nothing I can't figure out on my own."

After that, Buzz had never doubted his right to step in between mother and daughter—no matter that he wasn't her biological father, no matter how attached Tess was to Ruby. His devotion to Tess alone entitled him to protect her, to make choices for her safety; blood had shit to do with love.

He'd expected Ruby to hate him for it, but strangely she'd never fought him when he'd insisted Tess return to school. It had been his suggestions—his *pleas*—that she get medical help that Ruby had vehemently rejected. Just as Tess had said, Ruby claimed to have tried medication once before, explaining that it had left her hollow and numb, unable to paint. He'd consequently backed off on his demands, and eventually Ruby's depression had lifted, replaced with the feverish passion that he'd fallen in love with years earlier, when he had never thought there might be something harmful in that free-spirited lust for life.

"I'm not a doctor, Buzz, but I'd say she's manic-depressive," Frank had suggested soon after when Buzz had confided in his brother-in-law. "She should be under a doctor's care."

"I'm trying," Buzz had said. "I'm trying."

After that first episode, Buzz had found himself watching his wife differently, any shift in mood, no matter how slight, suddenly cause for alarm. And while the change in his demeanor might have been dismissed by Ruby, it wasn't by Tess. From the start, Buzz felt her resistance to his growing curiosity over her mother's daily well-being. Once, knowing how often she wanted to ride the wave of her inspiration for as long as she needed, he might never have worried if Ruby had gone two days without leaving her studio, and he'd have let her, gladly. Now if more than a day went by, he would knock on her door, refusing to leave until she'd let him see that she hadn't fallen into a despondent hole. And always, there'd be Tess right there, rushing in ahead of him, like a lawyer ready to tell her client not to answer any questions. Over the years, Buzz's instincts grew strong, or maybe it was just that Ruby's bad days began to fall into a dependable pattern. Whatever the reason, his heart broke each and every time he found her struggling.

Stop looking at me as if there's something wrong with me. People get sad all the time.

Sometimes it's more than that.

It's not. Tessie knows it's not. Don't you, lovey?

How many times had Buzz waited for Tess to shake her head, to just once see her mother's depression for what it was? But Buzz came to understand that for Tess, admission would have meant betraying Ruby, or worse, abandoning her. And as old as Tess got, as bad as Ruby got, she never could.

And while Ruby hadn't said so in her suicide note, Buzz had always believed that she'd taken her life so that Tess might get on with hers. Had Tess never thought so too?

The sun burst through the clouds, startling Buzz from his thoughts as he came over the rise in the road. Squinting against it, he caught the shimmer of a car's roof along the shoulder, a white sedan with rental plates. As he neared, he saw the familiar statuesque woman standing primly at the front end.

He pulled over, seeing Beverly's face brighten briefly.

"I tried calling for a mechanic, but I couldn't get a signal," she said, meeting him where he'd parked behind her.

"Even if you could, I doubt you'd have much luck getting someone out here before dark," said Buzz, already moving to the sedan's trunk. "The guys who run the body shop are in charge of the floats, so unless you plan on driving this in the parade, I doubt they'll be in any hurry to help."

Beverly folded her arms. "I'm sure it was from that awful road down to the Point," she said, watching him unload the spare. "I'm surprised no one has sued over those potholes. They're criminal."

He would bet she'd do that, Buzz thought with a grin as he knelt down in front of the flat. Sue Mother Nature over a frost heave.

"This won't take but a second," he told her, twisting off the lug nuts. "You're welcome to wait in my truck if you'd like."

Beverly glanced over her shoulder at the rusted yellow pickup, her eyes narrowing on the stretch of papers and crumpled fast-food wrappers that littered the top of the dashboard.

"I'm fine," she said decisively.

"Suit yourself." He slipped off the flat, leaned it against the car, and put on the spare. "So, what were you doing down at the Point?"

He'd only been trying to make conversation, but when he glanced up, Buzz found her looking down at him as if he'd accused her of something.

"Sightseeing. Just sightseeing."

"Good place to do it," he said, threading the lug nuts back on. "You get a look around the lighthouse?"

"Good enough," she said.

"Be glad you did. In a few days there'll be a line up the road to get a peek."

She nodded, letting the air quiet between them as he finished up.

"Thank you," she said as he rose, done. "Really, I owe you a good deal."

Buzz grinned, clapping his hands clean. "Buy me an early dinner and we'll call it even."

She looked at him, startled.

He chuckled. "I'm just kidding. We'll split the bill. You can keep me company."

Still, her expression remained dubious. "You should know I don't like seafood."

Buzz frowned, confused. "You came all the way to Maine, and you don't like seafood?"

"That's right," she said, unapologetically.

"We've got other stuff besides seafood, you know."

"All right," she agreed. "I suppose I could stand a bite."

"Good." Buzz returned the flat and the tools to the trunk, shutting it soundly. "We'll go to Pat's. You can follow me."

THE RESTAURANT WAS EXACTLY WHAT Beverly had expected from the outside: red-and-white-checked tablecloths, pine-paneled walls crowded with photographs of grinning patrons, silk flowers in plastic vases bookended by ketchup and mustard dispensers.

She could smell frying onions even before she'd stepped inside. It hadn't been a complete lie she'd told him; she *was* hungry, and while this sort of place wouldn't have been her choice under most circumstances, she would be willing to accept its menu today. After all, she did owe Buzz Patterson something. He had saved her a great deal of discomfort and inconvenience coming to her rescue. And yes, the thought had occurred to her—and she wouldn't apologize for it, either—that there might be an opportunity in this meal. She'd tried to get answers on her own and had no luck. Other than those brothers at the keeper's house, who knew better the truth of Frank's mysteries than her own host?

"Right this way." A woman took them past the quiet bar to a table in the back.

"Calm before the storm," Buzz said, gesturing to the empty tables around them as they took their seats. "By Friday this place will be mobbed. Just wait."

Beverly looked over the menu, thinking she'd have something light. Across from them, a couple feasted on plates of meat loaf and mashed potatoes, barely looking up from their food.

Their waitress arrived. Beverly ordered a house salad and a bowl of minestrone soup. Buzz ordered the fish and chips. "And I'll have a Johnny's IPA," he added, then glanced at Beverly and shrugged. "Why not, right? It's practically dinner."

"A beer for you too, ma'am?" the waitress asked.

"Oh no," Beverly said, unfolding her napkin. "I'll just have water. With a slice of lemon. No ice."

The waitress smiled at Buzz as she swept up their menus.

"That's Moira," he said when the young woman had left. "She's a great girl. She and Tessie used to be good friends."

Beverly caught the curious tense. *"Used to be?"*

Buzz sighed, resting his elbows on the table. "There was something about some guy," he said. "I could never get a straight answer. Tessie can be hard on people. Gets her feelings hurt so quickly." Buzz gave Beverly a sheepish look. "But then you probably already guessed that."

Beverly, nervous again, didn't answer, just neatened her silverware. She didn't know why she should feel so anxious, so exposed sitting there. It wasn't as if anyone knew who she was—least of all her dinner companion.

She glanced at Buzz, then watched him wave to an older man who had arrived at the bar.

Just ask him already, Beverly thought. *Don't be dim about it. You've come all this way. Now ask the man.*

Maybe she'd need a bit of help.

"On second thought," Beverly said to their waitress when she returned with Buzz's beer, "I'll take a glass of your house red."

"Good," said Buzz. "I hate to drink alone. I do that enough as it is."

"I don't usually drink," Beverly said, not sure why she felt the need to say so.

Buzz leaned forward, grinning. "It *is* legal here, you know."

She gave in to a small smile, thinking he did have

214

rather nice eyes. Underneath the burly exterior, there was a boyish appeal to him. Perhaps it was all the freckles. If he'd cut that absurd hair and put on a decent shirt, he might be quite handsome. She suspected he was once.

Their waitress brought her wine; Beverly sipped it, finding the peppery taste surprisingly pleasant and instantly relaxing.

"My wife was the same way, you know," Buzz said. "She couldn't bring herself to eat seafood, either. She said it didn't seem fair to swim with them, then turn around and eat them."

"I assure you that's not my issue," Beverly said. "I just don't like the taste."

A few minutes later their food arrived. Buzz salted his liberally, then asked for a second beer. The waitress pointed to Beverly's wine.

"Another glass, ma'am?"

"She'd love one," Buzz answered before Beverly could.

The truth was she had wanted another glass; she was very much enjoying the lightness it was providing. She couldn't remember the last time she'd felt this at ease. Ever since she'd found out about the men in the lightkeeper's house, her whole body had felt like a clenched fist. She could even feel the muscles of her face softening. How many occasions as of late had she caught a glimpse of her reflection in a mirror and thought, *Who is this person who frowns so much? I'm not this person. When did I become this person?*

Maybe it was the wine. She glanced across the table. Maybe it was the company.

Or maybe it was a little of both.

She drew up her fork. "Thank you again for your help," she said. "I'm sorry to have put you through the trouble."

"Are you kidding?" Buzz chuckled, dunking a piece of fish into a pile of tartar sauce. "Honestly, I'm grateful. I was feeling so lousy about everything—botching up your reservation, Tessie's fit over the quilt—now I feel like we're even." He saw Beverly's eyes flash, and he added softly, "You know what I mean."

She took another sip, thinking there was no harm in playing along. Around them the restaurant was filling slowly, patrons who seemed to know Buzz and vice versa. She watched them all as they filed by, wondering how many of them had known Frank.

"You have kids?" Buzz asked.

"Two boys," Beverly said, piercing a tomato with her fork and running it lightly through her side of dressing. "They're grown and living out West. I don't see them much."

"Must be tough, huh?"

She shrugged, cutting into a stack of iceberg leaves. "They have their own lives. It's how it should be."

"Doesn't mean you can't miss them, though. Doesn't mean you don't still wish you could find their dishes in the sink. You can miss that, I think."

Could you? Beverly considered the possibility, fairly certain that she didn't. She'd never been much of a homemaker. She'd put on a good show for Clark in the beginning, in the year before Daniel was born, but it was never heartfelt. Her own mother had been a terrible cook—so terrible that all throughout high school, Beverly's teachers had charged her with sneaking cigarettes, but Beverly would try to explain it was just the smoke from her mother's forgotten dinners stuck on everything she owned. Beverly's mother had blamed it on the divorce, but Beverly remembered plenty of charred food before her father had moved out.

It wasn't that Beverly *couldn't* cook; she simply didn't like to. So when Daniel was born, and Clark was so determined that his wife devote her every waking minute to their son that he'd gladly come home with premade dinners, pizzas, and chicken meals, she hadn't complained. Even after the boys were grown, they'd kept to the same regimen, much to Beverly's relief. She was more than happy to keep the refrigerator and the cabinets stocked with food so long as none of it required assembly. She was even fine with collecting Clark's shirts off the floor of his closet so long as all she had to do was drop them off at the dry cleaner.

For some reason, Clark never seemed to mind her lack of domesticity until she took the job at the makeup counter at Marshall Fields when the boys began going to school full days; only then did her husband began questioning the contents of the vegetable drawers and the load of laundry in the washer that had yet to be moved into the dryer.

No, Beverly didn't miss those chores—the dishes, the laundry. Who missed laundry?

But Buzz was insistent. "I know Tessie will get her act together one of these days and move out," he continued, "maybe get married, have kids, but I have to tell you, I don't like to think about it. She's everything to me. She's all I've got, especially now that my sister and my brother-in-law are gone."

Here it came, Beverly thought.

"You were all close then?" she asked as casually as she could.

"Not so much me and Joannie," Buzz said, smiling gratefully as their waitress returned with their fresh drinks. "But Frank—he was my brother-in-law—he and I were real close."

How was it possible? Beverly wondered as she watched Buzz over the top of her wine. She'd been in the man's company for three days now, and she still couldn't reconcile this relationship. But then, she couldn't reconcile much of anything about this place and her lover. Had Frank simply felt sorry for Buzz and his family? The Frank she'd known *had* been giving, loving, compassionate. Had he pitied Buzz? Surely he had. The man was sad in his own way, an open wound for the world to see.

"I miss him," Buzz said, picking up his beer. "I miss him a lot."

Beverly glanced down at her salad, afraid she might reveal herself. Feeling the wine, the quiet, the calm, she knew she should slow down, but still she continued to drain her glass.

"How long has he been gone?" she asked. "What did you say his name was, your brother-in-law?"

"Frank," said Buzz. "Not long. Just a few months."

She took another sip, needing a fresh burst of courage. "Is it true that he promised the lightkeeper's house to the town?"

Buzz glanced up at her, tartar sauce trimming his moustache. "Where'd you hear that?"

"I was at the museum earlier. The women didn't say much, just that they were promised the building."

"Of course they'd say that." Buzz dragged his napkin across his lips, then stuffed it back into his lap. "Those hens would say the moon promised them a few thousand stars too."

"They say there are two men living there. They seemed quite upset over it."

"They shouldn't be." Buzz's voice dropped. He reached for his beer and wiped at the beads of condensation on the glass with his thumb before picking it up, his expression turning wistful. "Those boys deserve a hell of a lot more than a drafty old house, trust me."

Beverly lowered her wine carefully, sensing the answers she'd longed for might finally be in reach. He knew something, she thought, her limbs flushing with heat.

"What do you mean by that?" she asked.

Buzz glanced up at her and smiled sadly. "Nothing.

Just that there's stuff those women don't know. Stuff no one knows. Oh man, listen to me. . . ." Buzz sat back, his palms flat on his thighs, his cheeks pink. "Two beers and I'm spilling my guts. And here I thought we were clearing our debts."

Their waitress came to check on them, offering them dessert. Beverly considered the opportunity, torn. If she pressed too hard, he'd suspect her. But she was so close, maybe it was worth the risk.

"I'll take a piece of your blueberry pie," she said, seeing Buzz's expression brighten at once. Maybe he thought she was enjoying his company too much to leave. After all, she hadn't finished her meal. Where would she find room for pie except as an excuse to linger?

"Pie for you too, Buzz?" the young woman asked.

"Sure. But I don't want ice cream on mine."

When they were alone again, Beverly took another fortifying sip of wine, eager to steer them back on the road he'd sent them down.

"You were saying," she began. "About those young men . . ."

"Just that there's a good reason they have that place, that's all."

"Were they family? Were they . . ." She swallowed, the words so close. *Say them,* she chastised herself. "Were they his sons?"

She'd done it. She'd put the question into the air, out

into the real world. Now she waited, the suspense every bit as agonizing as she'd expected.

Across the table, Buzz looked at her for a long moment, so long that Beverly feared she'd pushed too far. Her heart began to race. But then his brow relaxed and he said, "No. Nothing like that."

Beverly felt sure her breath had left her in an audible gasp. It was the rebuttal she'd been hoping for. So where was the certain and tidy sense of closure she'd been so sure she'd find on its heels? The answer had not calmed her. If that chestnut-haired man she'd watched disappear into the keeper's house wasn't Frank's son, then who was he?

"Why, then?" she pressed, too far in now.

"Why what?" Buzz asked, frowning.

"Why did they deserve your brother-in-law's house?"

Something caught Buzz's eye over her shoulder then, and his face spread in a deep grin. Turning to see what he saw, she found him smiling at the wall of photographs she'd glimpsed on their way in.

"Wait here. I'll be right back," he said, already rising. Beverly watched him approach the stretch of photos, hunting for one in particular, then finding it and carefully taking it off its nail. Somehow she knew what he'd gone to find, and her heartbeat hastened even before he'd returned. He slid back into his chair and handed her the framed picture.

"This is him. This is *them*," he corrected with a smile that could be described only as adoring. "That was taken right here, on their twenty-fifth anniversary. Joannie wanted to have some big to-do in Bar Harbor, but Frank wouldn't budge. This was where they had their first date, and Frank was determined as hell. As you can see from the picture, Joannie came around. This place was packed for them. It was one hell of a party."

Beverly nodded dully, but her eyes were fixed on the woman beside Frank.

It wasn't that she'd never seen a photo of Joan Hammond before this moment. Like most married men, Frank had carried a wedding picture in his wallet, and over the years Beverly had slipped it free while he'd showered or slept, studying the round-faced woman in the powder blue, Empire-waisted dress, thinking how unfortunate a cut it was for someone so short. No, it wasn't the woman herself that Beverly hadn't expected; it was something else.

Much heavier in this portrait than in the wedding picture, her brown hair shorter and frosted with gray, Joan Hammond sat pertly on her husband's lap, looking as light and carefree as a young girl. And for his part, his hands protectively and possessively wrapped around his wife's ample waist, securing her on his lap as if she might be in danger of falling off, Frank looked nothing short of enraptured.

There was no misunderstanding; it was quite simply the posturing of two people still deeply in love.

Staring up at Beverly, trimmed in a dusty plastic frame, was all the truth she'd been denied. Frank had lied to her, all right. He'd lied that he hadn't loved his wife; he'd lied that his wife hadn't loved him.

"It wasn't always an easy marriage, but it was a good one," Buzz said, leaning forward. "They'd wanted kids from the start, but she lost every one, every time. God, it was awful. Frank had this idea that it was his fault. I don't mean, you know, *mechanically*," Buzz clarified, flushing slightly. "I mean because he'd made unfortunate choices in his life—I won't get into it—but just that he thought it was the punishment for something he'd done, something bad. It wasn't true, of course. The doctors made it clear Joan couldn't carry a baby to term—and believe me, she gave Frank as many outs as there were days in a year to find someone who *could*, but he wouldn't take them. No matter his demons, he loved her. And it was the right thing to do."

Beverly wasn't even aware she was crying until she realized she couldn't make out the faces in the photograph anymore. That was how fast the moment of her reckoning arrived. There'd been no time to excuse herself, to push back the tears as they'd grown in her throat. In an instant, they spilled over, and there was no escaping them.

"Oh Jesus," Buzz said, looking startled. "I'm sorry—I didn't mean to make you sad."

"You didn't." Beverly pressed her napkin to her nose, then to her eyes to stop the tears from seeping out, as if putting pressure on a cut to stop it from bleeding. It didn't work; more tears flowed.

She set down her napkin and rose, excusing herself.

His expression worried and urgent, Buzz rose too, wanting to repair his blunder immediately but not sure exactly what it was that he'd done.

"But we ordered dessert," he said weakly, pointing to where Moira was already on her way across the restaurant with their pie.

"I can't," Beverly said. "I really can't. I'm sorry."

She tried to free the strap of her purse from the chair, tugging so hard that she knocked into the next table. She wanted only to run from him, from this place, this whole town. Somehow she made it to the door, made it outside, so grateful she had her own car, her own escape route, even if she was certain there would be no real escape now, not for a very long time.

Nine

DEAN INSISTED THEY EAT ON the back lawn, and, as was always the way, Tom's attempt to talk sense into his younger brother met with swift and certain disinterest. Tom had, however, managed to talk Dean out of lobster. They'd settled on pizza instead, which had of course required its own excessive spending: pizza pans, fresh mozzarella, fresh basil, and olives so big and blue-black, they might have been mistaken for tiny plums.

"I'm not even sure the oven works right," Tom had said as they'd walked through the small specialty shop outside of town, his nerves growing frayed watching Dean carelessly toss expensive ingredients into their cart like seashells into a child's bucket. "I'm just saying I wouldn't go overboard."

"It's pizza," countered Dean, eyeing a log of soppressata. "You can't fuck up pizza. Maybe we should get dessert."

"Tess said she'd bring something," Tom lied, just wanting to get them out of the store before Dean spent the entirety of their savings.

"STILL NOT SURE THE OVEN works?" Dean demanded, proudly swinging out a perfectly crisped pizza at six thirty. "What time's your mermaid coming over?"

"Soon." Tom glanced at the counter, noticing the scotch bottle was gone. Surely Dean hadn't polished it off already?

"Get a sheet," Dean ordered, rummaging through the pantry for plates, crashing several into a pile, and tucking them under his arm. "We'll use it for a blanket."

Tom did as he was told, knowing better than to try to derail Dean when he was like this, feverish with ideas.

When Tess arrived fifteen minutes later, they were already on the lawn. She came bearing two bottles of wine. Tom gave her a wary look, but she just smiled and dropped beside him, kissing his cheek.

"Hey, where's mine?" Dean demanded, thrusting out his unshaven jaw. "The cook always gets kissed."

Tess obliged him, then stepped out of her sneakers, pushing them into the grass. "A picnic? Whose idea was this?"

"Whose do you think?" Tom glanced at Dean who was already opening one of the bottles of wine. He'd come prepared, snapping open a corkscrew and twisting the tip into the cork, yanking it out in the next instant with a loud pop. Dean filled a pair of plastic tumblers and handed one to Tess.

"Aren't you having any wine?" Tess asked Tom.

"No, thanks." Tom looked disapprovingly at Dean. "Somebody has to be the designated driver."

"But we're not going anywhere," said Tess.

"It doesn't matter." Dean raised his glass to Tom. "Tommy's always got to be behind the wheel. Don't you, old man?"

An uncomfortable silence dropped. Tess glanced between the brothers.

"So, what's for dinner?" she asked, eager to diffuse the tension.

Dean grinned over his glass. "I thought you'd never ask." He handed Tess his wine, then moved to get up. "Be right back with the main course."

"Sit; I'll go." Tom rose and marched up to the house with his hands in his pockets before Dean could protest. Tess handed Dean back his glass, then watched him take several sips.

"So, when do I get to see this sculpture of yours?" he asked.

"Whenever you want. It's almost done."

She glanced back at the house. Dean added more wine to their glasses, even though Tess had barely touched hers.

"Don't mind Tommy," Dean said, sitting back. "He'll snap out of it. He usually does."

"What is it?" she asked.

"What *isn't* it?"

Tom returned a few moments later with the pizza and set the pan down on the sheet. He served the wedges, the smell of warm basil fragrant while they ate.

"So how did you and the warden meet?" Dean asked.

Tess looked at Tom, Dean's challenge too hard to resist. "He was spying on me in my studio."

"I wasn't spying," Tom said firmly. "I was looking to ask for directions."

"He was *spying*," Tess said again, equally firmly, grinning at Tom as she did.

"Busted!" Dean cried. "I'm going to start calling you Peeping Tom."

"Please don't," Tom said warily as he watched his brother scoop up the second bottle and deftly uncork it.

"So, how is it you can't swim?" Tess asked Tom.

"It's not that I *can't* swim. I just don't go out of my way to."

"Aw, that's bullshit—the real reason is that Tommy can't

stand to lose." Dean leaned over and thumped Tom on the back. "I beat the crap out of him one summer when we were kids, racing back from a raft in the lake, and he was such a goddamn baby about it, he never got in the water again."

"But *you* did," Tess said.

"I did more than that." Dean drained his wine. "Did Tommy tell you I was a shoo-in for the Olympic team?"

"What happened?" asked Tess.

She looked between the brothers, waiting for one of them to answer.

Tom's eyes fell to his plate. It was Dean who finally explained as he refilled his glass. "I was just kidding you yesterday about the rock climbing. It was a car accident. I limp because of the crash. Fractured my hip. I couldn't walk for months. Sure as shit couldn't swim. Ask Tommy. He changed my bedpan for weeks. It was fucking heaven on earth, wasn't it, old man?"

Tess looked at Tom, waiting for him to meet her worried gaze, but he refused to. Instead, he scooped up the pizza tray and said, "We should clear all this before it gets too dark."

"I'll help you," Tess offered, rising with him.

Dean fished the pack of cigarettes out of his pocket, lit one, and dropped down to the grass. "You kids have fun. I'll wait for you out here. Keep the fireflies company; chat up the crabs."

Tom and Tess stacked the dirty plates and walked up

to the house, the sunset washing the clapboards in a silvery pink.

"Why didn't you tell me?" she asked when they were inside.

"It's not the sort of thing you just throw out there."

"It must have been awful," she said, following him to the sink. "Were you in the car too?"

"We all were." Tom took the plates from her hands and set them under the tap. "My folks were killed instantly."

"Oh, Tom . . ." Tess reached for his hand where it rested on the edge of the counter. He watched her fingers slide between his.

"It's all right," he said. "It was a long time ago."

"How long?"

"We were in high school. I was about to graduate."

"What did you do?"

Tom glanced up to the window above the sink, searching the view of the yard, nearly cloaked in darkness now, where Dean had stayed behind. His brother was out of sight maybe, but never out of mind. "The same thing I'm doing now," he said.

Tess studied him in the harsh light of the overhead. She hadn't been imagining it; he was different tonight—uncomfortable, distracted. The frown line in the middle of his brow had been fixed there for hours. She had seen the way he'd watched Dean every time he'd refilled his glass.

"Is that why he calls you the warden?" she asked.

"He calls me that because he's a child," Tom said, "and he thinks all I ever do is come down on him." He turned to Tess. "You don't have to stay. He's exhausting; I know."

"I don't mind. I like him."

"So you've said."

She took up Tom's hand in both of hers, turning it, thinking, stupidly, how different his fingers were from Pete's. "I don't even know what you teach," she said.

"Biology."

"Do the girls leave you apples?"

"Cores, sometimes. From my class right after lunch. I don't keep them."

Tess smiled. "He's just fooling around, you know. He doesn't mean any harm."

She was doing it again, Tom thought, defending Dean when she knew nothing about him. He released her hands. "I'm all he has, Tess. I wish it were different, but it's not."

"Is that why Frank gave you this place?" she asked. "Because he felt sorry for you?"

Tom looked back to the window. "I should go check on Dean. He's liable to wander around in the dark and walk off a cliff."

Tess reached for him again. "You could come back with me," she said. "Just for a little while."

"I can't. I can't leave him." Tom cupped her cheek. "I'm glad you're here."

Tess put her hand over his. "Of course I came."

"No, I don't mean here now," he said. "I mean here in this town. I'm glad you're here in this town."

TWO HOURS LATER, DEAN'S CIGARETTE pack empty and the wind too brisk to endure, he finally went to bed. Tom closed down the house and came up to his own room. Under the sheets and staring a long while at the blue-tinted ceiling, he could hear the comforting sounds of Dean's heavy snores sailing down the corridor, proof that he was here and that he was safe. Tomorrow he'd take Dean to the clinic in Port Chester. Tom had managed to make an appointment on his cell phone while Dean had been trying to pick up a woman at the grocery store. Once there, he'd get Dean into a recovery program, get the list of local AA meetings, take him to one as soon as he could; he'd get his brother sober and finally keep him there.

Tom felt a deep and expanding sense of peace, an unfamiliar settling, like a breath let out after too long underwater.

Maybe there was some truth to the magic of this small town, he thought, closing his eyes.

Maybe he didn't have to drown like Linus Harris after all.

1887

THEY'D BEEN FOUND ON A small island almost seventy miles from the Harbor, a strip of land called Crow's Rock. To say the four men were found alive was clinically accurate, but to see them arrive at the wharf on that damp and gray morning, one might not have been so sure. Helped off their rescue boat, they shared a look of numb fatigue, their skin darkened and dry from the sun and the salt, their lips a chalky pink.

They were taken at once to the hospital in Port Chester, and that was where Lydia first saw her husband.

"Did they say what happened?" someone called out from the crowd that had gathered outside the hospital.

An officer raised his hands to quiet everyone. "They've not been in any condition to speak. All of that will come in time. Right now, they need to recover. They've been through a terrible ordeal and need a great deal of replenishment."

"He won't be able to return home for several days, Mrs. Harris," one of the doctors told Lydia a few minutes later when she'd been steered out of her husband's room.

"Is there someone you can contact, dear?" a nurse asked, looking genuinely concerned. "Family who could come and stay with you?"

PEARL ARRIVED AT THE POINT two days later. The sisters rushed to each other and held on for several moments while the driver hauled Pearl's bags down to the grass. Lydia began to cry at once.

"Why didn't you send word when he'd gone missing?" demanded Pearl, crying too. "I would have come that instant. I would have *walked*!"

"There wasn't time," Lydia lied. "It all happened so quickly."

"He must be a wreck."

"He's resting."

"*You* must be a wreck."

"I'm fine. I'm just relieved."

Pearl took her little sister's face in her gloved hands, studying her. "Are you fine?" she asked. "Are you really?"

"Of course I am." Lydia drew her sister's hands into her own. "Come on. Let's get you settled."

PEARL HAD BROUGHT CHEESE AND smoked meats, which they devoured at the kitchen table with tea soon after Pearl had unpacked her things. Rain fell, spraying the windows. The house crawled with damp. Lydia fed the woodstove until streaks of orange sparked and roared behind the grate, but it made little difference.

"And no one has any idea what happened to them?" Pearl asked.

Lydia shook her head. "And they can't locate the wreck. They've tried for more than a week now."

"You must be so anxious to know everything."

Was she? Lydia wasn't sure. The truth was a part of her had terrible dread for the moment when the real story of their journey would come to light—as if something had happened, something best left out there. But that was silly; Lydia knew it was. It was so silly that she didn't speak of it to her sister. She simply nodded and rose to clear their plates.

"You sit," Pearl ordered, standing. "I'll clean up."

Lydia smiled gratefully, watching as her sister carried

their dishes to the sink, setting aside the remaining ends of meat and cheese to be saved.

As she faced the window, Pearl's gaze locked on a figure in the distance. She squinted. "Who is that?"

Lydia stood up to see to where Pearl pointed. It was Angus, marching down the lawn toward the lighthouse. A surge of warmth filled her to see him. He'd kept his distance since news of the rescue, despite Lydia's attempts to speak with him. Not that she knew what to say now or what to do. Still, she wished to know what he was thinking, certain he had to be confused, maybe even sad. She only hoped he wasn't sorry.

"That's Linus's assistant," she said, afraid to say his name, afraid she would reveal herself if she did.

"Does he live on the grounds?"

"No," Lydia said, sitting down again, glad for the chair since she was suddenly unsteady on her feet. "He lives with his brother just below the hill."

Pearl smiled, pumping water into the sink. "You're lucky to have him."

Yes, Lydia thought. *Yes, I was.*

LINUS WAS BROUGHT HOME THREE days later. Officers helped him inside, though he insisted he didn't need their aid. Lydia stood in the corner of the parlor, feeling useless and lost, waiting for her husband to offer her a signal of his love, of how much he'd missed her, how happy he was to see her. But it seemed all Linus could manage was to get across the room and reach the stairs. His gaze remained low.

"Give him time, sweetie," Pearl said as she and Lydia prepared to part the next morning. Lydia knew her sister could see the distress in her face. She'd cried off and on for hours, anticipating Pearl's departure.

Lydia nodded bravely, wiping at her eyes. "He's home now; that's all that matters."

And it was, Lydia told herself as she gave her sister one last long embrace and waved her carriage away, slipping eventually behind the pines. In time, the last few weeks would seem like a dream. She'd have no memory of these strange days, these feelings of such absolute fear and worry that she could barely keep herself upright.

She walked back to the house, wondering how it was she could hope to see Angus and yet hope not to. Their time together had also been the stuff of a dream. But she was grateful to him, more than he could ever know.

Back inside, she paused a moment before ascending the stairs. She wasn't sure Linus would be awake, if she dared disturb him, thinking about the doctor's warning that he would need continued rest.

Still, she came into his room and sat beside him for a while, just to be near him, just to touch his hand, his jaw, not accustomed to the beard that had grown there in his absence, the light brown hairs flecked with white strands that shocked her.

"You're home," she said, not sure what to say, but the words poured out, the only ones that seemed important. "When you feel better, we'll talk."

Linus squinted at her, then swallowed. "I don't want to talk about it, Lydie. I just need to forget."

His eyes looked strange to her. She didn't remember them so dark a blue.

"Forget what, my love?" she asked.

But he'd closed his eyes again and turned his head away from her.

LYDIA WAS AT THE KITCHEN window, admiring the blanket of lavender that the setting sun had spread out over the lawn, when she saw Angus walking up the path from the lighthouse. She set down her dishes, tugged off her apron, and stepped out into the warm evening air, crossing the grass to meet him.

He looked up. "I was just leaving," he said. He shifted his gaze to the tower, squinting into the soft breeze. "It should be a clear night. I don't expect you'll have any trouble out there."

Lydia nodded. "I'm sure not," she said.

They looked at each other. Angus shoved his hands into his pockets. "He'll hear things. Once he's better, we both know he will. And I feel bad for that."

"He won't believe rumors. Linus is too good a man to

listen to gossip." Filled at once with regret, Lydia closed her eyes, knowing the foolishness of what she'd said.

Angus stared at the house. "I never should have—"

"No." Lydia moved to him, then stopped, realizing they were in plain sight and panicking that Linus might miraculously find the strength to climb out of bed, rush to the window, and see them there. "You were kind to me, Angus. You were there for me. It was natural that we'd . . ."

When Angus looked back at her, Lydia couldn't finish the thought; she couldn't say the words out loud. The longing in his eyes was so fierce; Angus must have sensed it too, because he turned from her again. This time she reached for him, laying just her fingertips on his left wrist where it hung out of his pocket.

"He'll be all right now," Angus said. "You'll see."

He smiled at her then, the sort of smile that one could describe only as halfhearted. Lydia wanted to press herself against him, to let Angus know that there was a piece of her, smaller certainly than her love for her husband, but a firm and defined piece that cared for him, that even missed him and the smell of warm earth that had filled her lungs those nights, and comforted her when she'd been certain nothing could.

She hadn't expected to feel anything more than relief at Linus's return, and now this. She wanted Angus to know that, but how could he understand something she didn't understand herself?

"Good night then." Angus tipped his cap and moved past her. He got several feet away before he stopped and said over his shoulder, "I know I should be sorry it happened, but I'm not. I'm not sorry I knew you. I couldn't be if I tried."

Lydia bowed her head, her eyes squeezed shut as tears seeped out the edges. Frozen, she waited for him to get all the way down the hill before she finally turned and made her way back to the house.

LINUS RECOVERED QUICKLY. It seemed to Lydia every day that as the burn of the sun drained from his face, he grew stronger. Soon he was back in the lighthouse, keeping records even more fastidiously than before. But inside their home, his recovery wasn't nearly as quick. When they made love, he seemed hesitant, as if he were learning her body for the first time. The same was true of their conversation. He inquired of things he'd once known by heart. Lydia told herself to be patient. She kept indoors, papering the downstairs in lattice and trellis designs, and making curtains and new spreads.

One Sunday evening, while they cleaned up from dinner, Angus knocked on the door.

"I can't stay," he said. "I just wanted to let you know I've taken a job at the cannery. Full-time."

Lydia's hands stilled reflexively, the news startling.

She could feel Angus's eyes shifting toward her; she didn't dare look up.

"Miles has put word out in town, sir. You shouldn't have much trouble replacing me."

"No need. I think I can manage without an assistant now." Linus extended his hand. "Best of luck to you, Angus. I guess you'll be moving into the village then?"

Angus accepted the shake. "Yes, sir. I've already got a place."

Lydia said nothing, then worried her silence might seem more suspicious than her congratulations. She lifted her gaze to Angus and found him already looking at her, his eyes pooling with affection.

Her smile came reflexively, her words too.

"Thank you," she said.

Angus nodded. "No need to thank me, ma'am. Just glad I could help."

But of course, he couldn't know the real reason for her gratitude.

There was a visit to the doctor that still remained, but a woman knew these things—even one as confused and scared as Lydia.

At last, she carried a child.

Thursday

One Day before the
Mermaid Festival

ONCE THE FOUR MEN HAD recovered, the authorities began an investigation in earnest, but without testimonies from the men themselves, there could be no resolution to the mystery, and so the case was finally abandoned, the men's health believed to be returned to them. But as the coming months would reveal, the four survivors weren't nearly as recovered as they appeared.

—The Mermaid Mutiny and More:
A Complete History of Cradle Harbor

Ten

EVEN IN THE MILKY LIGHT of dawn, preparations in Cradle Harbor were already under way. With only one day to go until the opening of the festival, the narrow streets of the village were teeming with activity. Shop owners stood in their doorways, accepting last-minute shipments of mermaid-themed merchandise. Bakers with blueberry-stained fingers rushed around their kitchens, stockpiling reserves of their trademark dishes and barking orders at sleepy-eyed high school students who were looking to make a few extra dollars during the busiest season of the year.

Down at the Point, morning rose through the keeper's house, cold and damp. Tom walked quietly past Dean's room and downstairs to make himself some coffee. He rubbed his chilled hands together, glancing to the cold woodstove; he didn't want to start a fire, knowing he and Dean would be heading out in a few hours. Memories resurfaced as he boiled water on the range. He remembered dinner on the grass, shared glances between himself and Tess as the sun had dropped. How beautiful she'd looked in that dappled evening light; how much he'd wanted to grab her when they were alone in the house and kiss her deeply.

"Morning, sunshine." Dean ambled into the kitchen, his hair crooked from sleep.

"I can make you some coffee before we go," Tom said.

Dean scratched at his stomach, squinting at Tom. "Go where?"

"The clinic. Today at noon. The consultation. I told you about it last night."

"No, you didn't."

"Yes, I did. You were smoking on the porch. You just don't remember." *Because you were drunk,* Tom wanted to say but didn't. Instead, he watched his brother carefully as he wandered to the counter.

"By the way, I need some money," Dean said.

Tom frowned. "What happened to the two hundred I left you with?"

"What do you think happened to it? I was on the road for two days, Tommy. Do you want me to go out to the car and dig up my gas receipts—is that it? Maybe I can find the one for the egg sandwich I lived off for eight hundred miles?"

"Okay, okay . . ." Tom fished out his wallet, fanning out the billfold and withdrawing a twenty. "It's just that we need to watch what we spend here, Dean. I don't have a job yet, remember."

"You'll get a job. You always do," Dean said, taking the money and pocketing it. He scooped up his keys. "I'll be back."

"Where are you going?"

"I'm out of smokes."

"There isn't time," Tom said as Dean stepped into his sneakers. "We'll stop on the way."

"There's plenty of time," Dean countered. "I'm not waiting two hours for a cigarette, Tommy. Not when there's a gas station just up the road. Relax. I'll be back in fifteen minutes."

Relax. Tom wondered how one word, especially one intended to soothe, invariably made him want to jump out of his skin every time Dean used it.

Still, he knew better than to push any more than he had. He was just grateful Dean hadn't refused to go to the appointment. Maybe the night's magic had worked its spell on Dean too. Maybe he saw the hope in this new start as Tom did.

247

Dean tugged on a Cubs baseball cap and twisted it into place. "Back in a flash, Captain."

IT WAS THE PROSPECT OF snow that had scared Tess the most. She and Ruby had arrived in Cradle Harbor in the heat of the summer, on a still and muggy day when winter seemed a million years away, but still Tess dreaded it. It had been hard enough to watch the leaves, bursting with color for a short time, crinkle and drop, leaving gnarled, naked limbs in their place. What would it do to her mother to look out one morning on a world of white? Tess had wondered fearfully. All the paint in the world couldn't compensate for that.

Amazingly, their first winter on the cove was blessedly mild. Only a handful of snowstorms came, each producing barely enough to cover the ground. Where it did, the flakes were so heavy and wet, they took on the hues of the ground beneath them. Browns and grays—dingy colors that on any other day would have seemed disheartening, but Tess was grateful for them. On those cold and blustery January mornings, those shades might as well have been psychedelic.

When her mother had made it through that first winter, Tess had felt certain they'd be fine. Even more than the temperatures, they'd weathered the gossip, the rumblings about Ruby's fondness for wearing bikini tops into

Puffin's ("This *is* a beach town, isn't it? *Isn't it?*") or her frequent sales calls, with Tess and armfuls of her paintings in tow, to get the local businesses to display her work.

Though the rumors had flowed slowly at first, like cold honey, their bite had been swift and deep once the town's teeth had finally been bared, but it was Tess who lost the greater amount of blood.

"Don't listen to them," Buzz had said when she'd been sent to the principal's office for squirting ketchup into a classmate's face after he'd taunted her all through lunch.

"They don't even know her," Tess had said, glaring out the truck's window on their way home.

"That's right; they don't. And people who don't know people say dumb things about them instead of admitting they don't know. So what? It's not worth getting into trouble over it."

But it was, Tess had decided. In her opinion, it was worth any amount of trouble to defend her mother, to champion her talents as a painter, her abilities as a parent— both of which were constantly in question, no matter how much Buzz beamed in Ruby's company.

For her mother, however, the gossip was fuel. From the first indication that she was now the source of speculation and gossip in the small town, Ruby seemed to thrive on the attention, a charge that had frightened Tess at first, then eventually buoyed her.

"If you can't join 'em, beat 'em," Ruby used to whisper when they'd take Buzz's truck into town on a hot day to lay out their towels on the end of the pier, settling in just to the right of the lobstermen's footpath. They'd smile innocently behind their sunglasses until Buzz would arrive in a borrowed car to bring them home.

"It's not that kind of pier," he'd tried to explain. "You can't spread out on it and get a tan."

"We weren't in the way," Ruby had argued, finishing the last of the egg salad sandwiches she'd packed them. "Were we, lovey?"

Tess had shaken her head. Buzz had shaken his head too.

Of course, the content of her artwork—her propensity for nudes, usually couples in a variety of suggestive poses—hadn't sat well with the residents, either, nor had her request for male models at the town meeting in late September. She was planning a large canvas, a portrait to honor the men of the Mermaid Mutiny, she'd explained. She envisioned them as mermen and was looking for four volunteers who wouldn't mind posing shirtless. Several men had raised their hands, keeping them aloft until their wives had tugged them down.

"It's art, for God's sake," Ruby had defended afterward. "Don't they know anything about art?"

She had even offered to bring her work to Tess's school, but the board had refused her, claiming her work was too provocative for children. Ruby had been crushed.

"You could always paint something else," Buzz had suggested as they'd sat around the picnic table, eating burgers and steak fries. "Something, you know, *quiet*."

"Buzzie, there's nothing harmful about the naked body," Ruby had said. "And I won't subscribe to all that Puritan crap. I won't."

For the next few weeks afterward, Tess was sure they would leave Cradle Harbor, sure her mother would wake her in the middle of the night, a garbage bag stuffed with their clothes hugged to her chest, and point them to the road, but she never did.

Now, as she stood in front of her sculpture, sixteen years after she and Ruby had arrived, a fierce sense of closure came over Tess. *Wish you could be here, Mom. Your daughter's sculpture on display for the whole town to see. Just let them snub us now.*

Was that why she'd wanted Pete so badly for so long? Tess wondered. Was that why she'd needed the town to see them together, no matter how many months would go by between their public reunions? It had meant something to be wanted by Pete Hawthorne: acceptance, approval, maybe even something to be envied. She'd believed that was love once—had she been a fool in that way too?

Her thoughts turned to Tom. She imagined him waking in that house, shaving at that chipped sink and using that spotted mirror. What was he having for breakfast, or was he just sipping coffee, maybe staring out the window, maybe wondering the very same thing about her? The desire to see him swept over her. They'd made no concrete plans for the day since she had the sculpture to finish and he had Dean to settle in, but she craved something certain, something to look forward to.

She was thinking about Tom again when she heard the tap behind her. She spun around to find Dean in the window, his face pressed up against the glass, eyes crossed, tongue out.

She grabbed a handful of shavings and hurled them playfully at the window.

"I figured I'd try Tommy's trick," he said, coming into the shed. "See what it would get me."

Tess set down her tools and let him give her a fierce hug.

"God, you smell good," he said, sniffing her neck until she laughed and wriggled free.

"What are you doing here?" she asked.

"I was just out, and I figured I'd come by and see the great sculptress at work." Dean stepped past her, moving toward the mermaid. "Look at that! Hot damn, you're talented."

"Thanks." Tess looked expectantly at the doorway. "Where's Tom?"

"He had to run some errands," Dean said, his hands already on the sculpture, caressing the curves of the wood as if they were flesh. "He said we should meet back up with him later this afternoon. He asked me to come over and keep an eye on you."

Suspicious, Tess glanced at him as she retrieved her chisel. "He did, huh?"

"It's true—I swear." Dean followed Tess to the workbench. "So, what do you say I keep an eye on you over a beer?"

"A beer? It's not even ten."

"So?"

"So the pub in town doesn't open till noon."

Dean shrugged, undeterred. "Then we'll go buy a six-pack and get drunk on the beach."

"We could go back to the Point," Tess suggested. "Bring food."

"No, I want to see the town." Dean took the chisel from her hand and set it on the bench. "Give me a tour. I'll drive; you tell me where to go."

"It's a small town, Dean. There's not much to see."

"So we'll go to another town," he said, undaunted. "I've got a full tank of gas and nowhere to be. We'll get lunch. We'll get shit faced." He tugged Tom's crumpled twenty from his pocket and snapped it in the air. "My treat."

Tess considered him a moment, thinking there was something strange, something off in his expression. He seemed nervous, jumpy. Or maybe it was just excitement. Sometimes it was hard to tell with people. How many times had she tried to read the flashes of expression that had crossed her mother's face, sometimes a dozen in an instant, and she'd clung to each one.

She wiped her hands on her seat. "I'll get shoes."

HE WAS A TERRIBLE DRIVER, Tess thought as Dean steered them up Route 9. He was distracted, driving too fast, braking at the last minute, and never using his turn signal. It was a wonder he'd made it from Chicago. Several times his phone rang, but each time he squinted at the small screen and quieted it, finally just shutting it off and tossing it into the backseat. Tess said nothing, not wanting to pry. She could only imagine the sort of affairs Dean must have enjoyed in Chicago, the besotted hearts he'd left behind.

They stopped at a roadside market an hour up the coast. Tess ordered sandwiches while Dean made fast friends with two men pumping gas into their truck. Tess watched him as she gathered chips and a six-pack of beer, thinking again how wrong Tom was about things and how much her mother would have loved Dean. Back in the car again, she pointed them to a state park. She took the food while Dean slipped four of the six beers into a sweater he'd dug out of the trunk, rolling the cans into the braided wool and tucking the package under his arm, assuring Tess when she raised an eyebrow pointedly that no one would think twice.

As it was, they needn't have worried. The beach was empty. They settled on a patch of sand, pulled off their shoes, and began to eat. Dean opened a beer and nearly drained it before he reached for his sandwich, peeling off the wrapping in one long strip. Tess watched him as she ate. It was hard not to marvel at the differences in the two brothers when time allowed the comparison. As much as she had wanted to work on her sculpture, as close as she was to being done, she was grateful for the reprieve, grateful for this second chance alone with Dean. She had a feeling he was like her, ready and willing to reveal things, deep and raw things, things that someone like Tom would never confess, someone too secretive, too controlled. A part of her hoped Dean would offer those confessions *for* his brother. She craved knowing things about Tom, little things, big things, anything at all.

But her first question was one that had been tugging at her since their dinner on the lawn.

"Do you always lie about your leg?"

Dean gave her a sheepish grin. "I prefer to think of it as *embellishment*."

"You must have been terrified."

"It was a blur, really. That's what they always say about those things, and it's true. Your brain can't really grasp what's happening to it, I guess."

"And no one ever came forward?"

"Nope."

"Surely there was an investigation to find out who the driver was?"

"I guess there was. I don't really remember. I was

pretty much numb for a good year after it happened. And when I wasn't, I was just *wishing* I was."

He took a long sip of beer, studying the water as he swallowed. Tess watched him, a great rush of sympathy coming over her as she thought about his lost chance at Olympic glory and imagined him so young, so strong, then losing the thing that had mattered most to him. Not only had he suffered the death of his dream; he had suffered the death of his parents too. She knew better than anyone what that was like—to lose the piece of your world you were certain you couldn't live without.

"It must have been so hard," she said. "I'm sorry."

Dean shrugged, but Tess saw a faint sheen of tears when he turned back to her, an unconvincing smile fixed on his mouth. "Shit happens," he said. "What are you gonna do, right?"

"I lost my mom when I was I sixteen."

"Oh Jesus." Dean's smile vanished, concern worrying his pale eyes.

"She drowned in the cove."

"Shit, I'm sorry. That must have been hell."

"It was. It still *is* most days. She was my whole world."

"Of course she was."

"It sounds crazy, but I still see her everywhere," Tess said, picking up a piece of shell and tracing the smoothed edges with her fingertips. "Everything I do, every time I make something, she's the first person I think about. It doesn't matter if it's a carving or a cake. I think how I wish she could see this. I wish she could see *me*." Tears rose along her lids; Tess blinked to dry them, smiling at her confession. "Crazy, isn't it?" she asked.

"Hell, no." Dean reached for her hand and squeezed it. She met his eyes, seeing the sincere empathy in them, his usual teasing gone now. "You want to know how many nights a week I wake up on the floor because I was swimming so hard in my dream? How I can still feel my arms hitting the water, how I can still taste the chlorine?" He smiled. "I bet she was amazing."

Tess nodded gratefully. Of course he would understand. "It was just the two of us until we met Buzz," she said, reaching for a napkin to dry her eyes. "Mom and I had our own way of doing things. It used to drive him nuts."

"Sounds familiar," Dean said.

"Tom worries about you a lot, doesn't he?"

"Tommy?" Dean shook the can to hear the faint sloshing of a last sip. He drained the beer, twisting the empty can into the sand. "It's not just that. He thinks the accident was his fault."

"Was he driving?"

"No, our dad was driving. Tommy thinks it was his fault because the only reason we were even out on the road was because he wanted to go to some fucking party, which he *never* wanted to do."

"That doesn't make it his fault. It was an accident."

"Yeah, well. That's the thing you have to understand about Tommy: He likes living on his hook. I've tried to help him down, but he won't have it. He'd rather quarantine himself like some kind of leper, put both of us in little plastic bags, and seal us up from infecting the world, I guess." Dean winked at her. "He opened the bag a crack for you, though. I never thought he'd do that for anyone. Shit, he won't even do that for *me*."

"He should," Tess said. "He should do it for you most of all."

Dean shrugged. "Now we just have to hope he doesn't close it back up, don't we?"

Tess looked over to see a large group moving down the beach, thinking of the hour. They'd been gone for a while now. "We should get home," she said.

"Not so fast." Dean rose slowly, favoring his leg. "You promised me a swim."

"I did not. Besides"—she gestured to their empty wrappers—"everyone knows you aren't supposed to swim right after you eat."

"Then I guess we won't swim."

His grin was all the warning Tess might have needed, but she wasn't fast enough to scurry out of his reach in time. Before she could protest, before she could do anything but scream, Dean tugged her to her feet and pulled her down the shore and into the surf.

THEY WERE SANDY AND SLIGHTLY damp when they got back an hour later. Dean had agreed to let Tess drive home, falling asleep shortly after they'd pulled out onto the road, and she was glad for the quiet. It gave her time to think on their conversation, to enjoy the fierce sense of relief she had in it. Her feelings for Tom were even stronger now, her desire to see him almost an ache. She wouldn't reveal what Dean had said, what they'd shared, but she'd gladly confess to Tom how much closer it made her feel to him, how much it deepened her wanting of him. Not that it made that craving any more logical. If anything, it made it less so. The more she understood how different she and Tom were, the more she felt herself drawn to him.

When they came down to the Point and rounded the turn, she saw him right away, waiting on the porch, and her breath caught with excitement. Drawing closer, she could see his strained expression, his rigid posture against the column, arms folded, and a strange ripple of dread traveled her arms.

He was already halfway across the driveway by the time she had climbed out of the car, leaving Dean to sleep, and walked to meet him.

"He didn't tell you, did he?" Tom demanded when he reached her, his voice sharp enough to slow her advance.

Tess looked at him, confused. "Tell me what?"

"He had an appointment at noon. It was important."

"No, he didn't say a word about it."

"Of course he didn't. He never had any intention of going." Tom glared at the car as he spoke. "I never should have let him leave the house."

Still giddy with sand and sun, Tess had to laugh at that, sure he could be cajoled into better humor. "What would you have done?" she teased. "Tied him to a chair?"

But Tom's expression didn't soften. "This isn't a joke, Tess," he said evenly. "He needs help."

She relaxed her smile. "Help for what?"

"What do you think? He's a raging alcoholic."

"Why? Because he had too much wine last night?"

"This isn't about last night. This has been going on for years, and he needs to be in treatment."

"I was with him all morning, Tom. He was fine."

Tom frowned at her. "Why do you do that?"

"Do what?"

"Defend him."

"I'm not defending him," she insisted, but even as she said it, Tess could see Tom's mind was made up. She watched his eyes swerve to the car again, then return to hers after a moment, looking wounded and hardened all at once.

"You have feelings for him, don't you?"

"What?" Tess stared at him.

"Let me guess—you went home and consulted your charts or cards or whatever it is you use, and it turns out Sagittarius is your perfect match. Is that it?" Tom said. "Well, congratulations. I wish you both a long and happy life together." He turned from her and headed back toward the house.

Tess stood frozen with shock at his accusation for only

a moment before outrage took over. Racing to catch up to him, she came around to block his path, stopping his charge at the edge of the lawn. "I don't want to be with Dean, you jerk!" she sputtered. "God, I wish I did. At least he isn't afraid to live his life!"

"And I am. Is that it?" Tom demanded.

"I think you're *terrified*," Tess said. "And I think you're terrified that if you let him live his life, he won't need you."

"If I let him live his life, Tess, he'd be dead."

"You can't know that."

"You bet I can," he said firmly.

"Why?"

"Because I live in the real world, not some fantasy land where I base my every move on the stars or some crackpot legend about mermaids because I don't want to see what's staring me right in the face."

Tess knew at once that she should leave, that what would come next would only make things worse, maybe even ruin them beyond repair, but she couldn't stop herself.

"You're just like Buzz, you know that?" she said. "You think you know what's best for everyone, and you're too stubborn to admit that you don't!"

"I'm not the bull here, Tess. I'm just the boring, responsible guy, remember?"

"You can't change people who don't want to change, Tom."

"So why even try, right?" he asked, gesturing lamely to the car. "Why not say the hell with it and just let them fend for themselves? Why not let them drive into a ditch or end up at the bottom of the ocean?"

Tess sucked in a sharp breath, the words like a strike. At once, Tom's brow twisted with regret. He sighed. "Tess," he whispered. "Christ, I'm . . ."

She shook her head fiercely, the tears already soaking the edges of her eyes as she whirled away from him and began up the driveway. For a moment, she wondered if he'd realize she didn't have a ride and come after her, but she knew he wouldn't. The damage was done, and they both knew it.

She marched up the dirt road, her view so blurry she could barely see where the shoulder slipped into the trees. It was just like Dean had said: Tom had unsealed himself for her, and now he was closing the gap once again. He liked to be in control too much to let anyone in for long.

Fine, Tess thought, dragging her hand across her wet eyes and down her cheeks. He could have his control. He could eat dinner with it, count stars with it, make love to it.

She was going home.

DEAN WOKE A HALF HOUR later and sauntered into the kitchen. In his growing fury, Tom had paced the house, wanting nothing more than to fill a pot with cold water, carry it out to the car, and douse Dean with it. His parting words to Tess haunted him; yet he still wished she could have seen his side in it all. Maybe it served him right for letting go of his routines, his commitments, for wanting things to be different. Let the rest of the lunatics lose themselves in this festival nonsense, Tom thought; he had responsibilities, and he'd shirked them long enough. Now that Dean was here, life would get back to its order. Tom would make sure of it.

"I don't know what you expected," Dean said, shaking out a cigarette. "I told you I didn't want to go, and you made the appointment anyway. That's what you get for trying to run my fucking life, Tommy."

Tom said nothing from his seat at the table. While Dean slept, he'd tried to work his way through the dauntingly thick file that had come with the house, trying to decipher the ancient receipts and legal documents. He'd given up after only a few pages, unable to concentrate.

Dean looked through the doorway. "Where's Tess?"

"She's gone," Tom said tightly, rising from the table and moving to the counter.

"You mean she left?"

"I mean she's gone."

Dean shook his head. "I knew you'd do this. I knew you'd fuck it up."

Don't bite the bait, Tom thought as he dragged a sponge over the trail of Dean's ashes. *Don't do it.* When he looked up, Tom spotted a taxi steering down the drive. He dropped the sponge into the sink and moved across the kitchen to the room's other window, the one that had a better view of the driveway. By the time he got there, the car had stopped and a woman with long black hair had climbed out, clutching a redheaded infant to her shoulder.

"Dean . . ." Tom's voice was thin. "Why is there a woman with a baby in our driveway?"

Dean came to the window and stood beside his brother, his face falling.

He sighed.

"That's Petra."

1888

SOMETHING WAS TERRIBLY WRONG, AND Lydia knew it.

In truth, she'd known it far longer than she'd let on. The instant Linus had labored off the rescue boat, the very first moment their eyes had met across the landing, Lydia Harris had known her husband was no longer her husband; that something within him, something deep, something binding, was now missing.

"What do you expect?" Annabeth Owen whispered

condemningly when Lydia had finally suggested it in the months following the men's return. "God only knows what they endured out there. They might have died. Who can know that sort of terror? Pray we never do."

But his eyes, Lydia had wanted to say. *They're not the same blue. I know how that sounds, but they're not. They're haunted. His are the eyes of a haunted man.*

"It's the baby, dear," Mary Bartle answered. "I remember how it was. I wanted to cry at the drop of a hat. It's a hard enough time carrying a child—and you've been through so much."

"They just need time," Annabeth said, baby Joseph on her hip, little Elizabeth tugging on her skirt. "They're back now. That's all that matters."

But it wasn't all, Lydia told herself. What did it matter that they had returned when she lay beside Linus and grew more and more certain that the man who had come back to her was changed, and changed forever. No amount of time could return something that had been stolen, that now resided in that awful, treacherous sea. Did no one else understand that?

Yes, she thought. There *were* others she could reach out to. Even Millicent Banks, wrapped as she was like cut crystal in her mansion on the green, must have noticed an alteration in her own husband.

Surely Lydia's heart was not the only one about to shatter like satin glass.

———

THE KEENES ALWAYS TRAVELED TO town on Thursday mornings. Lydia had no trouble making up an excuse to ride with them. She needed more yardage for the baby's crib bumper; she'd miscalculated. And there was no harm in getting more molasses while she was there; why wait until they'd run out?

She didn't dare tell Linus the truth of where she was headed when the buggy came down the road for her. She didn't even tell Sarah or Miles Keene, too afraid they would think her mad. In the weeks following Linus's recovery, the gossip had hushed to the faintest whispers, quieted by the news of her pregnancy. Whatever discomfort Miles had shown in Lydia's company during those feverish weeks when Linus had gone missing had faded away, her neighbor's courteous and mellow smile returning. Lydia didn't dare draw fresh suspicions all over again.

Feeling the warm spring air on her face as she sat beside Sarah, Lydia wanted badly to inquire into Angus's well-being, but she didn't. She couldn't possibly. She hoped over the course of the long ride that Miles might mention his brother, even in passing, but Angus's name never came up, and Lydia told herself it was for the best. Wherever Angus was, she only hoped that he was happy, maybe even loved. Yes, she hoped that very much.

———

THEY REACHED TOWN SHORTLY BEFORE ten and parted ways near the wharf where Miles meant to purchase paint. Lydia waved the younger couple off, making certain they were out of sight before she turned down the street toward the green, where the town's most prosperous residents, shipbuilders and merchants, lived in massive brick homes.

She forced her racing heart to slow as she climbed the steps of the Banks's Italianate mansion and stood under the columned portico. After a moment, a maid arrived at the double doors. "Is Mrs. Banks expecting you?" the young woman asked.

"No," said Lydia. "I don't suppose she is."

The maid considered Lydia a moment, then disappeared for several minutes. When she returned, Millicent Banks arrived with her, dressed in a burgundy tea gown. The woman looked noticeably older—and far less congenial—to Lydia than she had that frantic day on the wharf many months before, and it was clear that Eli Banks's wife didn't recall Lydia. Her eyes landed at once on Lydia's stomach, narrowing with panic.

Lydia knew what the woman must have thought.

"What is this about?" Millicent demanded curtly.

"My name is Lydia Harris, Mrs. Banks. My husband, Linus, is the lightkeeper. He was captain of your husband's boat. I'd like to discuss something with you."

"Now look here. If you've come to demand some kind of compensation . . ."

"Hardly," Lydia said sharply, not about to play the lowly commoner. "I just wanted a word. About the incident. About our husbands."

Lydia saw the briefest flicker of understanding flash across the woman's pewter eyes, just enough that Banks's wife stepped back and said, "Only a moment. I'm very busy, and I'm expecting guests within the hour."

Millicent Banks led Lydia through the foyer, past the twisting grand staircase and into the parlor, where she instructed the maid to bring them tea, which Lydia had already decided she would decline, no matter the chill under her skin. Had the Bankses any children? Lydia couldn't tell. Looking around the large room, appointed as it was with gold-leafed wallpaper, columned door surrounds, and so much gleaming china, she saw no evidence of a child's curious touch anywhere.

Banks's wife set her hands in her lap, but still her fingers worried the silk twill of her gown. "You should be made aware that I suggested my husband press charges."

Lydia stared at the woman, startled at the confession. It had never occurred to her that anyone held Linus responsible for what had happened, especially since there was yet to be any clear admission to the events that had transpired. Due to the fear of putting the men through any further trauma, the case had been closed months earlier.

Or had it?

"I don't see how that would be at all fair," Lydia said, shaking her head when the maid arrived with tea and offered to pour her some. "Linus was doing your husband a great favor." In the weeks following the incident, the Bankses had never sent as much as a token of apology to the Point. Perhaps the other two men had received some sort of kindness for their trouble? They were, after all, fellow businessmen—one a merchant, the other a banker. Had Eli Banks made sure to compensate *them*?

"Be that as it may," said Millicent, "your husband presented himself as someone who could handle a boat of that size with little or no aid. Clearly, he overinflated his abilities."

Lydia drew in a calming breath. She hadn't come to defend her husband, and she'd be damned if she would do it a minute more.

"I'm not here to discuss blame, Mrs. Banks," she said evenly. "I only want to know if you have found your husband changed. That is all."

"Changed? Whatever do you mean?"

I mean are his hands now freezing to the touch. Does he smell of salt water all the time, not like someone who might have stood in the path of an ocean breeze, but like a man who has sunk deep under the sea and slept there, so deeply that when he kisses you, you can taste seaweed on his breath.

"I mean," said Lydia, "if he seems different to you than when he left on that sail."

"Well, of course he's different," Millicent snapped. "What a foolish thing to even ask. One would expect an episode like that leaves a man changed. I'd sooner worry if my husband *wasn't* changed. Is that all you mean?"

No, Lydia thought but didn't say, *and you know it's not, you impossible woman.*

But when Millicent Banks rose and departed, leaving Lydia to follow the maid back to the door and outside, Lydia began to wonder if it wasn't something shared among the men, but rather something unique to Linus. Riding back, quiet beside the Keenes, a new fear bloomed within her. What if somehow Linus had known of her time with Angus? Had her face betrayed her when she'd met Linus on the landing? Had he known even then? How could he have? It had been all he could do to put one foot in front of the other, his body gaunt and slow, his eyes floating numbly over the crowd in which she had been swallowed up. But what of the gossip? Had he believed it, believing the whispers of strangers over the affection of his own wife?

"I want to go to Rachel's," Lydia said later that same week, meeting her husband on his way to the lighthouse. It seemed he never came indoors anymore, and when he did, it was merely to sleep for a few hours before sunset or take a bowl of soup. He'd lost so much weight. Some days when she'd see him slip past the window, he looked spectral to her, his eyes always fixed on something far away. "Pearl will be there," she added, "and I would very much like to see my sisters."

"All right." Linus answered her as if she were a stranger at the window of a train station, requesting a ticket. His voice was even and utterly without opinion. Didn't he want to know how long she intended to be gone, or when she planned to leave? Didn't he worry for the safety of their unborn child, unfounded as any worry was? The Linus she used to know would have teased her about his needing to come too to make sure Rachel's brother-in-law didn't flirt with her as he was wont to do after cribbage and bourbon; he would have tickled her until she'd screamed for mercy. The Linus she used to know would then have sat down on the grass and pulled her into his lap, telling her which of tonight's stars he would claim for her.

"This baby is everything we've wanted, Linus," she whispered.

"I know it is."

"Then why don't we ever talk about it? Don't you ever think about our baby?"

"All the time, Lydie. I can't think on much else anymore."

His words should have soothed her, but they didn't. Lydia waited for him to say more, to say anything, but no words followed. He simply shifted past her and continued down the path.

"YOU'RE AS WHITE AS A ghost," Pearl announced, taking her sister's hands as soon as she stepped off the train two days later, "and your hands are like ice."

Lydia never had to say a word. No sooner had she walked into Rachel's house than she was swept up in their care, nestled and pillowed like a featherless bird accidentally tipped out of its nest. She drank tea and even a few glasses of sherry. They made her roasted chicken and sponge cake scented with rosewater, but she couldn't keep anything down.

"He's so pale," Lydia whispered. "He's so *thin*."

"Forget about him," said Pearl. "It's *you* we're worried about."

Lydia shook her head. "He used to read me his log book every night. Now he hides it as if it were full of secrets. Sometimes he doesn't even come in for meals. All the other wives think I'm mad," she confessed, Rachel and Pearl on either side of her on the sofa. "They say it's just what can happen when you carry a child. That your mind isn't your own sometimes."

"What absolute nonsense," said Pearl. "It's a child, not opium. Have you tried talking with Linus?"

"He won't talk to me," Lydia said. "I've tried; I've *begged*." She closed her eyes, tears seeping out the corners; Pearl dried them with her fingertips. "He's my whole life, Pearl," Lydia whispered. "He's everything to me."

Rachel had asked her husband, Edward, to make a fire, even though it was still warm enough to keep the windows open through the night. "She can't get warm," Rachel explained. "She's chilled to the bone."

"Call a doctor," Pearl ordered Rachel's husband, without waiting for Rachel to concur. "Call one now."

Dr. Farnsworth arrived within a few hours; Lydia tried to stay awake, but her eyelids failed her.

"She hasn't a fever," Farnsworth concluded, briefing the sisters after his examination. "It's likely that the pregnancy could be the reason for her confusion, her condition. It's common for women to react so."

"Useless," hissed Pearl as she stood at the window and watched the man climb back into his carriage moments later. "I hope he doesn't expect to be paid for that rubbish."

"Pearl," Rachel scolded, "Dr. Farnsworth is a good man."

"Has it not occurred to anyone that something might be truly wrong with Linus? I mean, be sensible, Rachel. It's lunacy. That not a *one* of those men can remember what happened the entire time they were shipwrecked? And that old goat says our sweet sister is the one who's confused?"

"Keep your voice down," Rachel whispered, feeling Lydia's forehead for fever again, even though the doctor had assured her there was none. "It's not as if I have any answers, either, you know."

When Lydia woke several hours later, she smiled to see her sisters still at her side. She reached for each of their hands, gripping them tightly.

"I'm going back with you," announced Pearl. "You can't go home alone in the state you're in. I won't let you."

Lydia shook her head, terrified at the thought. How could she bear to have her sister see the anguish on Linus's face? Lydia knew she would never be able to contain her guilt. It would all come rushing out—and no matter how much Pearl might promise to keep her sister's secret, Lydia knew she couldn't ask Pearl to carry such a burden.

"No," said Lydia, biting at her lip to keep from crying. "I'll be fine; I promise. You'll come after the baby's born."

But Pearl kept her eyes leveled with Lydia's, not yet ready to agree.

"Really, you'll see," Lydia said, pressing her sister's hand to her cheek. "I won't let you leave."

A FEW DAYS LATER, LYDIA boarded the train and returned to the Point just before sunset. She was sure, *so* sure, that Linus would be there to meet her, but the house was dark, the only spot of light in the whole property that of the tower.

When she saw the door to the oil house ajar, she walked across the lawn and stepped in the doorway, finding Linus there, his back to her.

"I've missed you," she said, certain he would turn to her, but he kept on with his inventory, offering her a brief glance over his shoulder.

"Have you eaten?" she asked. "I can make chowder."

"I'll be in later," he said. "I've got too much to do just now."

She squeezed her eyes shut. "What's happening to us, Linus?"

He paused in his stacking, letting his hands drop uselessly to his side. Lydia stared at those hands, those hands that used to find her flesh at every opportunity, those hands that once couldn't be apart from her body. How long had it been since he'd touched her?

It was true. He knew. The distance between them, his

275

coldness, had nothing to do with his wreck and rescue. It was Angus. Linus knew what she'd done; he knew the child she carried wasn't his. He'd heard the rumors, and to her despair, he clearly believed them. And why shouldn't he? Had she thought she could keep her betrayal from the man who had known her better than anyone?

"Take me away, Linus," she whispered. "Take me somewhere new. Somewhere far away from here. We'll have our baby in a new house, in a new place."

He turned to her finally, his eyes drained of interest, of concern. "Don't be foolish, Lydie. We can't possibly leave here now. You know that."

Then, without a word, Lydia turned and stepped out of the doorway, fighting through a biting wind to get back to the house, sealing herself in, shivering even as she drew a chair to the very edge of the fire she'd stoked in the parlor, close enough that sparks landed on the hem of her skirt. She watched them brighten briefly, then die, thinking it might not be so awful if one caught, to feel something other than the pain of this heartbreak.

Sometime later, while she was putting away the chowder Linus never came to eat, she heard a creak in the kitchen doorway and turned to find her husband standing there. Her blood ran cold. He was looking at her as if he hadn't seen her for some time.

No, she decided, as he turned and walked back out into the night. No, that wasn't it.

Linus was looking at her as if he had no idea who she was.

Eleven

THE WOMAN HOLDING THE BABY was named Petra, and the baby was named Mia. Dean explained all of this while Tom stood stiffly at the mantel, tearing absently at a soft section of the wood with his thumbnail, sure he could have dug down to the pith.

"Mia," Dean said conversationally. "It's short for Maria."

The woman looked up at him with enormous black-blue eyes, saying nothing.

"She's shy," Dean explained, steering Tom into the kitchen. "She's just really shy. And her English isn't great. She's been in this country only a year and a half."

This wasn't happening, Tom thought as he and Dean walked out to the backyard, the air so sour with the scent of low tide, Tom believed he might actually throw up.

Dean took out his cigarettes, his hands shaking as he lit one. "You met her once actually. I brought her home after Thanksgiving last year."

Tom closed his eyes, then swallowed. *The breeze. Think about the breeze.*

"I don't remember," he said dully.

"She had bangs then. And these crazy red streaks."

"I don't remember, Dean."

"Fine, then screw it." Dean exhaled, squinting through the smoke.

Tom just stared at him. "A baby. Jesus Christ, Dean."

"I was going to tell you eventually, Tommy. You know, at some point."

"What point would that have been? When she started college? When she got married?"

Dean sucked hard on his cigarette, forcing the smoke out his nostrils.

"That's where you were, wasn't it?" Tom asked. "The last time you disappeared, you were with her, weren't you?"

"I didn't *disappear*, Tommy. Don't be so fucking dramatic. Just because you don't know where I am every second of the day doesn't mean I disappear."

"Do you love her?" Tom said.

Dean took a long drag; Tom watched him, waiting.

"Do you even *like* her?"

"Sure," Dean decided. "Sure, I like her."

But do you like her like I might have liked Tess Patterson? The question flooded Tom's mind, feverish and sharp. *Does she make you forget who you are, make you want everything all at once?*

"Listen to you," Dean said, letting the butt of his cigarette drop to the lawn and squashing it out with a few turns of his heel. "Since when are you the expert on love, old man?"

I'm not, Tom answered to himself as he watched his brother make his way back to the house. He dropped to his heels and plucked the discarded filter out of the grass, rolling it in his palm.

There was a time he might have had a chance to be, but not now.

IT HAD BEEN YEARS SINCE Tess had walked home. As a teenager, she'd done it almost every Friday night, sneaking out of the trailer, determined not to miss a chance to meet up with Pete on the green or at a bonfire on the beach. Sometimes she'd catch a ride, other times she'd bike it, but invariably when it came time to go home, she'd find herself walking, following the sandy shoulder in the dark and stepping farther toward the woods when a pair of headlights would appear. Sometimes, *most* times, it was Buzz looking for her. He'd pass her slowly, turn around in the road, and pull alongside her. She'd get in, and they wouldn't talk about it; they wouldn't say a word the whole way. She would look out the window, away from him, glad for the dark so he couldn't see how much she'd been crying.

Now the road was packed, and she was far from alone on it. The festival crowds were finally arriving, the flow of traffic thick and constant, headed for town and the larger inns farther up the road. The cottages would be filling up now. Buzz would be rushing around, probably panicked at her absence. She might have felt bad if she had had room for a thought other than the persistent and crushing memories of her fight with Tom. For the last half mile, she'd tried to avoid replaying every painful word, but she couldn't. What was there to distract her but the rush of hot air from passing cars, the skinny pines on either side that provided her no shade? She was wilting from the humidity rising from the pavement, but then her deflated state had little to do with the weather.

She looked up in time to see a van, painted emerald green, its passengers—a young couple—waving wildly as they passed her. Behind them came another stretch of cars with out-of-state plates. Tess smiled in spite of herself, waving back. This was it, what she waited all year for— the magic of the Mermaid Festival. And she'd be damned if she'd let Tom Grace or Buzz or anyone else who refused to believe in it steal that singular joy from her. Her mother certainly never did.

Rue, you do realize nobody from the Harbor actually dresses up for the festival; only tourists do.

Buzz had made the announcement moments after he'd walked into the trailer that first summer and found Ruby and Tess in a sea of blue and green tulle, lengths of it draped over his recliner and the TV, strands of tinsel everywhere.

"Who says?" Ruby declared as she painted purple stars across Tess's forehead. "Don't make it wrinkly, lovey. Try to keep it flat." And Tess had tried, but fits of giggles had ensued. "Besides, we've only just got here, so we can do whatever we want," said Ruby, planting a finishing kiss on Tess's nose when she was done.

"Yeah," agreed Tess, rushing to Buzz and leaping into his open arms in a small tornado of tulle and curled ribbon. He pulled her down with him into the couch, seeing a familiar clump of canvas on the floor by the TV.

"What's the tent doing out?" he asked.

"Tessie and I are going camping."

"In the cove!" Tess had squealed. "We're going to sleep on the beach so we can hear the mermaids, like you said."

"Now, hold on a minute," said Buzz. "I never said anything about being able to hear them. . . ."

"Well, of course you can hear them!" said Tess. "They sing. Everybody knows that."

He chuckled, letting her weave a piece of tinsel through his beard. "Everybody, huh?"

"Yup. We're going to make a bonfire and roast marshmallows. Isn't it great?"

Buzz gave Ruby a concerned look. "It gets cold as hell on the beach at night here, Rue."

"That's why we're bringing the tent, Grump-a-lump," Ruby teased, blowing him a kiss, her lips spotted with loose glitter. She crossed the room and joined them on the couch, snuggling up to Buzz just as Tess had done.

"Maybe I should come with you," he said, putting his arms around them both.

"No boys," said Tess firmly, playfully swatting his nose with a piece of her green tulle scarf.

"No boys, huh?" he asked.

"Nope. Mom's been reading all about mermaids, and she read that if you hear mermaid song, you'll leave her. Just like Linus Harris and all those other men did."

"Aw, no chance. No mermaid could make me leave your mom, kiddo." Buzz had leaned over to kiss Ruby then, finding her already turned to him. Tess had watched their embrace, feeling a warm sense of peace and belonging. She'd worried at first, concerned that Buzz would ruin what they had together, would come between them like a saw, cutting them in two.

Tess wasn't sure why the memory of that first festival had returned to her now as she arrived at the cove and came down the driveway to the cottages, seeing the property as busy as she'd expected. It was always a shock to see the cottages lived in after so many months of their sitting empty, such a joy to hear the sounds of voices blending from porches that were now full. But as soon as she stepped up the stairs to her own cottage, the delight faded. She'd left that morning with such hopes, such excitement for Tom Grace and the unexpected romance she'd found with him. Just hours later, it was gone.

No sooner had she crossed the room and gone to the sink for a glass of water than she heard Buzz arrive at her door. He rapped twice but didn't wait for her to respond before he came in, winded from his advance.

"Where have you been?" he demanded. "I've been going nuts here. Everybody showed up all at once. I was counting on your help."

"Sorry," Tess said, shoving a glass under the tap and draining it.

"What's the matter with you? You look like you've been dragged behind a boat."

"Good guess." She set down her glass and moved past him for the couch. She fell into it, grabbed a pillow from the end, and buried her face in it. Buzz came beside her, staring down at her, hands on his hips.

"What's going on, Tessie?"

"I don't want to talk about it," she mumbled through the pillow.

"Too bad." He snatched the pillow and tossed it beside her. "I can't fix it if I don't know what's broken."

Tess glared up at him. "You can't fix this, Buzz."

"How do you know?"

"Because you can't." She climbed to her feet, moving past him to the front door and stepping back outside. She hated when he got this way; he was always thinking he could change things, always thinking he could control every damn thing in the universe.

He followed her onto the porch. "Is this about Grace?"

"I don't want to talk about it." Tess could feel tears crawling up her throat. Across the driveway, guests moved in and out of their cottages; screen doors squealed and slammed. Someone was blasting the Chieftains. Someone was already grilling fish.

"I thought you said things were going well with him."

"I thought so too."

Buzz frowned. "What is that supposed to mean?"

"It means I changed my mind, okay?" Tess said.

"You did or *he* did?"

"What difference does it make?" she asked. "It's over."

"Since when?"

"Since just now."

"And this is how you're taking it?" Buzz folded his arms and stared at her. "You give that creep Hawthorne a hundred and one second chances, but you have one fight with Grace and you just give up?"

"Give up?" Tess whirled around to face him, the accusation cutting deep. "You're a fine one to lecture me about giving up. You mean the way you gave up on Mom the minute things got too tough?"

"That's not true, Tessie," Buzz said, his voice softening. "You know that's not true."

"I know you pushed her until she couldn't take it anymore."

"I didn't push her. I was trying to help her."

"By telling her she had to take pills or you'd leave her? Some help!"

"She couldn't manage her depression by herself, Tessie. What was I supposed to do?"

"That's how you want to remember it." Tess marched back into the cottage.

"You want to talk memories?" Buzz followed her inside, slamming the door behind them, ready to have it out once and for all. "Okay, let's talk about memories," he said. "Let's talk about the time your mother thought it would be fun to take that old canoe out, and I had to get Bill Cotswold's boat to bring you both back in, shivering like a pair of newborn pups. You remember that one?"

"Leave me alone," Tess whispered.

"Or how about the time she took you out of school and hitchhiked with you to Boston because she'd had a dream about the Swan Boats, and I had to come get you two in the middle of the night at South Station? You call that giving up, huh?"

Tess wanted to cover her ears. She wanted to sing

loudly like a taunted child. She wanted to slug him and break every dish in the cabinet. Instead, she just began to weep, big salty tears that ran straight into her mouth.

"Why couldn't you just let her live her life?" she said. "She and I were doing okay before you came along. We were fine!"

"No, you weren't, Tessie. Oh baby, no you weren't." Buzz reached for her, but Tess stepped away.

God, she still didn't get it, he thought. From the time she'd poked her head out from behind that row of paintings, sunglasses as big as saucers, teeth and gums coated with chocolate, and told him that her mother's paintings were going to be worth a million dollars someday so he had better buy one now before she got too famous. That was how long he'd loved her—from that instant.

Would she never understand that?

Buzz walked to the door, feeling like a cat toy banged around the floor, in and out, back and forth. They couldn't seem to make up their minds, he and Tess. Fix it or break it even more. But then, he hadn't been much of a mender lately. Beverly's crying rush from the restaurant came back to him, making him feel even worse, if that was possible. He'd gone over twice to check up on her, but she hadn't answered her door. What had come over everyone?

Goddamn festival. Once upon a time he'd enjoyed it. Now all it did was bring him grief and remind him of things he couldn't change. He'd be glad to see it end. There was nothing mystical in a set of wind chimes, no mermaids to call you into the surf in the middle of the night. Linus Harris was just a crackpot who'd taken in too much mercury and caused three other men—and his own wife—to perish for his delusions. Buzz was tired of being the only one who saw those men for the selfish fools they were. It was Lydia who was the real tragedy, Lydia who'd been left to pick up the pieces, Lydia who'd decided, poor thing, that she couldn't.

THERE *HAD* BEEN SOMEONE ELSE once in Beverly's life.

His name was Barry Harmon and she'd met him through the PTA, the year after she'd started seeing Frank. Like her, Barry had been widowed; he even had two boys, his a few years older than hers. He was an orthodontist with a timeshare in Naples. He'd taken her to dinner and, over a shared plate of calamari, told her that she reminded him of Kim Novak. He'd given her a magnolia bonsai.

Beverly hadn't thought about Barry Harmon in a very long time.

But she did now. As she watched Buzz march back up the lawn to his trailer from her cottage window, it seemed the choices she'd made in the years she'd known Frank were all she could think about. She'd watched Buzz and Tess's fight from the back window of the cottage, then heard a good deal of what she couldn't see when they'd moved inside, her heart breaking. That was what it was to be a parent; she understood that listening to Buzz. It meant putting your children above everyone else and turning away the love of your life if needed to protect them. She'd never done that; she had never believed that she should. She'd made loving Frank her focus, and that choice had cost her sons dearly. How many weekends had she dragged them away from their friends, from sport commitments, from school events, simply because Frank had rented them all a house on Lake Michigan, or surprised them with tickets to the Field Museum and a pair of rooms at the Sheraton? Or was it more than that? Maybe, just maybe, she'd never given her children the time they were due, never been truly comfortable as their mother, and Frank's invitation had merely been the excuse she'd wanted to slip free of motherhood.

No wonder she'd felt so undone being here, so anxious. It had nothing to do with hurt. It had everything to do with guilt. She realized now that she was every bit as accountable as Frank. Just like he'd done, she'd lied to people she'd claimed to love, lied to herself. And as for thinking that she'd been denied a choice in how Frank had kept her out of his life at the end, how he'd kept her out of it really for the entirety of their fifteen-year affair, Beverly couldn't have been more wrong. It had been her choice to get into that taxi, her choice to take those phone calls and flowers, to miss her sons' ball games; it had been her choice to turn down Barry Harmon when he'd asked her out on a second date.

The people who'd been without a choice were her sons; Joan and Buzz and Tess; and maybe even those brothers in the keeper's house, whoever they were—Beverly wasn't even sure she cared to know anymore. It wasn't important.

That was how swift and startling it was, her shame, her apology. She'd come here, believing she was entitled to her truths, but she was so wrong. She had a right to her mourning, but she had no right to her anger.

But there were those who did, she thought as she lowered the curtain, her eyes fixing on the spots of paint scattered on either side of the frame. As she joined them with her index finger, she saw at once they weren't nearly as random as she had first thought; rather, they comprised a map of sorts, points of starlight so that someone might always find their bearings under any sky.

She'd been a fool—blessed and so ungrateful.

Some mothers and their children didn't get enough time.

TOM SAT ON THE BACK porch, staring out into the night.

Dean had a child.

A child.

Dean, who couldn't take care of himself, had allowed another human being—a child and her mother—to come into the world to depend on him. Dean knew nothing about raising a child. Tom himself had barely done more than hold a baby before.

He thought about all the things a baby needed, then a child; how little he and Dean had, how little they could expect. He thought about the guests in those colorful cottages down at the cove, carefree people lost in the celebration, deliriously happy and unaware.

But most of all, he thought about Tess.

Even in the thickness of the mess Dean had delivered to them, Tom still managed to find space to miss her. He'd hurt her, and he hadn't meant to. Any chance they might have had to get closer was gone now. But maybe it was best this way. Even now, Tom had no idea how he might explain to her that seventeen years earlier he'd caused a disaster that he could never correct but had vowed to spend the rest of his life trying. How could he have faced her with that confession? Those eyes of hers had undone him that first day in her woodshop. The grassy smell of fresh basswood he had sworn had attached itself permanently to his skin.

Was she missing him too? he wondered. The fierce and irrational attraction he felt for her had been so certain to him—he'd thought she'd felt the same. He glanced up at the roof of black, the pinpricks of light, trying to recall the constellations she'd shown him. They'd been so clear when her fingers had directed his eyes. Now it was all a scattering of spots, unbound and unjoined.

What did it matter? In another few months, leaves would brown and crisp and fall, leaving stark, wiry branches. And he would convince himself to look forward to chilly autumn nights, cold gray days that offered no hint of joy, early dusks and wind so frigid people had to keep their heads down to protect their skin, eyes down too, not meeting their neighbors'. He'd try for a teaching job, take whatever he could. Snow would fall, maybe so much sometimes that he wouldn't be able to leave the house at all. Yes, he would embrace that isolation, that numbness of cold, the way he used to in Chicago—the only way he knew how.

IT HAD ALL STARTED BECAUSE Ruby couldn't find a pen to draw Cassiopeia. She and Tess had been sitting in their cottage, the one called Pink, one unusually warm November night, and Ruby had decided then and there that it was the night Tess would finally learn the stars.

Unbelievably, they'd had the windows open for three days straight—unheard of most Novembers in Maine (or so Buzz had claimed) when evening temperatures could easily dance toward frost. Best of all, they'd been able to shake off their heavy sweaters for a while, moving around in bare feet and bare arms.

"A hundred brushes and not a single pen," Ruby had exclaimed as she'd scoured the paint-splattered drawers of her studio.

"You could always just *paint* the stars on a piece of paper," Tess had suggested, nearly halfway through a bag of potato chips she'd brought down from the trailer, her fingers traffic-cone orange from the powder, try as she had to lick them clean. She and Ruby had been living with Buzz for several months by then, and even if Tess wasn't crazy about school or the kids in her class, she had to admit she liked living by the ocean, liked finding treasures on the beach such as mermaid purses and horseshoe crab shells. But most of all she liked seeing her mother smile so many days in a row that Tess would lose count, or cease to keep count at all.

"I think he looks like Poseidon," Ruby said as she rummaged. "Don't you think? His great big beard and that mane of red hair. I can just imagine him standing in the middle of a whirlpool, calming the seas."

Tess could too maybe. She wasn't sure she wanted to. Her mother had loved men before; she had loved them quickly and entirely.

"Do you like Buzz better than Eddie?" Tess had asked.

"Oh God, yes. Don't you?"

"I didn't like Eddie," said Tess. "He yelled at me once because I ate two of his cookies. He showed me the empty slots in the tray."

"He yelled at you?" Ruby stared at Tess, her face falling. "Why didn't you ever tell me that?"

Tess shrugged. "Because you said he was your destiny."

"Eddie was born on the cusp." Ruby sighed. "I didn't know that when we met. I didn't know a lot of things about him, apparently." She moved then to the window with a brush and a small dish of violet paint. She considered the petal pink wall just to the right of the frame, tilted her head, wrinkled her nose, then set down her first dot.

"Which star are you making?" Tess asked.

"All of them," said Ruby. "If you want to learn the constellations, you have to know where they live in the sky. It's not enough to pick out just one."

Tess watched, enthralled, as her mother made careful dots with the paint. Only a few times did she lean over to double-check the placement of her "stars." Soon, the wall was a mass of purple spots.

Ruby stood back, considering her work.

"Maybe we should label them?" suggested Tess.

"Oh, we can't do that. Then it won't look like the sky."

"But how else will I learn them?"

"You will—you'll see." Ruby returned to add a few more stars. After a moment she turned to Tess and said quietly, "He wants to marry me, lovey."

"That could be good, I guess." Tess reached into her bag of chips, considering it as she crunched down on a handful. "So we could stay here a long time then, huh?"

"We could. We could stay here forever if you wanted to."

"Forever isn't real."

"Isn't it?" Ruby winked at Tess. "How do you know we're not the two people on the planet who get to live forever? It's as possible as anything, I think. Or maybe we're more like the Phoenix, this one here." Ruby pointed to the middle of the wall and connected the dots of the bird's wing with her finger. "Maybe we burn up and then get to start all over again in the morning."

"I don't like that one," Tess said firmly. "I don't want to burn up. I don't want you to burn up, either."

"We all burn up, lovey."

"You and I won't," said Tess. "Promise me we won't ever burn up."

"Oh, I don't know. . . ." Ruby looked to the window, smiling wistfully into the night. "I think it would be nice to go that way. Like a star. An explosion of light and heat and love. I really do."

"Promise," Tess demanded again. And this time Ruby appeased her, no doubt hearing the panic in her daughter's voice.

"I promise, lovey," Ruby said. "You and I will never burn up like stars."

But she had. As much as she'd promised not to, Ruby had burst out of Tess's life without warning, and it was that singular broken vow that Tess had thought about over and over in the months after she came home from school to find the police at the cove. She saw Buzz first, standing with the state trooper, the skin above his beard the color of clam flat mud. Shaking her head, Tess went straight up to the trailer, dropping her books and her coat on the way, certain that if she could just keep walking, if she could keep Buzz from reaching her, then the truth couldn't reach her, either. She called for her mother, louder than she might have needed. The trailer wasn't big, but still she tore through it; then she came back outside and marched across the driveway to the cottages. Buzz was there to head her off. "Come here, Tessie," he pleaded, his voice like something heard underwater, liquid and blurry and faraway. "Come here, baby."

"I need to find Mom," she said. "I just need to find her and tell her something."

"Tessie, you have to listen to me now."

But she wouldn't listen; she wouldn't slow, either, not for anything. Never in all her life had Tess wanted to keep going as much as she did in that moment. Her heart pounded; her lungs burned. When Buzz finally caught up to her, she fought him for a moment, thrashing like a fish, until he managed to get both of his arms around her, stilling her like a top that couldn't stop its spin.

For several days and nights afterward, they'd lived on the beach. Since Ruby's body had not been found, Tess had refused to believe her mother was really gone. She had also refused to believe the letter Ruby had left in Buzz's truck, and Buzz had not once argued the point. Instead, he had just dragged down the old tent and set it up wordlessly in a stiff wind.

"We should make a fire," Tess said. "Just in case she isn't sure it's us, okay?" And he'd done it, building her a peak of flames that could have rivaled the lamp of the lighthouse.

They kept at it for almost a week, practically living out of the tent, bringing down their meals from the trailer—if cold cereal and wrapped cheese slices could be counted as a meal—leaving only to use the bathroom or get more blankets. Buzz wrote a note to the school to explain Tess's absence—not that they should have needed one, for Christ's sake, he muttered, handing it to a neighbor's daughter to deliver.

For three nights, Tess wouldn't let Buzz close the flap, afraid her mother might call out and she wouldn't hear, but when the temperature dropped to near freezing, which it often still did in early May, she consented to let Buzz zip them in snugly. He told her stories to distract her, but he would always drift off first, snoring deeply, sometimes weeping in his dreams.

But Tess would be wide awake. For hours afterward, once her eyes and ears had trained to the darkness, she watched the wind ripple the nylon, imagining each sweep of surf, each rustling of the hedges to be Ruby returned from her ocean adventure. In those moments, her senses became so acute, Tess swore she could hear the scurrying of hermit crabs halfway down the beach, their shell houses whispering trails through the sand. She felt more alive and more lifeless than ever—found and lost. But mostly, she just ached.

Now, nine years later, standing in front of the sculpture that would award her so much more than a three-hundred-dollar prize, Tess felt every bit as lost. For the last few hours, alone with her thoughts in the milky light of dusk, convictions had crumbled, stripped away like the basswood beneath her chisel blade. Everything she'd held dear and firm now felt as rootless and tumbled as seaweed in the curl of the surf.

She'd wanted to believe—*needed* to believe—that her mother hadn't been ill, that Buzz had pushed Ruby to do what she'd done, and that she, Tess, had every right to blame him.

She'd wanted Pete Hawthorne for so long, but why? Being his chosen one—even temporarily—had given her the acceptance the Harbor had always refused her mother. But was that love? Wanting him had made sense once, but as she stood there now, it wasn't Pete she missed. It was Tom Grace.

She didn't know how it was she could miss someone she barely knew, but she did. For all the years she'd craved adventure, now it seemed all she craved was someone who wore the same white shirt, who neatened the edges of sheets drying on the lawn, as if the man in the moon might look down and call him a slob. Women always fell for Dean, Tom had said. But Tess didn't think she could. Not the way she thought she could fall for Tom. And it made no sense, not even the littlest bit. She thought how Buzz would wag his finger in her direction, his eyes flashing with satisfaction.

Regret rose up in Tess, fierce and biting, like something sour you couldn't wash down. She thought of what Tom had said, how quick she'd been to defend Dean. She thought she knew what it was like to stand on the other side of that glass, to have to be the one to pick up the pieces of someone who was determined to shatter. She didn't.

She looked to the hill where she could just see the very top of the trailer, her tears rising, then overflowing. Buzz wasn't the one she was mad at; he never was. But it hurt so much less to be angry with him instead of her.

Tess dragged her sleeve across her eyes and nose, the guilt and regret choking her. She'd been so unfair to Buzz, so terribly unfair.

She needed him to forgive her.

But maybe first, she needed to forgive herself.

AS THE LAST LAVENDER THREAD of sunset was swallowed into the horizon, Wallace Mooney stood with his hands on his hips in the middle of his gift shop and gave the place a final look. Shelves were stocked, floors were swept, displays were tidy—six months of work that would be undone in a matter of minutes as soon as the doors opened the next day. Such was the first day of the festival. He'd come to expect it.

"Don't know why we bother," his brother, Terry, griped, emerging from the stockroom with one more box of sparklers. "It's all gonna look like hell ten minutes after we open."

"Let's hope," Wallace said.

"Supposed to be a full moon tomorrow night."

Wallace nodded. "Heard that."

"You remember what happened the last time there was one of them during the festival."

"Of course I do."

Terry chuckled. "Think Vera Blake does?"

"Now cut that out," scolded Wallace, shoving Terry's baseball cap at him. "She'd been drinking. She didn't mean anything by it."

"Maybe you'd rather it had been Mary Sturgis?"

"I mean it. One more word about it and you're walking home."

Terry Mooney chuckled as he set his cap over his thin white hair.

Wallace turned off all the store's lights except the four bulbs in the window. The brothers stepped out onto the street, the night air crisp but still.

"A little cool tonight," Wallace said, squinting up at the sky.

"No wind, though," said Terry. "You know what that means. No wind, no chimes."

"Listen to you." Wallace turned the lock on the store and pocketed his keys, shaking his head. "You keep hoping, Terr."

"I'm telling you, Wall. One of these days. One of these days, they just might show up again."

Wallace grinned, his gray eyes pleating at the corners.

"They just might," he teased. "And you, with that god-awful haircut."

1888

HENRY SHELTON HARRIS CAME INTO the world on a warm May evening. He nursed well from the start, which relieved the midwife, a nervous young woman, barely older than Lydia, who lived at the end of the road. Soaked with sweat and feeling so drained that she believed she could have floated away if someone had pushed the sash up any higher, Lydia cradled her new baby in the lamplight, his tiny, crinkled body like a fiddlehead, refusing to unfurl.

She wanted to tell him over and over that everything

would be all right now. He was here and he was safe, and nothing would ever change that. She wanted to tell him not to mind the roar of the surf beyond the window, or the flash of light.

She wanted to tell him that no matter what came next, he would always be loved. Completely. More than he might ever know.

AS PROMISED, PEARL AND RACHEL came within the week, arriving in sweet-smelling silk and velvet brocades.

"Oh, he's perfection," marveled Rachel as the three sisters stood around the bassinet, smiling down at Henry as he lay swaddled in sleep.

"What did you expect?" teased Pearl, gently pushing her older sister out of the way to get a closer look at her nephew. "What a color to that hair. It's so dark."

"Auburn," said Rachel. "Like Uncle Teddy."

"Yes," Lydia agreed quickly. "You're right. His was that color exactly, wasn't it?"

"Not that it means anything," Rachel added. "Babies rarely keep the color they're born with. Oh, I love them all scrunched up this way in the beginning. Does he eat well?"

"Very," said Lydia. "I nurse him every other hour."

"Every other hour?" Pearl said. "When do you sleep?"

"She doesn't, you ninny," teased Rachel, smiling at Lydia.

Pearl rolled her eyes. "Modern medicine is absolutely

useless if it can't come up with a tonic to make men pro-
duce milk."

"Oh, Pearl," scolded Rachel. "What of the neighbor
woman, Lydie? Does she help?"

"Sarah's been a lifesaver," Lydia said. "She comes over
daily to help with the wash. And she has children of her
own to take care of. I'm indebted to her."

"And Linus?"

It was the question Lydia had been dreading. In the
days leading up to her sisters' arrival, Lydia had recalled
with piercing and painful clarity the state she'd been in
when they'd last seen her. They'd observed her so fearful,
so undone when she'd come for her visit—fled her home,
truthfully. Maybe even fled her husband. Now she was
calmer. She'd watched Linus hold their son, seen the flush
of wonder cross his face, briefly washing away the tension
he'd worn for so long. It was the silent absolution she'd
been craving.

"It's better," she said, looking between them. "*He's*
better."

Pearl stepped to the window, looking out at the tower
while Rachel and Lydia stayed at the bassinet. "Whatever
became of that young man who was helping you?" Pearl
asked wistfully.

Lydia looked up, startled by the question. "He moved
away," she said. "He took a job at the cannery."

Pearl nodded, but Lydia swore she could see in her
sister's warm eyes something suggestive, and for a strange

moment, Lydia thought Pearl knew, thought for certain her sister knew that the child they'd adored in an instant wasn't Linus's at all, but Lydia told herself there was no way Pearl could have known. It simply wasn't possible.

THE SUMMER WEEKS SLIPPED BY, and, with their passage, Lydia's worries seemed to fade. Though Linus remained quiet and often distracted, she'd grown used to the man her husband had become in the year since he and the others had survived their shipwreck. She found endless comfort in Henry, who seemed to change with each day. Every development, no matter how small, enchanted her. And the weather! There'd never been such a flawless summer; Miles Keene had confirmed so when he came with supplies one balmy July afternoon. For a while, Lydia watched her neighbors' expressions each time they were around Henry, wanting to see if Miles or Sarah might have carried suspicions. If they did, they were careful to hide them, and Lydia was grateful to them regardless. With Henry snug in a field basket at her side and delighted with a set of measuring spoons she'd hung from the handle, Lydia planted lavender with the sun warm on her cheek.

SHE WAS SURE SHE HEARD the baby cry. That was why Lydia woke in the darkness. In the weeks since Henry's birth, she'd ceased to sleep in any sort of real way. Her eyes closed and her breathing slowed, but her mind could do neither. She would instead experience miniature sleeps, something altogether different. But that was how Sarah Keene had said it would be. Babies required attention all day and all night, and a mother's mind knew that, which was why Sarah had assured Lydia that she would never sleep in any true way for the rest of her life.

So it was not at first surprising to her that she should find herself sharp and awake in the dark. Instinctively Lydia rose from bed and moved across the room to Henry's bassinet. She had set his bed just shy of the beam's path so that she could always find her way to him. When she arrived, she found her baby asleep on his stomach, tucked under himself, his tiny wrinkled fists hidden.

She turned back to the bed, aware suddenly that she and Henry were alone. Linus's side was empty; Lydia could tell by the air, the lack of his breathing. She moved to the window, seeing the tower, the lantern room empty but for the lamp.

Had there been an emergency? She didn't see how it was possible. Surely Linus would have woken her, would have told her if he'd had to go onto the water, or leave the Point for some reason. But what reason could there be?

Lydia reached for her robe, tying it snugly around her waist. She came downstairs, expecting to find Linus milling about, but the rooms were empty. Seeing the faint thread of pink when she passed the window, she realized it was dawn, and her heart settled with relief. That explained it. She'd overslept, and Linus had wished to get an early start. She'd do the same, grateful to find herself not yet too heavy with milk.

She was setting their table when she saw the log book. It wasn't unusual that Linus might have left it there to record something he'd forgotten, though he'd grown so terribly secretive with it that Lydia found its display startling. But there was more to it; she could tell. Even from where she stood, she could see the end of a piece of letter paper peeking out from between the pages, crisp and clean against the purple dye of the book's deckle edges.

She walked slowly to the leather-sheathed book and carefully pulled the paper free.

Her first thought was that it was a strange color: a pale blue, a sort of paper she'd never seen, one she knew they did not keep in their house. She freed it tentatively, not sure what sort of news could possibly require her husband to use such a formal page, or write so much (already she could see the lines of text through the thin parchment).

Don't open it, was her first thought. *Burn it instead. Turn to the woodstove, to the fire you've just stoked. The flames are stretching and hungry; the page will burn in seconds.*

Instead, she lowered herself into the chair that was thankfully already there. Her hands shook as she drew the folds apart, facing the words.

She read them several times, enough times that the blue light of dawn began to fill the room around her, pouring in like an enchanted smoke. And each time she thought, no, it was all a mistake. She wasn't reading it correctly; she was missing something. Linus had forgotten a paragraph, maybe even a whole page.

But he'd already confessed to his omission, which was why he'd left her the log book.

Lydia's fingers were slow with dread, but she opened the book, the binding cracking, the sound like a slap in the silent dawn. She recognized the first few entries. The handwriting was tidy, flawless; the words she could still recall from Linus's reading to her at dinner about the warbler sighting and the pair of harbor seals that had stayed all afternoon.

But she knew those weren't the passages her husband wished her to read.

Those were farther in, where his handwriting was no longer neat and erect, but loose, choppy, pointed instead of curved.

May 1, 1888:

I am so weary of my deceit. Many months have passed since our unfathomable disappearance and our equally unfathomable return; yet the town seems to have already moved on from our lapse. Would that we four could. But climbing the stairs to face the sea and her secrets only makes my heart swell with disgrace, with shame, with terrible longing. The entries I have made thus far have been false. That is not to say I have not done my job, or done it with the same honor and commitment that I have always tendered this magnificent tower, knowing the magnitude and responsibility of my position. But the heart and the head can work in remarkable opposition. My hands and legs operate of their own engine; my thoughts float away untethered, and it is my dearest Lydia who seems the most in danger of being adrift. Any day now she will deliver our child, the miracle of life we forged in the days after my return; yet where my heart should be filled with eagerness and joy, I have only longing, and try as I do to hide my betrayal, I know my wife can see this bereavement plainly. I find more chores than ever to keep me from her nervous eyes, to keep me in the tower, close to the source of my confusion, my joy. I only wonder how much longer we four can keep our secret.

May 6, 1888:

My son arrived yesterday: Henry Shelton Harris. Lydia rests. The midwife has departed, and Sarah Keene, our neighbor, has come to help with the house. Holding him was the first moment of peace I have had in so long. It was as if the instant Lydia delivered him into my arms, a rush of wind blew my mind clean. But it was a short-lived reprieve. Try as I did to think on my child as I walked back to the tower, to keep the image of that pink and beautifully wrinkled face in my sight, my thoughts betrayed me, and now I fear I will never know that perfect calm again.

Lydia's sisters, Pearl and Rachel, plan to come soon. I don't know how I will conceal my

distractions from them without their thinking
me rude, or worse, simply unfeeling.

June 15, 1888:

I saw Duncan Spaulding in town today, this
being the first time our paths have crossed in
months. We did not stop and talk, merely
glanced at each other across the street. It is
as if we are contagious, as if distance will keep
the virus of our secret contained. But the
symptoms of our ailment are unmistakable. I
wonder if I wear the same shade of shame on
my cheeks as he does.

June 28, 1888:

Eli Banks came to me this afternoon. I was
cleaning the lens, and he kept me company,
pacing around me. I worked the rag as he
spoke, stopping only when he began to sob. This
great big man who can command a company

of hundreds weeps now like a lost cub. He told me he hears the mermaids call every night now, and he is sure they are waiting for us to return to them as we promised we would. He thinks I must summon them back, that I must keep watch, that I alone can work the light to guide them into the cove. I tell him we can't act so rashly, but I know he's right. I know too that it was my failing to steer that boat expertly, as I vowed I could, the failure that has brought us to this place; and I am desperate for my chance to correct it.

July 15, 1888:

The guilt is consuming. I give in to it only when I am in the tower, which is nearly all the time now. When I hold my son, the anguish is unimaginable. Tiny as he is, barely able to keep his eyes on me, I feel certain he can sense my grief. I have failed them both—my son, his mother. Lydia observes me now with

relief, and the effort to keep this small flame
of hope and peace in her eyes is taking its toll.
Perhaps Banks is right that we cannot hold
off any longer.

July 26, 1888:

Banks wants to hurry our departure, but I
managed to calm his haste. I told him the
songs are not yet close enough, that all our
efforts will be wasted if the sea maidens are
still too far out to sea, that we will drown in
the darkness without their guide, their breath—
as we nearly did the first time. Banks got up
several times in the meeting, went outside, and
came back in. Timothy Orchard said nothing.
Duncan Spaulding swigged from a flask and
talked incessantly. These are not the same men
I set sail with nearly a year ago.

That night, I am proved wrong. I take leave
of the tower to stand at my son's cradle,

watching him sleep in a ribbon of moonlight,
and I am too ashamed to even touch the
downy nest of brown hair that lies against his
tiny scalp. I close my eyes to force the sound
from my head, but it's no use. Even with the
window closed, I can hear their calls, so close
now I am certain the whole of the town can
hear them too.

August 2, 1888:

The time has come. This will be my last entry,
for tomorrow will be our last day on land.
There's no choice in the matter now. I cannot
bear the fear and worry that veil my wife's
eyes any longer; nor can I subject my son to
a father who feels such shame and guilt that
he can't bear to hold him. I have reconsidered
the words I've crafted in these previous pages,
and I feel no confusion over them, no shock,
though I know whoever reads these in the days,
or perhaps years, from now will. It is time

then, if today is my last here, that I reveal the truth in the same fashion.

There is no point to recording what is known of our journey that day. Our departure, our course, our weather: all that is well documented. I wish I could say we were concealing the truth of our collision and our subsequent wreck, but that truth escapes even us. One moment the sea was pleasant and yielding: the next we found ourselves tossed beneath it, scrambling and clawing at drenched wood and sodden sails, our eyes and throats burning with salt as we cried out to one another in our panic, even as the sun bore down on us.

It was Banks who saw the first one. He called for us all to see, turning our heads in the caps, even as our vessel pitched to its doom. They glistened like harbor seals, their bodies curving in the water like porpoises, their hair—all shades of gold, pewter, and green—so long it seemed to be

made of the sea itself. They swam up around us,
close enough that we could feel the tickling of
their tails. We twisted in the water, trying to
follow them, and soon their laughter rose high,
and I cannot tell you how sweet the sound was.
Imagine five months of winter under blankets of
silencing snow, and waking one morning to the
crisp song of a scarlet cardinal, a sound so joy-
ful and pure, you think you might cry from it.

Whoever reads this will wonder if there was
any moment of clarity between us, if for any
moment we doubted what we saw. But of
course we did. For who surrenders willingly to
madness, to a vision so impossible? And yet,
as we looked on, and the truth of our eyes
sharpened into focus, we saw the impossible
swimming beside us, taking our hands as if we
were no more rooted than seaweed, steering us
deeper out to sea, and we let them.

God forgive us, we let them.

IT WAS HENRY'S CRY, SHRILL and piercing, the way only a hungry infant can sound, that brought Miles Keene up the path at such a pace.

Lydia could hear the rapping on the kitchen door clearly, for she hadn't moved an inch since she'd sat down to read. Still she just stared at the wide wood panels, watching them shake, too numb to answer.

After a moment, Miles's face appeared at the window, squinting in. She looked back at him. His eyes rounded with confusion, but she didn't rise to let him in.

SEARCH PARTIES LEFT THE HARBOR at first light, the news of the letters moving quickly through the village. It seemed each man had left a similar confession, Eli Banks himself even using the word *mermaids* in his, a fact known only because Mrs. Banks had fainted before having a chance to dispose of the letter, and the authorities had confiscated the note, much to her outrage.

"Evidence," the sheriff had said.

"Evidence of what?" Millicent Banks had cried, her eyes wild with panic. "My husband's been tricked into some sort of madness! Can't you see it? That's not even his handwriting. He's obviously been kidnapped. These other men are to blame!"

It was a theory that took root quickly, inciting more

frenzy in an already anxious town and sending officers in a mad hunt to query the other wives, to demand proof of their abandonment. Lydia had delivered them the letter, but she had known enough to hide the log book, stuffing it in a basket of Henry's changing cloths.

"Had you noticed anything strange about your husband, ma'am? Anything at all?"

This was the question that undid her. Until then, Lydia had nodded dully through them all, determined to neither let the officers defame nor discourage her husband's condition, determined to hold on to the chance that this had all been a grave misunderstanding and that Linus and the others would return from their fantastical leave within a few days.

She began to chuckle, the sound so unexpected that the two officers who sat across from her glanced at each other.

"Is something funny, ma'am?" one asked, frowning at her.

"No," Lydia said, her tired chuckle fading and tears creeping up behind her eyes.

"Mrs. Banks said you came to see her several months ago," the second officer announced. "She now has suspicions that your visit was part of some kind of scheme. That you came for compensation and that when she denied you that opportunity, you left with ill will. She also said she informed you that Mr. Banks was considering pressing charges for Linus's negligence. Perhaps your husband feared arrest and concocted a plot to bring harm to Mr. Banks and the two other men?"

Dear God, what fools, Lydia thought, looking them squarely in their faces. Was this really what they believed? She'd tried for months to convince them all that something was terribly wrong. And when they'd told her it was only nerves, the exhaustion of carrying a baby, she'd convinced herself that Linus had withdrawn from her because of what she'd done with Angus.

Now four men were gone again. And that woman, that insincere, spoiled woman, had the gall to accuse Lydia of being false.

A third man came into the room, moving close enough to one officer to whisper in his ear. When he left, the officer turned to Lydia. "The log book is missing."

"I'm sure I don't know where it is," she said evenly. "Linus never let me see it."

The men shared a narrowed look.

"Perhaps it left with him," Lydia suggested.

But in the hours that followed, when no word came of a ransom request, thoughts of wrongdoing seemed to fade with the daylight. And with that dimming light, Lydia felt something shift within her too. Something that had trembled and faltered briefly once before but righted itself just in time. She'd been so certain the dark interlude of the last year was finally over; now, collapse was imminent.

AS THE ONE-WEEK MARK APPROACHED, there was speculation—hope, really—that there might be something to the anniversary, and that perhaps this two-week duration was becoming routine for the men's disappearance, but when week three came and went, and with it, a fifth search party that returned with no evidence of the missing men, the town grew attached to its fate.

For Lydia, the days were a series of moments out of focus, food without taste. She was aware only of the constant filling and emptying of her breasts of their milk, of Henry's fingernails, tiny white crescents she studied as he nursed, of the swirl at the top of his skull where his thickening hair coiled like a miniature tornado. Everything else, everyone else, was a blur.

When she received a letter from Pearl that her sister had heard reports of a strange incident and wanted to come to make certain all was well, Lydia didn't hesitate, knowing if she did, she would lose her nerve. She wrote a letter of her own, one she would not have imagined ever writing in her whole life; yet the words came with ease, just as Linus's confession had flowed, unhampered.

But perhaps this was what came with accepting life's twists and ruptures. The truth.

IT WOULD BE A WARM day, clouds hugging the skyline, though babies could never be too warm, Lydia thought as she dressed Henry in layers, glancing every now and then to the window to make certain the Keenes' buggy had not yet left its station. She didn't have to worry about the man in the lighthouse the coast guard had sent; that officer had already informed her of his plan to check the channel markers and that he would be gone till noon.

The chimes lay on the bed. She'd made them herself out of her wedding silver, tethering them with a heavy cord she'd found in the shed. They weren't much to look at, but they clamored fiercely, glinting like icicles in the path of the sun, just as the book had instructed. She carried them in one hand, Henry in the other, snug against her chest, down the road to the Keenes' shingled cottage. Sarah was in her kitchen, bunching herbs for drying, when Lydia stepped into the fragrant room.

"I was hoping you could watch him for me," Lydia said. "I won't be long."

Sarah brushed off her hands on her apron and took Henry into her arms. "Of course." The woman's eyes dropped at once to the chimes. "What do you mean to do with those?"

Lydia studied her son for several moments before she answered, her heart aching to watch him twist restlessly in Sarah's arms. "Hang them from the gallery," she said at last.

"Hang them? Whatever for?"

"For the sound, of course."

Sarah Keene looked nervously at Lydia, as if wanting to know more but not feeling right to ask. "Miles can do that for you, you know. He'd be more than happy."

"That's all right." Lydia stroked her son's warm cheek,

his skin as soft as a leaf of lamb's ears, her touch calming him at once. "It's something I need to do myself."

Looking back in the years that would follow, Sarah Keene would recall that moment more than all the others, the few seconds of quiet, of pause, when she could have reached for Lydia and stalled her neighbor, her friend. Instead, she said nothing, just stepped back to watch Lydia walk out into the bright day as the tinkling of the chimes trailed after her, drawing Henry's eyes, round and blinking, toward the sound.

IT WAS EASIER SOMEHOW THIS time, Lydia thought as she climbed the curved metal stairs. Maybe it was holding the chimes, maybe it was the distraction of their ringing, or maybe she'd just made peace with so many things, that fear no longer had its hold on her. Only when she stepped out onto the gallery and felt the wind pick up, snapping her hair around her face, her skirts and sleeves like sails, only then did she feel a short rush of panic. Her fingers shook as she tied the end of the cord to the railing, knotting it twice.

She gripped the stretch of iron to steady herself, letting the song carry and imagining the clamor, like a ribbon of sound, trailing across the sea. She would miss this place, she thought, sweeping her gaze over the land, the grass she and Linus had rolled over like children when they'd first arrived, the garden she'd meant to see grow wild and tall, so lush that she'd have needed a wagon to harvest it.

But those memories were gone. Not even memories, really. Only dreams.

Saying good-bye would be the best thing for all of them; she knew that now. Her beloved sisters, Pearl and Rachel. Her precious son, Henry, whose eyes were finally losing their blue, turning brown now, like his father's.

Of all people, Linus would understand.

Sometimes in life, you simply did what you had to do.

Friday

First Day of the
Mermaid Festival

AND SO IT CAME TO be known as the Mermaid Mutiny, for the men who chose to abandon their posts in life to heed the calling of their hearts.

—The Mermaid Mutiny and More:
The Complete History of Cradle Harbor

Twelve

OPENING DAY OF THE CRADLE Harbor Mermaid Festival arrived with a sky so clear, someone would have been hard-pressed to find the line of the horizon. Though the opening ceremonies wouldn't start until that evening, by ten the center of town was already packed with visitors, the narrow road that circled the green and looped around the four blocks of shops crowded and filled with noise.

Down at the Point, traffic hadn't yet begun to the lighthouse, but as he stood at the sink looking out onto the driveway, Tom knew it was only a matter of time before cars began to snake down the road, slowing as they passed the keeper's house and rolling on by, bound for the lighthouse.

It had been a long night for all of them in the keeper's house. He'd barely slept, catching short, restless stints of sleep, only to be woken by the frequent cries of Mia, then the hurried padding of Petra's bare feet up and down the stairs. Tom had risen at four and stumbled into the hall in the shapeless blue light, offering to help, but Petra had declined, twisting the baby away from him each time as if he'd come at her with flames jutting from his fingertips, then closing herself and her baby inside Dean's room, her eyes bright with suspicion. For Dean's part, he'd taken the stairs even slower than usual, though never with the baby. As far as Tom could tell, the child had never left her mother's arms.

Hearing the creak of the stairs, Tom looked up to see Dean arrive in the kitchen doorway. His brother's eyes were bloodshot, his hair wild.

Tom moved to the coffeepot. "I'll make more," he said before Dean could reach the empty carafe. "Where's Petra?"

"She refuses to come down. She says this place scares her."

She scares me, Tom wanted to say but didn't. Those huge black eyes spooked the hell out of him. But she was young and plush with swishing ribbons of jet-black hair, and that was just how Dean fancied his women. How amazing it was that the baby had come into the world with Dean's bright red hair, Tom thought. Despite all that dark, she'd still come out glowing like a clementine.

Dean settled in to the table, pulling the saucer he'd been using as an ashtray in front of him and retrieving his cigarettes. Tom scooped out the grinds and saw his own hands shaking slightly.

"I can't stay, Tommy," Dean announced.

Tom turned to his brother, panicked at the thought. "What are you talking about?"

"Petra has family in Philadelphia. We can live in her grandmother's house. She's in a nursing home, and they're just sitting on it."

"Dean, you're not leaving here. You can't even take care of yourself; you think I'd stand by and let you ride off into the sunset with a *baby*?"

"What do you know about what I can do, Tommy? Shit, I don't even know myself."

"No one's going anywhere," Tom said firmly. "Not you. Not that woman. Not that baby. We live here now. This is our home."

"*Says who?*" Dean demanded, his eyes fierce. "I never agreed to stay here. I said I'd see how things went."

"I think we can both see *how things went*, Dean," Tom said, nodding to the stairs.

Dean pushed back his chair, hard enough to send a shriek across the linoleum. "What is that supposed to mean?"

Tom shoved the carafe back onto its plate and turned to Dean. "'What is that supposed to mean?'" he repeated slowly. "Which part, Dean? Which part isn't clear to you?"

"Don't start with me, Tommy," Dean warned, rising and moving to the counter. "I'm this close to packing up right now."

Tom just stared at his brother. "You'd do that, wouldn't you?" he said. "After everything I've done for you, you'd just pick up and take off without a second thought, wouldn't you?"

"What you've done for me?" Dean turned to face Tom. "What the fuck have you *done* for me, Tommy, besides drag me out to this dump?"

"I put my whole life on hold for you, that's what. I lost sleep; I lost jobs. I took blood money for you, for Christ's sake."

"You did what?"

"Forget it," Tom said, pushing past Dean and heading for the front door.

"No, I won't forget it." Dean followed his brother out of the house and down the steps, the screen door slapping the clapboards behind them. "What the hell do you mean *blood money*?"

Tom stopped at the edge of the lawn and turned around, finding Dean there, rigid and waiting. Here it was, he thought—his chance to finally get it all out. And what difference did it make now anyway? Everything he'd tried to protect, everything he'd worked so hard to secure for them, Dean had washed it all away in an afternoon.

"This *dump*, as you call it," Tom said, pointing behind them. "This whole damn place. Everything. Frank Hammond wasn't a friend of the family, Dean. He was the son of a bitch who ran us off the road."

Dean blinked with confusion. "What are you talking about?"

"He found us," Tom said, not afraid now, the confession he'd been dreading for so long suddenly no heavier than smoke. "He found out where we lived and he started sending money every month and I took it. I took it because I *had* to."

"You're lying," Dean said quietly. "Tell me this is a fucking joke, Tommy. . . ."

"It's not a joke." Tom swallowed, keeping his eyes leveled with his brother's. "I didn't have a choice. You needed treatment and therapy, and there was no money, no insurance."

"Bullshit," said Dean. "There was the trust!"

"There was never any trust. I made that up. All the money came from him."

Dean stared at Tom, the truth sinking into his features and twisting them. "And so you bring me here?" he said. "You bring me to live in *his house*, and you tell me he's some saintly friend of the family? How could you do that? How could you be so fucking selfish?"

Anger flared in Tom like a lit match. All the times he'd put Dean's needs first, and never complained, never dared to, and Dean called him selfish? "I took that money for *you*," Tom said. "Everything I've ever done has been to take care of *you*."

"Take care of me?" cried Dean. "You fucking *suffocate* me is what you do!"

Tom came toward Dean, his hands fisting at his sides as he uttered slowly, "You think I wanted this? You think I wanted to take care of you my whole goddamn life?"

"Don't you dare," Dean warned, thrusting a finger in Tom's face. "Don't you fucking dare pity me, you sanctimonious prick."

"Why should I pity you?" Tom demanded. "You live like a king! I'm the asshole who gets to follow you to the emergency room once a month while they pump out your stomach. I'm the asshole who brings your one-night stands home in the morning because you're too hungover to give them a ride. Pity *me*, you thankless shit."

Dean's eyes were wild. He lunged at Tom, palms out, and shoved him hard. Stunned for only a second, Tom went at Dean and shoved him back, using enough force that his brother stumbled. When Dean recovered, he came at Tom like a linebacker; bent at the waist, he tackled Tom to the ground, sending them both into the driveway.

Out of the house came Petra with Mia pressed to her. She screamed for them to stop as they continued their wrestling, rolling over each other in the dirt, but they didn't slow their match. Dean got on top of Tom and pinned him down, socking him in the eye. Managing to free his left arm, Tom swung and landed a punch to Dean's mouth, sending his brother backward. Tom struggled to his feet, stumbling a few steps until he found his balance. Sitting up, Dean touched his lip and saw blood on his fingers. He scowled at Tom, but Tom wasn't looking. Drained, numb, Tom lurched forward, just wanting to escape, to be gone from everyone and everything. He didn't dare drive, too afraid his eye would swell shut behind the wheel, so he headed for the only place he could think to go on foot.

Thirteen

THE COTTAGES WERE WHITE WHEN Buzz and his first wife took over the business. He'd fallen in love with the property at once, reminded of the seaside cabins his grandfather had tended in nearby Port Chester when Buzz was a boy. Beth'd had a decidedly different reaction. "They look like a row of rotted teeth," she'd grumbled, swatting at a greenhead fly. Buzz should have known then and there that Beth wasn't long for the cove, or him.

For Ruby, the buildings' bleak decor had been a matter of great and urgent concern.

"You don't mean to keep them that color, do you?" she asked within days of their arrival at the cove.

"They've always been white," Buzz said.

Ruby blinked at him. "And people still stay in them?"

He chuckled at that, though he could see she was seriously worried over it, so much so that by the very next morning, Buzz was standing in the paint aisle at Harbor Hardware, shaking his head in delight while he listened to Ruby try to explain what shade pomegranate was to the store's eighty-two-year-old owner, Harvey McKee.

"Now, let's not get too crazy," Buzz had said gently as he watched the elderly man mix up gallon after gallon. "Paint's expensive. We'll take it one cottage at a time, okay?"

But within the first three months Ruby and Tess lived there, all six cabins wore fresh coats of paint, in colors so blinding, Buzz was quite sure they could be seen from the moon.

Now in the pale light of morning, Buzz surveyed them, thinking of all the times he'd just wanted to say to hell with it and repaint them all the same shade of white, but he could never go through with it. He knew how Ruby had felt about white.

The grounds were quiet, but that would change in a few hours. Guests rarely slept in on opening day, too eager to start in on the festivities, those in town and those of their own making, so Buzz set out the boxes of cider doughnuts on the porch, then started the coffeemaker.

He had never been much for sleeping in, either, not even when he was a kid. Even though his own dad hadn't risen before noon on a Saturday, Buzz couldn't keep his eyes shut against the early sun. His internal clock had been a source of great despair for Ruby who had loved nothing more than staying up until three and four in the morning, then sleeping well into the afternoon. Oftentimes she'd cajole Tess into keeping her company through the night (not that it took much cajoling), and Buzz would walk down to the cottage the next morning to find Tess and Ruby curled up asleep on the daybed like a pair of cats, Tess's fingers and chin still streaked with melted chocolate, the half-eaten bag of baking chips she'd been devouring still beside her on the quilt. Buzz would carry Tess back and bundle her up on the sofa while he made breakfast, the smell of pancake batter always rousing her. Together they'd stand beside the stove and see who could pour his closer to the shape of Maine, the winner, who always ended up being Tess, getting to add a handful of M&Ms. She loved to watch the candy coating melt off into her batter, then try to swirl the puddles of color into a recognizable shape. *Look, Buzz—it's a sailboat. Look—it's a fish.* Everything had to mean something, and always something desperately important. Buzz had recognized that about his stepdaughter even then.

There was hardly any breeze this morning, barely

enough to jostle the chimes as he walked down the lawn and across the driveway. He saw Beverly's white sedan pulled around, the trunk up. All night he'd thought about her abrupt departure from dinner, feeling lousy for making her cry, still not sure how he'd managed it. Had the mention of an anniversary made her miss her late husband? That had to be it, yet they'd spoken of him before, and she'd seemed to weather the subject just fine.

He assumed she was heading into town for the festivities, but as he came closer, Buzz saw her bags peeking out of the opened truck, and he frowned. Surely he hadn't offended her so badly that she meant to leave before the festival even started?

He made his way to the cottage, but Beverly was already on her way out. They met at the bottom of the porch steps.

"You're not leaving, are you?" he asked.

She nodded. "I'm afraid so. My original flight out was for tomorrow, but I moved it up a day. I spoke with my son. He's been called out of town on business at the last minute. I offered to help out with the boys while he's gone. I don't see them nearly enough."

Buzz studied Beverly a moment, trying to decide if she was telling him the truth, but she wouldn't meet his eyes. All along she'd been planning to leave early. He didn't understand it; he thought she'd come for the festival.

Beverly motioned to Tess's woodshop. "I'm sorry I didn't get to see the artist at work," she said cheerfully.

"There's still time," he said, looking wistfully at the shed; he knew Tess was likely inside.

"That's all right," said Beverly. "I'll take your word for it."

Buzz nodded. "She's damn good. Better than she realizes."

"She'll find her way. We all do. Some of us take longer than others; that's all."

It was a curious statement, Buzz thought, certain she meant to implicate herself with it, but again her gaze drifted out of reach.

Remorse tugged at him. He rubbed the back of his neck and sniffed. "I hope this isn't because of something I said the other night. . . ."

"No," Beverly answered quickly, gently. "It's nothing you said. It's just time for me to go, that's all." She smiled at him, a warm smile that he hadn't seen on her before now. "I do apologize for leaving the restaurant like that. It was rude of me. It was awful of me, really. I'm truly sorry."

"You don't have to be sorry," he said.

"Yes, I do. You've no idea how sorry." Beverly leaned over to kiss Buzz on the cheek, lingering a moment against the prickly hairs of his beard to whisper, "I miss him too."

When she pulled back, Buzz saw her eyes had filled with tears. He stared at her, confused. "Who?" he asked.

Beverly stepped past him for the car. "I left the key on the table inside," she said. "And you might want to have someone look at the bathroom sink. It made the most awful noises when I turned on the cold water." At the driver's door, she hesitated, giving the view of the cottages and the sea beyond a last look before she tugged open the door and climbed in. Settled in her seat, she rolled down the window. "You know, I may just have to come back next year for this festival of yours, Buzz Patterson," she said as she turned on the engine.

Buzz came close, peering into the passenger window. "I hope you do. I promise I won't screw it all up if you give me another chance."

Beverly slipped on her sunglasses. "Good," she said, smiling up at him as she shifted into gear. "I promise I won't, either."

THE RICH, CLEAN SCENT OF tung oil was thick in the woodshop, but Tess never tired of the smell, any more than she could tire of watching the smooth wood soak up the finish. It had taken her most of the night—with the exception of a two-hour nap between three and five—and now the sculpture shone an even golden blond.

There could be no more tweaking, no more second-guessing. The past two months had all led up to this moment, and now she was done.

Exhausted and giddy, Tess stood back and admired her work. The nose wasn't quite right, but the almond-shaped eyes were, their edges turned down just a bit. She'd had plenty of pictures she might have used as reference, but it had been important to her to recreate the face from memory.

"It looks just like her, kiddo."

Tess turned to find Buzz in the doorway. She gave him a small smile before looking back at her mermaid, her eyes misting as she considered the sculpture. "I was so sure I could remember every inch of her face," she said, "but I can't."

"Nine years is a long time, Tessie."

"So why does it still feel more like nine days?"

Buzz came all the way inside and walked to where Tess stood. She looked up at him. He reached out; Tess gave him her hand, and he squeezed it.

Her voice was thin, soft. "I used to worry you'd come between her and me. Did you know that?"

"Did I?" Buzz snorted. "You put me through my paces. Man, you were worse than one of those detectives in the old murder movies. I swear you would have shone a flashlight in my eyes that first night if you'd had one handy."

Tess smiled, recalling the night they'd met at the music festival. She remembered how she'd sneaked out of their tent after her mother had gone to sleep and found Buzz by the bonfire, how she'd peppered him with questions, how he'd kept telling her he was sure she must be tired and she'd told him no every time.

"I *was* kind of rough on you, wasn't I?" she said.

"Rough? Hell, I dated girls in high school whose fathers were pussycats compared to the grilling you gave me."

They both chuckled at that, but somehow it only made Tess cry. Her sobs needed no time to build their steam. They came out mournful and deep at the start, so hard that Buzz strained to make out her words when she finally could talk.

"She didn't let me say good-bye."

His eyes filled. "I know, kiddo."

"And I'm so angry at her for that. But I don't know how to be angry with her and not feel like I'm losing her. I don't want her to think I don't love her anymore."

It was a child's confession, but Tess didn't care. Saying it felt like stepping out into daylight, like landing in something soft and safe after falling for so long. Buzz had only to tug gently, and she collapsed into his embrace, burying her sobs in the warmth of his flannel shirt.

He put his hand on her head, trying to smooth down what a restless night had done to her hair, trying to smooth away so much more. He thought about watching her when she was a little girl and how he'd looked forward to the days when she would be grown, bigger, as if after a certain size he might cease to worry for her, as if it were only a matter of weight that kept a parent's heart so tied to his child. But of course it was just the opposite: The bigger Tess grew, the more Buzz had feared for her, because there was less he could do to keep her safe.

"You need to let it go, Tessie," he whispered, his voice hoarse with tears. "All this stuff inside you, this grudge, trying to make people love her, trying to prove how wrong they were about her. It doesn't matter anymore. It never did. You and I loved your mother enough for the whole world, and she knew that. Being angry for her won't bring her back, and it won't keep her here—it'll just keep you sad."

The tears came harder, and Tess didn't try to get ahead of them. He was right. Somewhere along the way, in spite of the chilly reception she and Ruby had first received, Tess had carved out—figuratively and literally—a life for herself in Cradle Harbor. It was a good life, with friends and people who cared about her.

Buzz rocked her a few moments in the quiet, studying her sculpture.

"She'd be so proud of you, Tessie," he whispered against her temple. "Don't throw it away."

Tess looked up at him, sniffling.

"Grace," Buzz said, though he could see she knew whom he meant. "Whatever it is that makes you think Hawthorne's the only one there is, let all that go too."

"It doesn't go away overnight."

"I never said it did. But you make it so hard. It doesn't need to be. Do you like Tom Grace or not?"

She smiled. "I like him."

"But . . . ?"

"But he doesn't know her, Buzz," Tess said. "He doesn't know anything about her."

"So you tell him. So you build new memories. You're allowed to do that, you know."

Tess glanced up at him again, her eyes narrowed dubiously. "I don't see *you* building any."

"I know," he consented. "And, you know, I've been thinking about that."

"Good," Tess said, rolling in his embrace, twisting enough so that she could see her mermaid too. She said it again, and this time she meant it. *"Good."*

Fourteen

TESS WASN'T EVEN SURE TOM would want to see her. She nearly turned around a dozen times on the ride over, vowing to pull over every time a driveway spilled into the road. After all, shouldn't he be the one to apologize to her? Did it make her look desperate if she ran back to him? Maybe it did. And so what? She didn't care. She *was* desperate. She was desperate to let him know she'd been wrong about so many things and she needed to see him. She *needed* him. And she didn't want to wait anymore. She knew better than anyone how life could steal your chances from you, how much danger there was in thinking you had a thousand hours to find your moment.

Her heart pounded as she pulled into the Point. A soft breeze feathered the air as she stepped out of the VW and crossed the driveway to the house. When she climbed the steps to the front door, she saw a dish towel that had been left on the top stair. The towel was stained red. Picking it up, she saw it looked like—oh God, it *was*—blood.

"They fight."

Startled, Tess glanced up and found a woman in the doorway, her shiny hair falling over one shoulder like black taffy, a red-haired infant resting against the other. The woman made a sweeping gesture with her hand, rolling her dark eyes. "One goes that way; one goes another way. Horrible. Like little lions. Growling and snarling. Dumb."

Tess stared at the woman, confused. But there was no confusion in the color of the baby's hair, a familiar shade of cherrywood.

"Who are you?" Tess asked.

"Who are *you*?"

"I'm Tess."

"I'm Petra. She's Mia." Petra paused, sizing Tess up before she said, "So, which one you want?"

"Excuse me?"

"Dean or Thomas, which one you want?"

Tess smiled, liking the woman at once. It was as if

they'd met at a clearance rack and both eyed the same pile of jeans, only to realize they needed different sizes.

"I want Tom," Tess said firmly.

Petra smiled slightly. "Good."

"Your daughter's beautiful."

"I think too," Petra said, bouncing Mia gently in her arms. "You have babies?"

"No. No babies."

"You want babies with Thomas?"

"Oh God, I only just met him."

Petra shrugged. "So what?"

So what, indeed, Tess thought, smiling too.

Mia stretched out a tiny fist, like a little apricot; Tess reached for it, the baby's pink fingers curling over her thumb. Why hadn't Dean told her he had a child?

Tess recalled her complicity in their earlier battle, the weight of guilt heavy again, flattening her smile. Whatever had happened here was her fault too.

"Where's Tom?" she asked.

Petra pointed down the road, to the lighthouse. "There."

TESS COULD SEE THE TOWER door was cracked from the far end of the walkway as she sprinted down the wooden planks. She stuck her head inside, smelling the cold, wet brick, and called up into the darkness, seeing the trapdoor closed.

"Tom?"

345

She waited, hearing nothing.

"Tom, please. I need to see you."

After a long moment, there was a creak, then a loud bang as the trapdoor opened, bathing the steps in light. Tess advanced, moving quickly up the curved metal stairs and poking her head into the bright expanse of the lantern room. The half door to the gallery had been opened, letting in soft bursts of sea air and the insistent clang of the chimes.

Tom sat on the other side of the circle crouched against the curved wall, his legs drawn up and his hands drooping over his knees.

Tess came all the way in and closed the trapdoor behind her. When she came around to see Tom fully, she gasped at the stain of color trimming his right eye. He wouldn't look at her; his stare remained fixed on the gallery and the sea beyond.

She dropped down to her knees.

"I can't do it anymore." His voice was flat, faraway. "I can't fix it. I kept thinking I could, but I can't." Tom swerved his gaze to hers then, his pained eyes pooling with regret. "I hit him, Tess. I hit him hard."

She scooted over to him, taking his hands into hers. "You were upset."

"I never should have brought us here."

"Don't say that."

Dropping his head back against the metal wall, Tom closed his eyes, forgetting his swelling, and winced at the immediate jolt of pain. Tess winced too.

"I know I could make it right if he'd just let me, but he won't let me," Tom said. "All I want to do is save him from himself, and he won't *let me*."

"Who ever said he needed saving?" Tess reached up to stroke Tom's brow, just above the maroon crescent of skin.

"I didn't mean that about your mother," he said. "I didn't mean to hurt you."

"You were right," she said.

"Don't be so sure."

"I am."

Tom took her face into his hands; her eyes filled at once.

"He wants to leave," Tom said.

"So maybe he will." Tess saw panic flash in Tom's battered eyes. She drew closer, arching up against him, his hands lowering to hold her.

"I can't go back there, Tess. I don't know what to say to him."

She combed her fingers through his hair, dropping gentle kisses along his hairline and down the middle of his brow.

"Say good-bye."

WHEN THEY WERE YOUNG, SEVEN and eight, Dean had found an injured luna moth in the backyard. It had been covered in ants, and Dean had flicked them off, only to find the insect's pale green wings streaked with its own blood. Still, Tom had been certain they could save it.

"You can't hold him like that; you'll crush him," Tom had chastised when Dean had arrived, the failing moth cupped tightly in one hand.

"Just let me do it," Dean had said, shoving Tom's hand away. "I'm gonna put him in my bug box with some fruit."

"That's butterflies. Luna moths don't eat fruit. They don't eat anything."

"Just let me do it my way, Tommy, okay?" Dean's face had scrunched up like the knot of a balloon, and Tom had stayed back, watching from the doorway as Dean had raided the refrigerator, tearing the peel off an orange and stuffing wedges into the mesh container. But that night while Dean slept, Tom rose to examine the moth. Finding it still clinging to life, he carefully replaced the orange pieces with bark and dried leaves and watched it for almost an hour, sure it would now recover.

In the morning, the luna moth lay unmoving at the bottom of the box.

"Why couldn't you just let me do it my way?" Dean had sulked at breakfast.

Because he'd been so sure he knew better, Tom thought now as he strode through the hedges, bound for the beach, the memory returning to him sharp and clear. Because he'd been so sure Dean didn't know anything. Because it should have been easy to make it all right. Was that how it was for all siblings? Tom wondered as he walked. Was the order of things laid down in the womb, or was it built in pieces over time, brick by pathological brick?

Tom would never know, and what did it matter? He'd worked too hard to bend something that would never yield. Tess had helped him to see that. They'd spent the afternoon together, exploring the rocks, the boathouse, each other. They'd made love in the old skiff, its bottom gritty with sand, that the lighthouse keepers had used to check the channel markers. Then Tom had told her about the party, and about Frank. Tess had told him about her mother, the man named Pete she'd made the cheesecake for, about the first time she had laid eyes on Buzz and why the smell of bonfire smoke could always make her cry.

Now the sun was falling at last. Tom found Dean leaned against the rocks, bobbing Mia gently on his knees, the baby savagely gumming her own tiny fist.

Tom approached Dean slowly.

"I can't believe Petra let you bring her down here," Tom said.

"She doesn't know. She's sleeping." Dean motioned to the pebbled sand. "You can sit down, you know."

"All right." Tom dropped beside Dean, seeing his brother's lip was still swollen. Tom frowned at his handiwork and looked away.

"You look worse, you know," Dean said, catching his brother's study and his shifting gaze.

"Does it hurt?" Tom asked.

"Does yours?"

"Like a son of a bitch," Tom admitted.

"No shit." The brothers looked a moment at each other.

Mia burst into a fit of gurgling cries, twisting madly in Dean's arms.

"She wants to check you out," Dean said, shifting her around.

Tom watched the infant, riveted. The skin of her cheeks reminded him of a new mushroom, unblemished, barely touched. The wrinkled soles of her feet were so unbelievably clean, like blank sheets of paper. She knew nothing of what had gone on between him and Dean, nothing of the event they'd endured on that frozen, empty road—the loss, the disappointments, the useless rage. It was amazing to him, seeing someone so unaware, so blissful, so unfettered. No wonder people adored babies. They were the best proof of hope, the most potent reminders of innocence.

"Christ," Tom whispered. "She's perfect."

"You can hold her if you want," Dean said. "She's really light. It's crazy how light."

"How do I . . . ?"

"Just like this." Dean guided Mia into Tom's cupped arms. "You want to help her hold her head up. She's still kinda weak up there."

God, she *was* light, Tom thought, letting Mia settle against him. He'd expected something much heavier, more cumbersome, like a bag of groceries.

"She's your niece, you know."

Niece. In all the chaos and the worry, Tom hadn't let that one simple truth sink in. Mia stared up at him, a lacquer of drool glistening on her lips. He smiled at once, helpless.

"You're right, you know," Tom said, his eyes pained as he turned his gaze to Dean. "Everything you said about me is true."

"No, it's not. I'm an asshole of the highest order. I'm a fuckup and a piece of shit, and if I were my brother, I would have put a pillow over my face years ago."

"Shut up." Tom reached over and pulled Dean to him, hugging him fiercely and squeezing his eyes shut as the tears seeped out.

Dean gently pushed him off. "Watch it—you'll smother her."

"I won't," Tom said, sitting back. Mia looked up at him with continued delight.

"It looks like your mermaid and Petra are best friends."

Tom turned to see Tess and Dean's girlfriend making their way down the beach. Petra's outrage was audible in an instant, a breathless stream of Greek. Tess just smiled at Tom; he smiled back.

"She will freeze!" Petra scooped Mia out of Tom's arms and held her close, rubbing gentle circles on her tiny back, glaring between the brothers as if they had been feeding the baby sand.

"Just wait till I get her swimming, Pet," Dean said, climbing to his feet. "She'll turn into a mermaid, she'll love it so much. Just ask *her*." Dean nodded toward Tess and winked. "The water's full of 'em here."

There was another surge of Greek, but this time when she'd finished her tirade, Petra gave Dean a soft, curious look. Tom had never seen her so soft. Her eyes seemed almost liquid on Dean, her lips plump and inching toward a smile. Dean grabbed her at the waist, giving her a deep and hungry kiss until she fussed at him to release her, but when he did, she was smiling and blushing a fierce pink that made her eyes look nearly purple.

Tom felt Tess's fingers slip between his. She tugged. "Come on."

"Where are we going?" he asked.

"To the Dash," Tess said. "Petra and I agreed on it."

Tom blinked at her. "You did?"

Dean appeared between them, swinging an arm over each. "So you wanna do it?"

"I'm not dressed," Tom contested.

"Well, no shit." Dean laughed. "That's the point! You go in as you are."

Tom frowned, certain he didn't want to. He *couldn't*.

Dean pulled Tom to his feet. "Come on. We're going in together. All of us."

"I'm too tired to swim, Dean."

"That's the beautiful thing, Tommy." Dean smiled. "You don't have to swim," he said. "You just have to *float*."

1888

PEARL KNEW WHILE SHE SLEPT. She blinked awake in the darkness, as if someone had shaken her. That was how it was with sisters.

The news came in anguishing pieces. Linus and three others had drowned themselves. Lydia had gone out on the gallery to hang a set of wind chimes in tribute to her lost husband and, in her grief, had jumped to her death. The baby, Pearl's beloved nephew, Henry, was with neighbors, a man and his wife.

Pearl traveled north in a state of numbness, the landscape from her train window a never-ending blur of sea and sky and balding pines. She'd come alone, Rachel's husband claiming he didn't dare let his wife go. "The doctor has given her a sedative," he'd told Pearl that morning. "She's barely come to since the news."

How barren the property looked to Pearl when she stepped out of the carriage. She hadn't thought it could look any lonelier than it had that first time she'd come to visit, her heart sinking in her chest when she thought of her beautiful baby sister, left to blow away on this grim and bleak point of land. Knowing there'd be a baby, a tiny fire of life to warm them all, had been tremendous comfort.

She didn't bother going inside the house; there was no point in it. There was nothing in it to keep. Even the pieces Pearl had recognized from their youth, the wall hangings, the love seat, the table with the chipped corner their father had accidentally snapped off trying to carry into the house only days after finishing it. None of it seemed to belong to her anymore. It belonged instead to the house, and so she would leave it all. All that could be saved now, all that mattered, was Henry.

The Keenes' cottage seemed to Pearl to be sunken deep into the earth as she walked toward it, the perimeter trimmed in wild hedges of white and pink sea roses.

I'll be fine; I promise. You'll come after the baby's born. Really, you'll see. I won't let you leave. . . .

Sarah Keene had already opened the door, having been watching the window frantically all that morning. She'd not put Henry down, not once, not even when she'd had to use the privy. She knew how babies felt things. Henry wasn't so small that he didn't know his mother was gone. Sarah was certain if she set him down, if she left him alone for even an instant, the child would never recover.

"It's so awful." Sarah wept as soon as Pearl stepped inside. The woman's sleeves and apron hem were damp. She'd been crying for so long, blowing her nose and wiping her eyes on anything she could. "I never should have let her go up there alone. She had made the strangest mobile. She meant to hang it, she said. God only knows why. I should have known then that something was wrong. Your sister barely ever set foot in that lighthouse, and then she went out on the gallery like that? Please believe me, if I'd known, I never would have . . ." Sarah clapped a hand to her mouth to quiet a sob. Pearl touched the woman on the arm.

"It's not your fault. You must never think that."

It was then that Pearl glanced to the window and saw Angus Keene step out of the shed. She recognized the man at once, the one who'd been such a help to Lydia and Linus, before things had gone so terribly wrong.

"I've got all his things," Sarah said, sniffling as she smoothed Henry's fine hair with her fingertips. "I've put in a few more blankets. Just in case. And if he doesn't take all his milk at once, don't worry. He's a careful one, is all."

Pearl hugged Sarah Keene and walked back up the

hill with Henry. She tried to keep her eyes fixed on the keeper's house, but she couldn't think straight for the sound of the surf. It was deafening, but more than that, it was intrusive; like an impatient child banging his chair for attention.

Fine, she thought, changing course when she'd reached the walkway to the tower. She'd indulge it this once. Did it wish to tell her something, this miserable sea, this white-tipped moving grave that had been the coffin to her sister's beloved husband? Had it known how much Lydia feared it? Had it driven her so mad in that moment on the gallery that she'd sacrificed herself to quiet it once and for all?

Pearl traveled the wooden bridge, Henry rooting use-lessly at her collar. She came as far as the door to the tower, not wishing to advance. She looked around, imagining her sister's last moments on this earth, her purposeful steps up into that glass room that saw all, her bottomless sadness that she hadn't dared share, the hopelessness she'd never given anyone a chance to repair.

It was then that Pearl heard them. Soft at first, gentle, as if someone had brushed past them with his shoulder, they then grew louder, as if they'd been pummeled with fists, twisted mercilessly by the wind.

She squinted up to where the sound seemed to origin-ate and caught the reflection of something silver, short shafts of light that looked strangely like flatware.

"She thought it would keep them away."

Pearl looked over, startled at the voice, and found

Angus Keene beside her. The young man looked exhausted, drained, and weary, Pearl thought.

"What do you mean?" she asked.

"The chimes." Angus nodded toward the gallery. "It was an old wives' tale she'd read. She hung chimes to keep them from coming back."

"You don't mean the men?"

"No, ma'am. The mermaids."

Pearl stared at him, bewildered. "I don't . . . I don't understand."

"You don't know?" he asked.

"I know my sister has taken her life. I know my brother-in-law has drowned."

"Mr. Harris left it all in his log book," Angus said. "They found it in her things when they went through the house. He said they'd been rescued by mermaids when everyone thought they were lost. Said they fell in love out there and finally went back to be with them."

"*Back?* But that's absolute madness."

"That's why everyone thinks she killed herself. But she didn't." Angus held out an envelope, the edges grayed with fingerprints, as if it had been opened and sealed a hundred times. "She just slipped. She was coming to be with me. She and Henry."

Pearl stared a moment at the letter, then at Angus, seeing his gaze had fallen to the baby, a faint smile tugging at his mouth, his eyes filling, and her breath caught. She'd suspected a long time ago, standing in her sister's kitchen, when she had asked about the man who strode down the path and had seen the flash of affection in Lydia's eyes. Pearl had witnessed it then and once again when they'd stood around Henry's cradle just a few weeks before. Didn't Lydia know that sisters could see inside each other's hearts?

"You can read it for yourself," Angus said, dragging his sleeve across one eye, then the other, and sniffing hard. "I haven't shown it to anyone. I can't, you know. But it's not true that she killed herself. She would never leave Henry. Not for anything."

Pearl gently pushed the letter back at Angus. She didn't need to read it. Instead, she came at him and hugged him fiercely, but only with one arm to keep Henry from being squeezed.

After a long moment, she let him go and stepped back.

"What will you do now?" she asked, blinking at her own tears.

"I put in for work in Connecticut," he said. "I leave in a few weeks. It'll be good. Get out from under everyone's feet. Get on with things."

When Pearl looked back, she found Angus watching Henry again, his eyes dry now but full with longing.

"You can see him," she said. "Whenever you wish. I promise you."

Angus looked at Pearl, his eyes flashing with concern, then in the next instant, with calm understanding.

"I appreciate that. I do," he said, but they both knew he would never see his child again.

Together they walked back to the house where the carriage was waiting, Henry's clothes and cradle stowed above. Angus waited until she and Henry were tucked safely inside before he began back down the hill. Pearl watched him as they drove away, turning her gaze to the lighthouse only when Angus had slipped beneath the rise, the cupola remaining in view until they rounded the turn in the road, daylight bouncing off the wedges of black like sunbursts, brighter than any beam.

Friday Night

The Mutiny Dash

YEARS PASSED, AND THE MYSTERY of the Mermaid Mutiny and the lives it stole gave way to other concerns, but the cloud of tragedy continued to hang over the town. Even the steady Cradle Harbor Light could no longer maintain its beam over the water. Complaining of Lydia's ghost, keepers left their posts after only a few months. Soon the coast guard dimmed the lamp for the last time in 1937, building a new tower in nearby Port Chester. It wasn't until 1943 when the town, looking to provide a distraction from the physical and emotional demands of wartime, decided to resurrect the legend and organized the first annual Mermaid Festival, a celebration that began as a simple town picnic and has since grown to a three-day event that draws tourists from all over the East and farther, to celebrate the story of four men and the mysteries of the sea that virtually swallowed them—and their loved ones—whole.

—The Mermaid Mutiny and More:
The Complete History of Cradle Harbor

Fifteen

THE VILLAGE GREEN WAS LIT up like a fairground and twice as crowded. A few amusement park rides, including an old-time carousel with purple and pink horses and a pair of emerald dolphins, had been set up on an adjoining stretch of lawn. Paper bowls of hot blueberry crumble, topped with quickly melting scoops of vanilla frozen custard, lined picnic tables, while musicians played in rousing clumps up and down the sidewalk.

Down at the town beach, the speakers sizzled expectantly into the soft night air, crossing the bustling crowd that lined the sand, braced and prone. The four of them—five including the baby—had parked at Pike's, as the owner always let Buzz and Tess do every year for the festival, and they made good time getting through the crowds to take their places on the cold sand. They'd added their shoes to the impossible mountain of sneakers and sandals at the top of the beach. ("We'll never find them again," Tom said, worried. "Not tonight, you won't," Tess had answered, kicking off her own and watching them be swallowed up in the pile.) It was indeed a banner year, Tess thought as she looked up and down the shore. There had to be at least four hundred people running the Dash this year, a striking increase from the handful there for the first Dash she and Ruby had attended when she was just nine, with Buzz watching from the sidelines, try as Ruby had to convince him to join the line of racers.

"You're not scared, are you?" Ruby had whispered, clutching Tess's small hand. "Because it's okay if you are."

"I'm not scared. Are you?"

"How can I be scared? I have you."

"Do you think *they* were scared?"

"Who, lovey?"

"Those men. Those men who loved the mermaids."

"No, they weren't scared."

"But how can you be sure?" Tess had asked.

"Easy." Ruby's eyes had filled then, glistening like jarred honey on a windowsill. "Because true love isn't scary, lovey. That's what makes it true."

"Look!" Tess turned to see the town manager taking his place on the podium at the end of the pier, his bullhorn raised to his mouth.

Then it had been like being poured out of a spout. That was how Tess would always remember it. The crush of people, the shrieks of delight, the rush of wind and cold water, the taste of salt spray as they'd charged into the ocean, splashing and cheering.

Now it was Tom standing beside her. He scanned the beach, his eyes drifting over to the pier where Edith Hawthorne and the rest of the town officials were lined up, beaming like jack-o'-lanterns under a canopy of lights.

"They won't quit, you know," he said. "They want me out of that house."

"Just let them try," Tess said.

Tom looked around. "Where's Dean? He was right behind us."

"There." Tess pointed down the beach to where Dean and Petra stood with Mia.

"He thinks it's going to be easy," Tom said, watching his brother blow raspberries on his daughter's fists. "Like a puppy. He has no idea."

Tess smiled. "He will."

But Tom's expression remained dubious, even when he turned his gaze back to her. "So, what do we do now?"

"Now we take the hand of the person next to us, and when the time comes, we all run in together."

"I didn't mean about the Dash," Tom said.

Tess reared up and kissed his cheek. "Neither did I," she whispered.

"*Dashers, ready?*" The town manager's voice crackled over the loudspeaker. Tom took Tess's hand and squeezed it hard. Dean appeared beside them just in time, sliding his hand into Tess's. The three of them smiled at one another, hands linked; then they faced the water.

"*On your mark, get set . . . dash!*"

It was like being poured out of a spout. That was Tom's first thought as he felt the rush of speed and energy blowing behind him, and he and Tess and Dean all allowed themselves to be part of the flow. They crashed into the water, hundreds of bodies whooping and flailing into the cold surf, getting waist deep before they finally slowed their advance. Tom couldn't believe how cold it was; Tess had never felt the water so warm. She submerged herself, tasting the salt. Bending her head back to float, she saw Tom above her. He was smiling even as he shook his arms to regain feeling in them.

There were clouds tonight; Tess could see them thinning. They'd hide the stars, those stars that were always there, even if you couldn't see them, even if you didn't know their names. Closing her eyes, she swore she heard chimes above the din of the crowd, colliding in a far-off breeze, a farewell tinkling, a shifting good-bye of salt-lapped metal, or maybe just a ringing of memory, of love, of new.

ACKNOWLEDGMENTS

I am so fortunate to work with such talented and gracious people at NAL. To my editor, Danielle Perez, who saw the early spark of this novel and gave it air and plenty of fuel to burn bright—my deepest thanks. I also wish to thank Jane Steele, Daniel Walsh, Rosalind Parry, Kayleigh Clark, and Mimi Bark for all they have done on this book's journey.

To Rebecca Gradinger, who always steers me in the right direction. I thank her—and my lucky stars to have her as my agent.

As someone raised in Maine, I came to realize that I knew embarrassingly little about lighthouses and sea travel when I started writing this book, so I am indebted to several people for sharing their expertise and keeping me from looking dim on the subjects: David Richards, Erma Colvin, and Thomas Tag from the U.S. Lighthouse

Acknowledgments

Society for detailed information on keeper's log books. Thanks as well to the lighthouse museums of Maine—and those all over the world—that tirelessly maintain these important historic structures so we can all be "keepers" of the magic and the majesty of the sea.

A NATIVE NEW ENGLANDER WHO was raised in Maine, **Erika Marks** has worked as an illustrator, an art director, a cake decorator, and a carpenter. She currently lives in Charlotte, North Carolina, with her husband and their two daughters. This is her second novel, after *Little Gale Gumbo*.

CONNECT ONLINE

www.erikamarksauthor.com

twitter.com/erikamarksauthr

The
MERMAID
COLLECTOR

ERIKA MARKS

This Conversation Guide is intended to enrich the
individual reading experience, as well as encourage us
to explore these topics together—because books,
and life, are meant for sharing.

A Conversation
with Erika Marks

Q. This is such a rich story of parents and children, and of lovers. In deciding to write it, were you accessing stories that you had wanted to tell for a while, or was it an inspiration of the moment?

A. I remember very clearly when the idea for this story came to me. I was reading an article about a seaside home, and in the house was a gorgeous mosaic of a mermaid and a man that was meant to commemorate a local legend about a sea captain who had fallen in love with a mermaid and left his wife and family to be reunited with her. It was that instantaneous for me. And while I knew the legend itself wouldn't be the main focus of the story, I immediately envisioned a novel driven by the inherent romance in such a legend, what it would be like to grow up in a place where life was impacted by that fantasy, how that would help to shape people's beliefs in love and their understanding of family and community.

Q. How did you decide to write the parallel narratives? Did you arrive at them at the same time, or did one time period or story inspire the other?

A. I always imagined Lydia's and Linus's voices in the story in some form, but in the early drafts it was mostly in journal entries. It wasn't until later drafts that I began to explore Lydia's narrative, and suddenly her story grew, and with it, new twists to the legend that I thought I already knew. I especially loved moving back and forth between the two time periods and the two stories. It felt seamless to me because even though there were more than a hundred years separating the two narratives, their setting (the town, but more specifically the lightkeeper's house) and some of the challenges facing the characters (loss of loved ones, isolation, unexpected desires) were so similar.

Q. Maine's atmosphere absolutely permeates these stories. What sort of memories or experiences of the state inspired you here? Were lighthouses always important to you?

A. There's no question that my growing up near the coast was at the heart of my inspiration for this novel. There is a ruggedness and a starkness to the Maine coast that I think is truly beautiful and haunting at the same time. I'm drawn to stories of people who build their lives in coastal places, and how that setting shapes who they are and what they want.

Lighthouses are such an intrinsic part of our image of the coast and I have always been fascinated by them, their architecture, and the histories of the individuals who took care of them—how remarkably demanding that life must have been.

Q. You evoke an incredibly intimate vision of a town in Maine, but at the same time you portray characters who grate against the smallness of their towns. Tess, for example, has a conflicted relationship with her hometown, yet she doesn't seem to want to leave it. How did your experience of Maine's small towns shape your portrayal here?

A. I was fortunate to grow up in a very close-knit and nurturing small town in Maine, so I wanted to convey the strong sense of community and comfort that comes from that setting, even for someone like Tess. In her case, her conflicted relationship with the Harbor reveals itself when she eventually sees how much support she does have in her town and that her sense of isolation has more to do with who she is than with who her neighbors are.

Q. In Tess, you've created a vibrant but often prickly heroine. How did you create this attractive yet often flawed character?

A. Tess revealed herself to me, not surprisingly, in fits and starts. She was often a hard character to pin down and I think that was part of what I loved about her. She is such a ball of inconsistencies—on the one hand she is passionate and highly emotional and very needy, but in other ways she wants to present herself to the world as a tough nut who is fine with being perceived as an outsider. Yet when the opportunity arises to carve the commemorative statue, she is determined to use the chance to win the town's approval. In reality, I think we all struggle with our own inconsistencies, and the parts of us that we want the world to see are often at odds with who we really are in our most honest moments.

Q. Some of the darker issues dealt with in the book include Ruby's bipolarity and Dean's alcoholism. Did you research these illnesses? Or did something in your personal life experience give you a sense of these issues?

A. Even though I have been close to people who have struggled with both bipolar illness and alcoholism, I did look to several mental health professionals in order to have a fuller understanding of the challenges of living with these illnesses. But Dean and Ruby's health challenges are only a facet of their stories—what was paramount to me in writing their narratives was how their illnesses impacted the people around them and how their resistance to treatment often defined them in the eyes of their loved ones.

Q. Tom and Dean are such an intriguing set of brothers. Having lived together for so many years, they obviously love each other, yet they are also codependent. What drew you to write about this unusual pairing?

A. After writing about sisters Josie and Dahlia in *Little Gale Gumbo*, I wanted to explore the relationship between two brothers and how that might be similar to and different from the challenges and joys that sisters encounter in their relationships. With Tom and Dean, much like Josie and Dahlia, there are huge personality differences, but there is still that basic sense of belonging that can come only from siblings.

One of the most interesting aspects of Tom and Dean's relationship is how mutually conflicted they are about their codependency. On the one hand, Dean imagines Tom as his "warden," but Dean knows—whether he will admit it or not—that Tom's overbearing concern allows Dean the luxury of a sometimes-reckless lifestyle. Similarly, Tom doesn't want to see that he condones Dean's dependency to avoid losing his brother's companionship.

Q. Lydia and Tom are both newcomers to the town (albeit centuries apart). Have you ever had that experience yourself? If so, did you draw from it in creating their arrivals?

A. Absolutely. Several times in my life, I have moved to new places—many times alone and often not knowing anyone. It can be a very empowering experience because it can offer—as it does for Lydia and Tom—a chance to make a fresh start. But too often we imagine a new setting will magically wash away the things we struggled with or that we think we left behind.

I don't think that's possible. Our personal challenges, if not confronted and resolved, follow us no matter how different our new home, which is the realization both Lydia and Tom eventually come to at the keeper's house.

Q. The characters in this novel often define themselves in relation to the ocean. In your life, do you feel that same sense of mystery and romance toward the ocean? How did that affect your writing of this novel?

A. Regardless of whether you grow up inland or right at the edge of the water, I think the coast has a strong effect on all of us and how we see ourselves in the world. For me, the ocean is instantly settling and a source of great joy. There is something humbling and peaceful in walking the beach and facing the surf and the expanse of the sea, in the sounds of the water, the texture of the sand, the smell of the tide. The characters in this novel have very complex relationships with the sea. Some see it as their livelihood, others as the source of a magical legend, and then others, like Lydia, feel its power in a foreboding way and struggle to relate to it. It was interesting to me, as someone who has no fear of the ocean, to explore a character who fears the sea— and ultimately the sea confirms her fears by taking away her most precious possessions: her husband and his love for her.

Q. I think one of the most enduring images of this novel is Ruby's bright pink house nestled along the coastline. Have you seen a house like that, or did something in particular draw you to that color or to that idea?

A. I think it's impossible to spend any amount of time in a city like New Orleans—where I lived for several years and met my husband—and not be transformed by the vibrant palette of the city. Since Ruby was an artist, and very attached to the properties of colors (even if those properties were of her own making), I loved the idea of using color as a way to symbolize the contrast between Ruby's bolder philosophies and the more subdued world of Cradle Harbor. Even though the town has a lively festival every summer, their day-to-day world is much more restrained and reserved. Ruby's arrival changes that—and her desire to repaint the cottages cements it.

QUESTIONS FOR DISCUSSION

1. To all appearances, Tom and Tess are an unlikely match—yet their attraction is immediate and insistent. What do you think draws them to each other?

2. The sea plays a role in both the present-day and historical stories. For some characters it is a source of joy and peace; for others it is a source of great fear. Choose a character and discuss how the presence of the sea impacts the way he or she views the world.

3. Beverly comes to Cradle Harbor with a mission for truth, but over the course of the few days she is there, it becomes clear that the truth she has been seeking may not be the one she wants to find. Discuss how Beverly's "mission for truth" changes over the course of her visit to Cradle Harbor—and how what she learns changes her as a person.

4. Everyone in Cradle Harbor thinks they know the true story of the Mermaid Mutiny, but it becomes clear through the course of the novel that the legend has been misunder-

stood. Do you think the townspeople would like to know the truth, or do you think they are too attached to their own versions? Do you think as a general rule people select their own truths in stories, depending on their own needs, as well as the timing?

5. It is clear that Lydia has strong feelings for Angus, even though she remains devoted to Linus and committed to their marriage. Do you think it's possible for someone to love two people with equal depth?

6. Both Lydia and Tom come to the lightkeeper's house seeking stability. Lydia seeks it for her marriage so they can finally start a family; Tom seeks it for Dean so he will stop drinking. Do you think Lydia and Tom ever attain that stability?

7. The residents and the attendees of Cradle Harbor's annual Mermaid Festival are all enamored of the mystique of mermaids even though the legend states that mermaids led Linus and the other men to abandon their wives. What do you think it is about mermaids that fascinates people?

8. By the story's end, Tom is not convinced that Dean is capable of taking care of himself. Do you think he is? Do you think Dean is as helpless and irresponsible as Tom believes him to be? Or is there codependency between the brothers? Does Tom need Dean as much as Dean needs Tom? Discuss how one brother depends on the other to function in his role.

9. It is evident that Frank had a deep love for his wife, and yet he engaged in an affair with Beverly for many years.

Why do you think he continued to see her? Do you think it had anything to do with the accident?

10. Tess grows up refusing to believe that her mother is mentally ill. By the end of the novel, do you think she has finally come to terms with the reality of her mother's illness? If so, how might it change her memories of her life—and the "fun" they had—with her mother?

11. One of the prevailing themes in the novel is the use of "legends" and perceived history. Just as the townspeople have unknowingly "rewritten" the details of their treasured Mermaid Mutiny legend to suit their festival, all the characters in the novel have personal histories that they have shaped over the years to suit their emotional needs. Tom and Tess are both guilty of this. Tom uses his perceived guilt to keep him bound to Dean, while Tess uses her perceived "outcast-ness" to keep the memory of her mother alive. Discuss how Tom and Tess help each other to confront their mutual retelling of their personal stories and face the truths from which they've been hiding. What other characters in the novel face a similar reckoning with their own personal legends?

12. By the end of the book, it is apparent that Tom and Dean's mysterious affiliation with the town will soon be revealed. How do you think the townspeople—in particular the prickly members of the Historical Society—will respond to this information?

13. While there are journal entries, letters, and plenty of local lore on the event, it is never entirely clear what happened to the four men between the time they left the harbor for their doomed sail and the time of their rescue. Discuss what you think may have transpired during those lost days on the water.